LOVER

D0514042

Also by the same author

The King's Pleasure

and available in Coronet Books

Lovers all Untrue

Norah Lofts

CORONET BOOKS
Hodder Paperbacks Ltd., London

Copyright © 1970 by Norah Lofts
First published 1970 by Hodder & Stoughton Ltd
Coronet edition 1972

Printed in Great Britain for Coronet Books, Hodder
Paperbacks Ltd., St. Paul's House, Warwick Lane, London,
E.C.4, by Cox & Wyman Ltd., London, Reading and
Fakenham.

ISBN 0 340 16216 3

Thy wars brought nothing about,
Thy lovers were all untrue.

Dryden

AUTHOR'S PREFACE

I adore reading accounts of actual crimes — mainly, I think, because only in the glare of a criminal investigation does one see other people's lives in such complete detail. To be truthful, Lizzie Borden's activity with the axe interests me less than that joint of mutton which in a hot summer week, before the days of refrigeration, went on and on, and finally turned up as mutton soup for breakfast!

And of course all the most fascinating cases are the unsolved ones, or at least those in which nobody is irrevocably pinned down. Julia Wallace; Constance Kent; Madeline Smith.

It is, alas, many years since I read Madeline's story. She lived — I think — in Edinburgh, was a member of a highly respectable family, was passionate, and articulate, took a lover, wrote love letters, and then, with the prospect of a suitable marriage before her, had those letters held over her as a threat. The lover died and she was accused of giving him arsenic in cocoa. The verdict, possible in Scotland, not in England, was 'Not proven'.

Marion Draper is not Madeline Smith; Mr. Draper — and let us thank God for it — never existed outside my mind; but the situation in which Marion found herself was that of Madeline — and of who knows how many more girls, passionate and eager and capable, doomed to live in claustrophobic, Papa-dominated Victorian homes?

Making bits of nonsense for a sale to raise funds to help women in purdah, Marion thought — *Who is in Purdah, if we are not?*

Who indeed? And the staggering thing is to think that the circumstances against which Marion battled, existed less than a century ago.

Madeline Smith — may the earth lie lightly upon her — gave me the germ of the story. Dryden gave me the title, 'Thy wars brought nothing about; thy lovers were all untrue.'

It was possible to say, 'Yes, I understand, Papa,' and to think — I hate you. I wish you would drop dead, there on the hearth-rug!

'What I fail to see,' Mr. Draper said, 'is why you should bring up the subject again. I thought I had made it clear, in September, that I had no intention of allowing you and Ellen to go running about the streets after dark.'

Running about the streets. What a way to describe a brief walk, out of Alma Avenue, into Honey Lane, across the Buttermarket, on to the Square and into the Guildhall.

'Mr. Marriot himself suggested that I should ask you again, Papa. The membership of the Musical Society has fallen below his expectations.'

'As I warned him. Mr. Marriot is in many ways an admirable man, but when a clergyman, who should know better, suggests forming a Society, the only qualification for membership of which is a fondness for music, he cannot expect support from decent people.'

Marion Draper felt her hands clench. Fortunately they were hidden by the voluminous folds of her skirt. She was aware that she was about to argue with Papa. She was careful to speak very meekly.

'Angela is a member, Papa. She has often urged . . .'

'That will do,' Mr. Draper said in a crushing voice. It irked him not to be able to deny that the daughter of the town's leading solicitor and related, through her mother, to a county family, was to be reckoned among the decent elements of the town.

'How Mr. and Mrs. Taylor permit their daughter to behave is no affair of mine. I do not intend to imitate it. You will oblige me by not mentioning the matter again.' He consulted his watch. 'Ring the bell. Supper will be late by two minutes.'

She pressed the white china handle inset in the crimson-papered wall, and the bell could be heard ringing at the bottom of the kitchen stairs. Betty, however, had been waiting in a state of palpitating agitation just outside the dining-room door, balancing a laden tray on her hip. As she entered she brought with her the good smell of roast beef. Mr. Draper

9

took his mid-day meal at a little chop house near his Maltings, so the evening meal, called supper except when there were guests, was always of a substantial nature. Marion went to the sideboard and took from the drawer a highly starched white cloth and spread it over the fringed red velvet one on the big table. She placed the heavy silver cruet in the centre and the decanter of claret within reach of Papa's place at the top of the table.

Presently I shall perform these actions in reverse and that will complete my day's work! Oh God, how long? How long?

She went out, across the black-and-white-tiled hall and up-stairs to the room which she shared with Ellen. Ellen had chosen not to be present when Marion made her request, but she looked up eagerly. Marion's face gave nothing away; it never did; she had learned to control its expression and was the fortunate possessor of pale, rather thick skin not unlike the best kid gloves in texture; it never coloured from any emotion and was equally impervious to outside influences.

'Well?'

'A point-blank refusal. And the subject never to be mentioned again.'

'Oh dear,' Ellen said, but she spoke with a comfortable resignation. 'I never had much hope. Poor Marion, it is worse for you. Angela is more your friend.'

'It was not for the sake of seeing more of Angela ... Nor for the music. It was the thought of one evening, just one evening a week, with something positive to do. Out of this house!'

'I know. It is a shame.' For herself Ellen minded little. She had a placid nature, was inclined to be docile and fitted quite easily into the way of life which Papa considered suitable for his daughters. She was not, like Marion, clever, or restless, or rebellious; but she could sympathise. She now said, 'Anyway, this evening we shall have something positive to do. The shells arrived and if we sort them beforehand it will save us time when the glue is hot.' She had already begun her orderly little preparations; on a vast *papier-mâché* tray she had arranged a number of containers into which the shells were to be sorted according to size, and the white linen sack full of shells — exotic ones from places far away. An enterprising young man in London was importing them by the ton and making a good income by pandering to the latest craze — the making of shell-encrusted boxes.

Downstairs, Betty, having placed a tureen of soup and four well-heated plates at the lower end of the table, beat upon the gong, a copper half-drum slung in a framework of bamboo. The girls hurried down and took their places. Mamma had appeared and as they all sat down she lifted the tureen lid, dipped in the silver ladle and began to serve. Mamma had vanished as soon as Marion had announced her intention of speaking to Papa, once more, about the Musical Society. To use the words appear and vanish was completely apt where Mamma was concerned. No ghost could be more elusive. In a house which though spacious was not rambling or many-roomed, Mamma managed to perform astonishing vanishing tricks, especially if any trouble threatened. On her plump little feet she could move without noise; no door she ever opened creaked or slammed, and she was completely impervious to cold. In the dead of winter when other people, however unwillingly, centred about the dining-room fire, Mamma could be anywhere, in the drawing-room where the frost had etched flowers and ferns on the windows, in the unheated conservatory where only the hardiest plants survived the cold season, in the seldom used room known as Papa's study or up in the box-room. The only time when her presence in any of these places was announced was when she played the grand piano in the drawing-room. She did it about once a week, or once in ten days, and then everyone knew; for Mamma played the piano with power, with authority, with something approaching violence; and never, at such times, any gentle, sentimental popular tunes, nothing in any way like the music she produced for the entertainment of guests after the rare dinner-parties. Marion, in the last two years, since she had left school and come home and begun to observe and form judgments, had often thought that Mamma's private sessions with the piano — Liszt one of her favourite composers — offered a clue to a real personality, suppressed and lost. But it was a clue that could never be followed; the trail was too thoroughly concealed by the plump, completely subservient and seemingly contented woman who was not only Papa's wife but also his willing slave; and who said things like, 'You must ask Papa', and 'Papa says', and who could do a vanishing trick and then re-appear, calm and incurious, and dish up soup.

The soup this evening was one of Ada's best; a smooth blend of chicken stock, sieved leeks and cream. Ada, with all her skill, her bulging book of recipes and her unpredictable temper had been, as Mamma had once said, 'One of my wedding presents.' And Ada was rare — most cooks, married or not, insisted upon being called 'Mrs.', Ada had no patience with such nonsense; many cooks refused to do anything that was not directly concerned with their culinary art, and some were oppressive to their underlings. Ada was unique, a treasure, and up and down Alma Avenue Mrs. Draper was much envied.

Only animals ate in silence. Papa spoke; he said, 'Excellent soup, my dear.' And to that Mamma said, 'The leeks were especially fine, Ada bought them at the door. A young man named Smith is attempting to establish a market garden at Asham. He is prepared to deliver daily and to take orders. Ada thought favourably of him.'

Papa remarked that enterprise should be encouraged. He then inquired how the girls had spent their day. His temporary displeasure with Marion had vanished and he had regained his usual paternal geniality.

'This morning we visited Nanny,' Ellen said. 'We took her a few things.' A harmless, indeed creditable way to spend a morning, but over the last of his soup Mr. Draper looked disapproving.

'I hope you did not stay long. All the hovels on that side of the Common are very insanitary. They should be pulled down. The old woman — and most of her neighbours — would be better off in the Workhouse.'

It sounded ruthless, but Marion, rising to remove the soup plates and to ring the bell to summon the roast, felt obliged to be just. Papa's rule was rigid, heavy, galling; but he was concerned for the health and well-being of his family. And over a few things, the old woman whom they called Nanny, for example, he was of divided mind. It was right that she should be visited, taken a half pound of tea, a dozen eggs, as well as her regular allowance of five shillings a month; but it was wrong that his daughters should be exposed, even for a few minutes to the atmosphere in which the old woman, after a lifetime of faithful service, spent her last days.

'I thought Ada visited Nanny regularly.'

'Ada,' said Mamma, gently, but sticking up for her own, 'is becoming lame.'

'I am sorry to hear it,' Mr. Draper said. It was quite a long time since he had seen the woman who twice a day provided him with well-cooked meals.

'She finds the stairs increasingly trying,' Mamma said. 'I am seriously considering turning that little room under the stairs into a bedroom for her.'

'An excellent idea,' Papa said, looking appreciatively at the sirloin now before him. He took up the carving knife and gave it the few strokes on the steel without which the knife, however well-honed below stairs, would not be considered quite serviceable in the dining-room. He carved swiftly and skilfully. Mamma, at the other end of the table, placed roast potatoes and brussels sprouts on each plate. The cruet, the gravy, the dish of freshly made horse-radish sauce went from hand to hand. After a few mouthfuls Papa made another contribution to the conversation. Clegg, his head clerk was away, ill again; the second time this autumn.

No real business details were ever discussed at home but illness, marriages, death and births among the workmen were often given mention. Now, hearing of Clegg's indisposition Marion's hands tightened again, for it called to mind an occasion, almost a year and a half ago when another clerk, named Thompson had gone for a swim in the river and been drowned. She had then been home from school for six months and was finding the boredom unbearable and she had said across this table, 'Papa, could I be of assistance? I am rather good at figures.' Papa's reaction to that suggestion had been one of shock and anger. 'Have I ever allowed you to set foot in the Maltings? When I cannot run my business without aid from my womenfolk, I will burn the place down.' The rejection hurt, but oddly enough the scarcely warranted violence of the second sentence had struck an echo from a deeply buried streak of violence in her own nature. She was also capable of strong feelings, preferences and prejudices, and occasionally made — in the company of Ellen or Angela — what were called sweeping statements.

'I shall have to think seriously about replacing him,' Papa said. 'Fortunately clerks are easily come by.'

Baked apples, done to a turn, fluffy within their neatly scored skins, their cores replaced by chopped dates, completed — with a jug of yellow cream — yet another of the good solid meals to which they were all so thoroughly accustomed that no gratitude was involved.

'And what is the work this evening?' Papa asked. He liked to see his daughters happily and busily employed. He always considered that the things they contributed to the Church Bazaar were superior to all others. On the actual day he would take an hour off and walk around the stalls in the Guildhall, saying with shameless self-satisfaction, 'Ah yes, I seem to have seen that before!' He would buy the teapot-stand painted by Ellen, the crocheted antimacassars made by Marion, the little shoulder shawl knitted by his wife. Then, with a benevolent air he would give them away, the purely decorative articles to ladies of his acquaintance, the more utilitarian ones to the humbler sort.

'The shells have arrived, Papa,' Ellen said. 'This evening we are going to sort them, ready for sticking on.'

'Good,' he said. He seated himself in the large leather chair, went through the evening ritual of selecting a cigar from a box of identical ones and opened *The Times*. Mamma took the smaller, tightly buttoned little velvet chair and put her feet on the beaded footstool. She began to knit. Ellen fetched down the tray.

On the black marble mantelpiece the black marble clock, shaped like a Grecian temple, showed the time to be twenty minutes to eight. Another interminable evening had begun.

Marion wished that on this particular evening there had been some occupation of a more demanding kind; or no work at all, in which event she and Ellen could have played some paper game. Ellen was not very good at supplying the names of twenty nouns all beginning with the same letter of the alphabet; once when the letter was S she had filled in the name of the river as *Sane* and she cheated over the book titles; unable to supply one when the letter was F she had written *Fanny's Birthday*. Marion said, 'There is no such book!' 'How can you know?' Ellen asked. 'Can you prove that in all the world there is no book called that?' 'No.' 'Then I get my mark.' After that she would often slip in a bogus title, and mild as the joke was, it served.

It was possible to think a little about the places from which these pretty things, all pearly and glistening, came; to imagine them being gathered by brown, laughing, almost naked boys from white beaches against which blue seas broke. Possible also to think that each once held a living creature. Now, empty and cleansed they awaited the moment when they should be rendered immobile for ever, stuck with glue on to boxes, large and small, around the edges of photograph frames. And all for the benefit of some unfortunate Indian ladies living in a state of purdah.

Who is in purdah, if we are not?

With her hands busy shell-sorting, Marion looked at Papa, master of this harem. He was handsome, not unlike one of his own well-fed, well-groomed cart horses; the same glossy look, almost the same colouring, a dark chestnut — her own hair was the same shade, but plentiful, whereas Papa's was receding, a fact that gave his forehead a height, almost a nobility. He was fifty. He had deferred marriage until he was properly established. And by that she knew his age, putting together things he said when lesser men married early . . . 'I was thirty before I thought of marrying.' Mamma had once said, 'I had begun to despair. Over two years.' So, now seventeen herself, the first-born, Marion could tell Papa's age. Fifty. But he had kept his figure and only the faintest hint of jowls under his clean-shaven jaw indicated that he was a day over forty.

A father to be proud of; had the slightest touch of fondness been involved. But he had disliked her from the start. It had puzzled her for years and then she had understood. Papa had wanted a son and been given a daughter. That daughter's resemblance to him, in all but sex, had been the final affront. Such a near miss! Oddly enough, he was fond of Ellen. One would have thought that the second failure on Mamma's part would have been even more strongly resented, but Ellen was fair, blue-eyed and meek like Mamma.

It would have been far better had Ellen made the plea to join the flagging Musical Society but Ellen had backed away — 'I never think of the right word.'

Marion's critical eye looked upon Mamma who had long since given up looking for the right word. Mamma never argued, or exercised persuasion and if she made a comment it was always of an uncontroversial nature. After Ellen's birth Mamma had retreated into a vague semi-invalidism which excused her from even the mildest social duties — it was understood, for instance, that the Draper girls never had birthday or Christmas parties; Mrs. Draper was not 'up' to any form of entertaining except the rare, staid dinner-party; she was not even regular in Sunday morning church attendance. Mamma was, in fact, what Papa had made of her, a plump placid bird in a comfortable cage, and if, at the piano, she beat frenzied wings against the bars it was when Papa was

15

out of hearing. Her very name was lost; when Papa addressed her he always said, 'My dear', when he spoke of her he said, 'Your mamma' or 'Your mistress'.

Mr. Draper was not unaware of the fact that since Marion had said something about Angela Taylor's membership of the Musical Society she had not said a word. Sulking! After downright defiance or giddy-mindedness, sulkiness was the worst trait a female could show and Marion had, from an early age, been sulky. Worse, not better, since he had withdrawn her from Miss Ruthven's Academy.

Sending her there had been one of his few mistakes — forced upon him by the fact that he could not find a suitable governess. He had tried. The capable ones were pert, if young, dictatorial, if old; the incapable — doddering old indigent gentlewomen — were a nuisance with their headaches, their backaches, their snuffling colds. So Marion, and presently Ellen, had been sent to Miss Ruthven's and too late Mr. Draper had learned that Miss Ruthven held and inculcated some extremely radical and modern views — that women were capable of earning a living for themselves, for instance. Marion, at fifteen, had declared her intention of going to a place called St. Hilda's and training to be a teacher.

Abruptly he had withdrawn both his daughters from this poisonous influence. Ellen who had had only one year of exposure to contamination was happy to be freed from routine and lessons. Marion had argued, pleaded and then sulked. In the intervening years she had argued less and less and cultivated a moderately meek demeanour, but she still fell into silences which Mr Draper always resented, feeling them full of unspoken criticism and now and again those lowered eyelids would lift and reveal a look that Mr Draper found distinctly unpleasant. However, she was still young and malleable; in the end she would conform.

Presently he lowered his paper and addressed her directly.

'Marion, have you written to Mr Marriot informing him of my decision?'

'No, Papa. There has been no time . . .' And he knew that perfectly well since she had been out of his sight only for a minute since he made the decision. 'I thought that Ellen and I could call at the Rectory in the morning and acquaint . . .'

'That would be to lay yourself open to further persuasion,'

16

Papa said. 'Write a note now. I need hardly tell you how to phrase it, need I? Miss Ruthven thought highly of your powers of composition.' Part of his power lay in his capacity for saying sarcastic, sardonic, hurtful things in a silky voice — the other part lay in his complete self-confidence: he was invariably right. It was not only his family and his business which he dominated. People who had no reason to be subservient to him, people completely independent of him felt their self-confidence ooze when faced with his.

Marion wrote with slightly tremulous fingers because of the strain of trying to set down something acceptable to Mr. Marriot and to Papa, who was sure to ask to inspect the letter. Impossible to tell the blunt truth — Papa will not allow; and uncivil not to offer some excuse. 'My sister and I have thought again ... Much as we should have liked to join ... The calendar always so crowded at this time of year.'

'It will do,' Papa said. It was just possible that had Ellen written it he would have said, 'Quite well put.' Since he could not fault the wording of the letter he attacked at a vulnerable point — the calligraphy which was distinctive, absolutely upright and inclined to spikiness. 'I still maintain,' he said, 'that Miss Ruthven is in error in abandoning the copybook.' Miss Ruthven held that girls could use their time better than in copying *Honesty Is The Best Policy* six times making the down strokes thicker than the up ones. Dear, dear Miss Ruthven — the one person, except Mamma and Ellen, whom Marion had ever loved; the only person she had loved *and* admired. She had been silly enough, at the end of her first term to let this esteem be obvious, and thus handed to Papa a weapon which he wielded with assiduity.

'Would you wish me to post the letter or deliver it by hand, Papa?'

'The answer must be obvious. If you deliver it the whole point in writing will be missed. You may take a stamp from my study.'

'Oh. Are you going to read,' Ellen asked.

'I must. Just for a little while. I won't disturb you. I will turn out the gas and manage with a candle.' Marion had taken, from under the neatly piled underclothes, the latest example of what Papa called trashy novels — Miss Marie Corelli's *Romance of two Worlds*. All evening as the clock lagged and her temper chafed, she had thought of this moment when, the dull day lived through, she could escape. She guessed — correctly—that Miss Ruthven would share Papa's opinion of most of the books she devoured these days, but she often felt that without them she would go mad. To obtain a supply was difficult. There was a little lending library at the back of Blake's the tobacconist's, but Papa had forbidden her to use it. Without having read a word that Ouida had written, he condemned her out of hand, together with Miss Rhoda Broughton, Miss Braddon and Miss Corelli. He never wanted to see a book by one of them, or by Mrs. Hungerford or Mrs. Henry Wood in *his* house. Hopelessly addicted, Marion was dependent upon Angela, who — and this was irony — never wanted to read anything that was not connected with clothes, but who was free to go into Blake's three or four times a day should she wish. Angela, soul of good nature, would borrow the forbidden books and Marion would smuggle them in.

In return for this and other lesser favours, Marion had lately been able to reciprocate, for Angela's freedom, though comparatively vast, was not absolute and since September . . . At the thought of the risks which Angela had been taking, connived at, alibied for, Marion broke into perspiration and the page blurred before her eyes. I must get out! But how? She could think of only one way . . . Realising that for once even Miss Corelli had failed her, she put the book under her pillow, blew out the candle and lying in the dark said:

'Ellen, are you asleep?'

'Nearly.'

'Could we go to Angela's to tea tomorrow? At least, arrange to and you go and make some excuse for me?'

'We can always go to tea with Angela. But suppose Mrs. Taylor should ask about you. What can I say?' Curiosity banished drowsiness. 'Where will you be?'

'I want to see Miss Ruthven.'

'Good grief! Whatever for?' A year of Miss Ruthven's governance had been enough for Ellen; she had left the school and its headmistress without a single regret. But she saw that it had been different for Marion, who had she stayed another year would have been Head Girl, and who had actually been already chosen to play Rosalind in the performance of *As You Like It* which was to mark the end of the summer term. 'And anyway, you couldn't get there and back in the time,' Ellen said. 'It's three miles.'

'Walking pace,' said Marion, who had read this interesting fact somewhere, 'is four miles an hour. I shall run, once I'm in the country. We could leave at half past three. If I run all the way there, and all the way back. And if you would tell Mrs. Taylor — should you see her — that I have gone to hunt for that special blue silk . . . but most probably you won't even see her. Now that Angela has a sitting-room of her own . . .'

'Well, all right,' Ellen said, not very willingly. 'But you know that Papa said . . .'

'I know; that is why I have to go this roundabout way. Will you, Ellen?'

'Of course. But I hope I shall not encounter Mrs. Taylor.'

'Thank you, darling. I'll do as much for you one day.'

'Not over visiting Miss Ruthven,' Ellen said with a chuckle. She flung herself over and went to sleep.

'But my dear girl,' Miss Ruthven said, thoroughly discomposed for once in her life. 'It is impossible. You must see that without your papa's consent it is impossible. You are under age, he is your legal guardian, you could not even make a marriage, however suitable, without his consent. How much less this that you propose?' Miss Ruthven had tested Mr. Draper's strength of mind at the time of Marion's removal; she had written urging, almost imploring that a girl with so much mental ability and with an inclination to study — all too rare — should be allowed to remain at least another year. To that letter Mr. Draper had not replied directly; but he had chosen to regard her plea as arising from concern because he had not given a full term's notice; he had sent a cheque for both girls' fees for the term between Christmas and Easter. She had returned the cheque to him, saying that his daughters' places had already been filled, from her long waiting list.

'Besides,' Miss Ruthven now said, 'there are other considerations. It is now two years since you ceased serious study; it would take a year's intensive work, probably more, before you could qualify for entry to St. Hilda's Training College. I'm sorry, Marion; the plan is simply not feasible.'

'It was the only thing that occurred to me, Miss Ruthven. But I would do *anything*. Any work at all. Could I become an *unqualified* teacher? Or a governess?'

'Not without your father's consent.'

'Need he know? If you could assist me to find some post, I could just walk out — as I have done this afternoon. As you know, we have never been allowed to come back here even when invited to functions. I could just walk away and never go back.' She saw herself transferring a few absolute necessities, one at a time to Angela's house; borrowing her fare to wherever it was from Angela ... She had no money of her own; Papa was very generous in his own fashion, bills for clothes were never queried, he liked his women-folk to be the best-dressed at any gathering; he gave expensive gifts at Christmas and on birthdays, but he thought two shillings a week ample pocket money for girls whose real needs were provided for.

'That is wild talk,' Miss Ruthven said rather sternly. 'Your whereabouts would be discovered within a week. Your papa would be fully justified in asking police aid in tracing you. And if I were known to have encouraged such a scheme there would be a scandal which would affect the school most unfavourably.'

She looked critically at her visitor. Marion's street wear, a knee-high, well-fitting jacket with full matching skirt, was a buff-coloured cloth, so fine and good that it had a silky sheen; her small round hat was of matching velvet with a brown feather; her long tippet, now loosened and thrown back upon her shoulders, and the muff which lay on her lap were of sable. Good shoes and gloves. At least the man was not mean! And the girl was now seventeen and though not pretty by the standards of the day, remarkably good-looking. Perhaps there was some reason, not yet stated, for this wish to break away.

'So you cannot help me?' Marion said.

'Not along the lines you indicate, Marion. But to talk over a problem is always useful. Tell me, have you any reason, any *personal* reason for wishing to escape from your father's control?'

'No. Only what I said at first, Miss Ruthven. The utter tedium, the emptiness, the complete futility of life as we are compelled to lead it.'

'You have not formed a romantic attachment?' Miss Ruthven wore her inquisitorial face and she put the question bluntly. She had had much experience in probing out truths from those anxious to conceal them.

'None at all, Miss Ruthven. We never see a man who is not Papa's friend. All old, all married.' There was something about the placid assumption that a romantic attachment could only be formed between people who had met socially, that convinced Miss Ruthven that the girl was telling the truth. That and the straight, candid gaze of the almost amber-coloured eyes.

'Unfortunately such attachments can be formed outside the family circle,' she observed – but more as a warning than as an accusation.

'I never think about it,' Marion said. That was not quite true. In every one of the smuggled books there was at least one handsome hero with whom she was in love so long as the book lasted; but such men were not real people.

Miss Ruthven made another effort to be helpful.

'I freely admit,' she said, 'that the life you describe sounds extremely dull — particularly for a girl like you, with an active mind. Is there no voluntary work you could take up? Something along the charitable line?'

'Papa has such a horror of infection. Even our old Nanny . . .' She briefly explained this allusion. 'And Mr. Marriot once suggested that we should help with the Sunday School. Papa would not even consider it. The children, he said, had perpetually running noses. And ring-worm!'

There was a little pause. Then Miss Ruthven said:

'I am afraid, my dear Marion, that all you can do, for the moment, is to exercise patience and cultivate resignation. And bear in mind that your way of life offers certain compensations.' A thought occurred to her. 'Were you contemporary with Louise Hayward?'

'For one term. She was older.'

'Now Louise did succeed in entering St Hilda's; and did well. She obtained a post in a Church School — it was always clear that Louise would be obliged to support herself. She is bitterly unhappy. The village parson sounds to be a most unpleasant character — straight out of *Jane Eyre*, and his wife exploits Louise to the extent of making her dressmake for her, write her invitations, cut her sandwiches and wash her hair! An incredible situation in this day and age; but the Church Schools retained their independence when the Board was set

21

up and a school-mistress who refused to be a general amenuensis would be quickly replaced. I have Louise's letter here. She complains of too much to do; you complain of having too little. I sympathise with you both, but I think, perhaps ... Probably Louise and many other young women would gladly change places with you, Marion.'

She could, in fact, have named a dozen. Miss Ruthven, an ardent disciple of the redoubtable Miss Beale, a believer in the education and the equality of women had within the past few years received some sharp shocks which made her see that in a world shaped and completely governed by men, the forward-pressing women if not actually martyrs, were misfits. She had her days of discouragement; days when she realised that it was only her grandfather's money which had enabled her to set up school and be independent enough to scorn — for example — Mr. Draper's cheque. As things stood, behind every woman who successfully broke away, there must be a man. Look at Elizabeth Garrett!

At the same time she was aware that Marion Draper who had come asking a crumb of bread was being sent away with a stone. And upon that thought, her spirit once ardent and lively, but now failing and dubious, sickened.

She said, 'And doubtless your father has some matrimonial plans for you, Marion.'

Marion gathered and fastened the sable tippet.

'I think not, Miss Ruthven. Papa's attitude towards us is *possessive* in the extreme.'

A man's walking pace was four miles an hour; a girl, holding up her skirts and running and running, except when not alone on the road, when decorum must be observed, could cover the three miles in under an hour; and she did it. She reached Angela's house just slightly late for tea, but not too late for a girl who had been hunting that particularly elusive brand and colour of embroidery silk. The coldness of her reception astonished her. 'Good afternoon, Marion,' Mrs. Taylor said, 'so you have got here at last. I am afraid the tea has cooled.' She did not, as she would have done in ordinary circumstances, ring for a fresh pot; nor did she smile. From Mrs. Taylor, usually easygoing about time, this was direct rebuke, and Marion hastened to apologise. Her breathlessness bore witness to her statement that she had hurried. There was an unpleasant tension in the room. Neither Angela nor Ellen spoke. They both looked pale, and Angela had been crying some time that day. She was one of those girls whose eyes remained red-rimmed for hours after the last tear had been shed.

Pouring and passing a cup of tea which was not only tepid but stewed, Mrs. Taylor said, 'You are in time to take leave of Angela. She is going to her grandfather at Asham tomorrow morning. For a protracted visit.'

Marion's heart, already beating fast from running and swift walking, gave a sickening thump. It could mean only one thing. She glanced at Angela and their eyes communicated. Fear confirmed! She tried to remember on how many occasions she and Ellen had covered up for Angela. She tried not to think about how Papa would act when he knew. Momentarily incapable of swallowing she held a gulp of the bitter brew in her mouth and waited for Mrs. Taylor to arraign her for treachery, lying and deceitfulness. *She* would be blamed, being the oldest of the three, she was two months older than Angela.

The attack never came. Angela said, 'Mamma, I beg you not to inform Marion or Ellen as to the way in which I have disgraced myself.' Oh blessed Angela, offering a pointer; brave, loyal Angela, under the frivolous manner. Marion swallowed the mouthful of tea.

'I have no intention of doing so,' Mrs. Taylor said in a chilling voice, not looking at her daughter but at Marion. 'I have no notion of the extent to which you and your sister have been in Angela's confidence and I do not propose to make inquiries. This I say, and I say it very forcibly — whatever you know, much or little, you are never to speak of it. Never. My faith in Angela's veracity has been severely shaken but she swears that nobody knows anything of this disgusting business. So, if a word of gossip is *ever* heard I shall naturally suspect you, her closest associates, of starting it. Is that understood.'

How, Marion wondered, would someone in complete ignorance reply to that speech. While she wondered and hesitated Ellen, who could not spell *Seine*, had the answer.

'Whatever Angela has done, Mrs. Taylor, we should be the last to talk about it — *even if we knew*. We are her *friends*.'

Ellen spoke with exactly the right touch of earnest innocence. In fact she made Mrs. Taylor wonder if she had not handled this whole thing clumsily. Perhaps there had really been no need to inform even the Draper girls that Angela *was* in disgrace. The truth was that the whole thing had been such a shock that all day she had hardly known what she was doing, or thinking.

'So long as you remember that,' she said with a marked decline in aggressiveness. 'Angela has been ... rather naughty.' She should have used that word in the first place. And to end the awkward interview she said, 'And now she must go and pack.'

The parlourmaid came in and said, 'Madam, there's the boy from the office; the master left some paper he needed ...'

Poor Alan, Mrs. Taylor thought, rising from the tea-table, he was upset, too, not knowing whether he was coming or going and not absolutely sure, from a legal point of view, whether he had been right, in giving the young man, found kissing Angela in the shade of the lime tree by the gate, 'something to remember', in fact beating him over the head with a heavy walking stick.

'I will come,' Mrs. Taylor said.

She had no sooner gone than Angela launched herself at Marion and, beginning to cry again, said, 'Will you tell him? Please, Marion, please. It was all so sudden and so dreadful. Please tell him I am sorry he was hurt and that I may not write or ever see him again ... He is so gentle and there was Papa, lashing away with his stick. I can't tell you how horrible. Tell him how sorry ... He's in Freeman's ... you know, the chemist's ...'

The parlourmaid came in to take away the tea-things. Marion managed to say, 'I hope you will enjoy your stay, Angela. The country is lovely just now.'

'Promise me ...'

Gratefully remembering that Angela, taken by surprise, shocked, made miserable, had not let one incautious word slip, Marion said, 'Yes. I will tell him. I promise.'

'*A shop assistant*,' Ellen said. 'After all the mystery about a well-connected Frenchman! Marion, honestly, when I went in, and Mrs. Taylor seemed to have taken a dislike to me, and Angela, I could see, had been crying, I could hardly *breathe*. I was obliged to sit there — Angela and I had no opportunity to exchange a word — and explain why you were late. I was so afraid, I felt quite *sick*. I thought of the two Sundays when Angela was supposed to be spending the day with us, and all the other times ... and until you appeared, I thought about you ... I haven't felt so ill since I had measles.'

'You managed to say exactly the right thing, darling. I am certain that the way you said *even if we knew* averted Mrs. Taylor's suspicion that we did know.'

'Shall you keep your promise to Angela?'

'I shall try to. Not being allowed to use Freeman's makes it rather difficult.'

Freeman's chemist's shop was under ban because he was a nonconformist and Papa suspected all nonconformists of being radical in their political views. He himself was such an extreme Tory that had he had the power he would have reimposed the Corn Laws. He never knowingly employed, or spent a penny with, anyone who was not prepared to claim, at least, to be Church of England.

'That can be got over,' Ellen said, after a moment's thought. 'I'll look up a few things in the advertisements, things Baxter's is unlikely to have yet, and that will be an excuse. When we made the pot-pourri, if you remember, Baxter's had no orris root.'

They were obliged to walk briskly, for the Taylor home lay on the opposite side of the town; and even when the girls had been out on such a respectable errand as taking tea there, or other reputable places, Papa liked them to be home, washed, tidied, changed from their street wear by the time he himself arrived. But even the pace at which they walked and the fact that they held their muffs high against the cold, frost-threatening air, did not account for Marion's silence. It suddenly occurred to Ellen that Marion was a little put out because she had not inquired how Miss Ruthven was. She did so.

'I found her somewhat ... changed.'

Ellen would have liked to say — For the better? But that

would give offence and the one thing which their manner of life had taught them was to maintain an amiable relationship with one another; so instead she asked, 'In what way?'

'She seemed older.' Neither of the words she had used to describe Miss Ruthven was exact, but they were the best she could find.

'Well, she is. It is two years since you saw her,' Ellen said sensibly. 'And she must be getting on.' Marion thought, *patience, resignation, matrimonial plans*; words that had not been included in the vocabulary of the Miss Ruthven she remembered.

'She seemed worried about a girl — you wouldn't remember her, she was before your time — Louise Hayward.' As they crossed the Market Square, hurried along the Buttermarket, turned into Honey Lane and then into Alma Avenue, Marion told Ellen about Louise's predicament, trying all the time to derive a little comfort from the comparison between their two lots, and failing dismally; better to have too much to do, better to be compelled to perform even menial tasks, than to have nothing, absolutely nothing to do.

Ellen, whom Miss Ruthven, disappointed at not having been presented with another Marion to instruct, had once called witless, said 'I expect she does all these things too well. I should blot the invitations or get the addresses wrong and cut horrible, thick sandwiches and pull the parson's wife's hair.'

'Louise has her living to earn,' Marion said. 'She would be dismissed ... Ellen, I've just thought of something. With Angela gone I shall never have another book from the Library.' With this simple statement, a recognition that life in future would be even more dreary and empty than it had been in the past, they were home.

Thirty years earlier a far-sighted builder had gambled upon the chance that with the coming of the railway, the building of the gasworks, the expansion of Draper's Maltings and Frewer's Iron Foundry there would be a tendency for prosperous men of business to move from Fargate and other similar areas, into more salubrious and prestigious surroundings. He had planned and built for the strictly middle-class man, not of the carriage class, the man who wished to reside within walking distance of his office or his works. So he had bought land on either side of what was then known as Goose Lane; left enough of the ancient trees to justify the name of Avenue, and

26

reared some buildings of a kind never before seen in the little country town.

A row of railings separated the tall grey houses from the footpath. Each house had two gates, one leading to the eight steps up to the front door, one leading to the rear where more steps led down into an area, off which opened the kitchen door, a coal and woodshed and a water-closet. The water-closets — there was a second one for family use wedged in half-way up the main stairway — the piped gas and water, were the selling points. The multiplicity of stairs was no disadvantage; willing, labouring legs were easily and cheaply hired. And the uniformity of the frontages was a spur rather than a deterrent; in the narrow front gardens an unacknowledged competition was waged throughout the year. Number Ten, into which, twenty years earlier, Mr. Draper with a feeling that he had arrived, had brought his bride, was distinguished by the four tubs of agapanthus lilies, two at the bottom, two at the top of the stairs that led to the door. All along Alma Avenue there were in due season displays of daffodils, tulips, geraniums, salvias, begonias, closely clipped bush roses; regular as the habits of those who had caused them to be planted.

The Draper girls sped up the stairs. Copper cans shrouded in towels awaited them. They washed. They put on their house dresses; Marion's brown velvet, Ellen's blue. As always they assisted one another in the twenty-four buttons down the back.

Ellen said, 'Marion, I have thought of something. Papa forbade *you* to set foot in Blake's. Not *me*. I can take your book back and fetch another.'

'Darling, that is splitting hairs. But if you only would, I should be everlastingly grateful.'

Almost ready they went, as one person to the chest of drawers that they shared and took, Marion from the left-hand top drawer, Ellen from the one on the right, a clean handkerchief. Marion first and then Ellen, sprinkled, from the wicker-encased flask that stood on a crocheted mat in the centre of the chest's top, exactly four drops of eau-de-Cologne. As they emerged on to the wide landing Mamma came out from the conjugal bedroom and smiled and said, 'Good evening, my dears. Did you have a nice visit with Angela?' She took precedence of them down the stairs and Papa, entering by the front door, looked up and saw them, velvet-clad, dove-grey,

27

brown and blue, their kid-slippered feet soft on the stairs, the sweet-scented aura meeting him. All present and correct! My family. He said, 'Good evening, my dears.'

The door at the top of the kitchen stairs was closed and would remain so until Betty came up to set the table; but the scent of roast pheasant, of braised celery was just discernible — Louise and many many other young women would gladly change places with you ... And I would gladly change places with any one of them, I would change places even with Betty ...

'Parson's Tonic Pills,' Ellen said, 'for colds, asthma and all pulmonic afflictions. Advertised *this* month, but not *last*, so it must be *new* and safe to ask for at both shops. We can go to Baxter's together, then I'll go to Blake's and get you a Ouida if I can, you go to Freeman's and give Angela's message.'

The threatened frost had fallen and Mamma had been apologetic about sending them out at all; but somewhere on the vast desert of the evening of yesterday she had come to the end of the wool she was using. 'I had no idea,' she said, 'it seemed quite a big ball, but it must have been *hollow*. You should wear your fur coats.' So, out of the muslin bags, smelling of lavender, thyme, rosemary and cloves — all moth repellents — they had taken the sealskin coats, the matching hats and the little ankle-high, sealskin-lined boots that constituted their winter wear. Well-clad, well-fed, most enviable, they pattered along. They bought Mamma's wool, carefully matching the two-inch piece she had given them as a guide to colour and thickness; then they went into Baxter's where Parson's Tonic Pills had never been heard of. 'We must buy something,' Marion said, recognising in Mr. Baxter's demeanour almost the identical sense of failure as she had sensed in Miss Ruthven.

Ellen said, 'Two pennyworth of liquorice, cut, please, and a packet of black-currant lozenges.' Mr. Baxter took the thick black strip of liquorice, cut it, weighed it, reached down the packet of lozenges and said, 'I trust that no member of your family is suffering from the prevalent cold.'

'Thank you. No,' Ellen said. 'We do a few errands for those who cannot get about.' She put sixpence on the counter and took up the little packages. Outside in the cold that could make itself felt through the sealskin, the silk lining and all the good woollen stuff, Ellen said, 'I don't suppose Freeman's have ever heard of it either. But it is an excuse . . . Be as quick as you can. It's too cold to wait about.'

On Freeman's forbidden door the bell jangled and from the far end, out of a kind of loose-box of polished mahogany and ground glass came the young man about whom Angela had been at once so reticent and so confiding. She had described him as handsome. This morning he was not looking his best, having a swollen nose, a black eye and above the eye a strip of sticking plaster; he also wore the slightly greenish pallor which a naturally swarthy skin takes on when its owner is not in the best of health or spirits. He wore a very clean, knee-length white coat.

'Good morning, Madam,' he said, and moved to the angle of the L-shaped counter, ready to hand down from behind the shorter one soap, scent or any toilet preparation, from behind the longer one anything in the medical line.

Brusquely, because she was nervous, Marion said:

'Are you Mr. de Brissac?'

'That is my name.'

'I have a message for you. From Miss Taylor. She asked me to tell you that she was very sorry, very sorry indeed. And that she has gone away and will not be able to see you, or to write. And that . . . that she was sorry . . .' It was difficult to look at only half a face. The young man seemed to sense the difficulty and before speaking lifted his hand so that it covered the bruised and swollen eye, the plaster and one side of the swollen nose. His hand was long and slender, an elegant hand. On his little finger he wore a heavy seal ring.

'I am most grateful,' he said. 'It was extremely kind of you to convey the message. Thank you.' With the injured half of his face covered she saw him differently, could see what Angela meant. His hair, very dark and glossy, grew beautifully from his forehead and then dipped in a romantic, Byronic curve; the visible eye was a clear grey, lustrous and long-lashed. 'May I ask you something, Miss . . . Miss . . . ?'

'My name is Draper.'

'Thank you. Miss Draper. Will you be in communication with Miss Taylor?'

No order had been issued. Angela had not involved them in

her disgrace; Papa and Mamma had received with mild interest the information that Angela was going to stay with her grandfather, Sir Miles. In the circumstances it would indeed seem strange *not* to write.

'I suppose so.'

'Then would you please be again kind and tell her that I also am sorry, very sorry. And that my injuries were slight.'

She saw then that his mouth was beautiful. As he said the word 'slight' it both smiled and sneered, mocking the word. Mocking — absurd thought — everything.

'I will do that. When I write,' she said. A feeling hitherto unknown to her, a warm, weakening, a yielding, a yearning, ran through her. She said a little breathlessly, 'Parson's Tonic Pills; have you any in stock?'

'They are on order. Friday, Saturday at latest.'

'I will look in again,' she said; and armoured in sealskin, in respectability, in virtue that had never been tested and in integrity only slightly tarnished, she was about to make for the door. Then she thought of Angela's words about Papa lashing about with his stick. What use to hustle Angela away, to forbid her nearest friends to say a word, with this possible source of gossip wide open? Had the Taylors thought of that?

She said awkward again, 'Your poor eye ... I have no wish to sound unkind; I hope it will soon be better ... but it would be a kindness to *her*, to Miss Taylor, if you would avoid telling the truth about how you came by it.'

' "What is truth, asked jesting Pilate",' the chemist's assistant said. 'Last evening I slipped on an icy patch and hit my face on a step.' The good eye said — Trust me! It also said — Those who will believe that will believe anything!

Outside, in the plain, straightforward, ordinary world, Ellen waited, cuddling a book. 'My trouble was I did not know what you had read and what you had not. *Under Two Flags* was the only Ouida there today. All right; then you owe me twopence. Did Parson's Tonic Pills work over there?'

'As an excuse, yes. But I am now more or less committed to buying some.'

'Mamma will pay — if we tell her we wanted them for Nanny.' Ellen said in her cheerful, practical way. 'And what did you think of Angela's *beau*?'

Marion tried to speak judicially. 'He is, in fact, more like Angela's mysterious French gentleman than a chemist's as-

30

sistant. In looks, in speech . . . and in demeanour. Mr. Taylor must have hit him very hard; he had a black eye and a patch on his forehead. I had the sense to ask him not to reveal how he had come by his injury. He understood.'

Ellen then voiced the doubt which Mr. Taylor was himself entertaining. 'You know, Marion, I'm not absolutely sure that you are allowed to hit a person with a stick even if he is meeting your daughter secretly. Suppose the young man made a fuss.'

'I don't think he would. He is not at all the type.'

'He seems to have made a favourable impression on *you*, too.'

'A shop assistant who uses one of Miss Ruthven's favourite quotations is something of a rarity. At least in this town.'

Marion wrote to Angela. Carefully, for now, doubtless, Angela's correspondence would be subject to the strict scrutiny which had always applied in the Draper household. The writing was rather a delectable task, calling as it did for some little exercise of skill. 'Old Nanny, whom Ellen and I visited on Tuesday has been advised to try a new remedy for her asthma, Parson's Tonic Pills. They *do* exist, but not in Bereham yet. We tried Baxter's first but without success so we were obliged to go to that horrid Mr. Freeman's shop. Fortunately he was not there himself and we were waited upon by his assistant who had had a fall and blacked his eye which gave him a somewhat sinister appearance. In contrast his manner was agreeable and he seemed to be intelligent. At least he had heard of the new remedy and was obliging enough to offer to procure it for us within a few days. We had had no time to obtain Papa's permission to go to Freeman's; we must do so before we enter the shop again, but I am sure it will be forthcoming since the errand is to benefit Nanny . . .' And that was sufficient. Angela would read between the lines and understand. Yet she found herself reluctant to quit the subject and paused for quite a while before relating how many shell boxes she and Ellen had assembled that afternoon, 'We cannot work at the gluing in the evening as the glue has an unpleasant odour.' She hoped that Angela was enjoying her stay with her grandfather. A letter that anyone could read . . .

On Friday, armed with Papa's permission — 'Well, we will make an exception, for Nanny's sake, though none of these new-fangled things work. She would do better with Friars' Balsam,' the girls entered the shop together. The young man's nose and eye were less swollen, but even more discoloured than they had been on Wednesday. The Tonic Pills, he said, had not yet arrived. There was no opportunity to say a private word because Mr. Freeman himself was behind the shorter counter, wearing the frock coat, green with age and much spilled upon, but a frock coat which marked him out as the owner of his business. He was surprised to see the Misses Draper in his establishment, and took it as a sign that a go-ahead business must, by God's law, outstrip its competitor. Parson's Tonic Pills, he said, interrupting, would almost certainly be in the shop by Monday; and could he send them as soon as they arrived? Marion said no, it was no trouble for them to look in again. He opened the flap in the counter and obsequiously bowed them to the door. All there had been time for was an exchange of glances. Above the young man's uninjured eye the narrow, clearly defined eyebrow had lifted in a question which she had answered by a nod of her head.

Monday brought, by the early post, a letter from Angela. All letters were placed by Papa's left hand, all were studied before being passed over. Marion, taking hers and recognising Angela's writing which had displeased Miss Ruthven so much that she had once called it a broken-down fence, felt her heart jerk. She hoped that Angela had been discreet. Papa was inclined, now and then, to ask whom letters were from and at unpredictable intervals demand to see them.

Angela wrote discreetly and meaningfully. 'You may have thought that the country, in October, would be *dull*. The contrary is true; there was a shooting party — twelve guns — here on Friday; two more are planned for next week. My grandpapa says he has long missed the presence of a female, "to do the honours" as he says in his old-fashioned way. He calls me *a minx* but when he says this I gather that he rather likes minxes; perhaps because, greatly daring, I made his *fearsome* old housekeeper bring out the proper dinner service. Why should he and his guests eat from plates oddly assorted and mostly cracked? He is too easy going in *some* ways. Seventy-three years old, Marion, not at all Victorian, though he saw her Coronation.' (That was the kind of sentence of which Miss Ruthven disapproved!) 'I am sorry,' the broken-fence writing ran on, 'not to be with you at the stall at the Bazaar. One of the men who came to shoot and is staying on for the next is a kind of relative, cousin once removed. Army, on half pay. Quite splendid. A V.C. at Kandahar and one day a title.' The broken-fence writing suffered a complete collapse and its meaning, patiently sorted out became incoherent; then it righted itself. 'I only wish my *dearest* friends to know this. Early days yet! But I think, perhaps by Christmas ...' Then there was a line heavily crossed out and the words, 'I wanted you and Ellen to be prepared, and to know what to say ...'

'And from whom is your letter?' Papa asked.

'From Angela, Papa.'

'Oh yes. She is staying with her grandfather.'

'Yes. And she sounds very happy.'

Mamma said, disconcertingly, 'She left very *suddenly*.'

'It would seem that her grandfather rather wished for someone to play hostess, Mamma. Would you care to read Angela's letter?' It was harmless, the term my *dearest* friends would mean nothing to the uninformed.

But, just as it was possible to feel hatred for Papa and wish him dead, so it was possible to feel a truly green-eyed envy of Angela. Discovered, disgraced, banished — to a doting old grandfather, to a new admirer, possibly to a husband; fortunate girl! While to me nothing happens, nothing ever will, and the only excitement, the only landmark in the stretch of dreary days, is the prospect of going again into Freeman's.

It then occurred to her that Angela had entrusted her with another commission — that of breaking the news of her new interest to Jean de Brissac. That was why Angela had underlined the word *dearest*.

A week ago she would have approached this business without any sympathy; the young man must have known that nothing could come of the clandestine meetings save disappointment. She might even have thought — Serve him right! But now that she had seen and spoken to him she felt differently; sorry for him. He was a foreigner, perhaps he did not understand the finer shades of class distinction in England; meeting Angela socially, at the Musical Society and being encouraged by her ... The confident, jaunty tone of Angela's letter was evidence of the progress she could make with a man in very short time ... and she had been seeing de Brissac regularly ever since September. Now, in addition to

33

having been beaten over the head with a stick he was to learn that he was virtually forgotten. Poor fellow.

It was a bright, invigorating morning and they had more shopping than usual to do. Mamma was again in need of wool and she also wanted hairpins, stockings and toilet soap; the girls needed velveteen with which to line the shell boxes and some stiff canvas from which to fashion another contribution to the stalls — some of those little pouches in which gentlemen hung their watches at bedtime. Marion, at any time a quick reader, had become so engrossed in *Under Two Flags* that she had read each evening until the candle guttered out, and now wanted another book. 'I'll go to the Library while you fetch Nanny's pills,' Ellen said.

The young man had discarded the plaster strip and so arranged his hair that the soft dark fall concealed all mark of the injury. His nose, aquiline and rather thin was its normal size and the bruise about his eye almost invisible.

'Good morning, Miss Draper. Your order has arrived. I am sorry, I have not yet had time to wrap it. Mr. Freeman is confined to his bed with lumbago.' She was relieved to hear it. Busying herself with the white paper and the little blobs of sealing wax, the young man said, without looking up, 'Have you yet been able to convey my apologies to Miss Taylor?'

'I took the first opportunity to do so. I think . . . I think you had better read this.' From the little pocket inside her muff she took Angela's letter and held it out. While he read it she turned away and studied some bottles of hair oil, each of which bore a picture of a hirsute gentleman who had obviously used the preparation with satisfactory results. Then the young man said, 'I am very glad to know that Miss Taylor is enjoying her stay in the country.' His voice was pleasantly conversational; his face bore no sign of emotion. She said, awkwardly, 'It was . . . the other part that I thought you should see.'

He smiled, his sharply curved, rather flat-surfaced lips moving again into the expression she remembered, a sweet mockery.

'If I seem stupid, forgive me. I do not aspire to be one of the dear friends to whom Miss Taylor wished to hint at such exciting news. Merely an acquaintance.' For a second Marion said nothing, but she looked at the still faintly discoloured eye. And Jean de Brissac thought — This one is *not* stupid! He put his hand to the side of his face, repeating the gesture she

34

remembered. 'That,' he said, 'was the absurdity. I think that Mr. Taylor — shall we say paid me an undeserved compliment? Suspected me of designs I had never once entertained. Miss Taylor extended to me, a stranger in a strange land, a friendliness as valuable as it is rare. I was grateful. But . . .'

The shop bell jangled, a heavy, shabbily clad woman came in. He said, 'Excuse me, please . . .'

'I want,' the woman said, 'a box of Beecham's Pills.' She was gratified to see that Mr. Freeman's new assistant, holding what looked like a long order, one item of which was already packed, white and red upon the counter, should break off to serve a chance customer; but why not? The other customer was obviously a lady, with time to spare, not like herself, with three children under four years old and a husband whose constipation made him bad-tempered and Beecham's Pills a necessity.

The little interruption had given Marion time to take from her purse elevenpence and the halfpenny, the price of the Parson's Pills. It had also given her time to recover herself, to retreat. The shop bell jangled.

'You have been so kind,' the young man said. 'So kind in conveying my apologies to Miss Taylor for a situation neither foreseen nor justified, but I am glad to know, culminating happily, that I wonder whether you would resent it if I tried to make amends? It is nothing much.' He reached down into the recesses of the counter and brought out a small parcel, wrapped in tissue paper. 'It belonged to my mother . . .'

She said, 'But I have done nothing . . .'

'Please. It is only a token.' She took it, unwrapped the paper and saw a little scent bottle, not like those most fashionable in England at the moment, either white or ruby-coloured glass with silver stoppers; this was of green glass, gilded, the gilding inside the glass, veins of gold.

'I couldn't possibly,' she said.

'Smell it, please.'

The stopper was not just a rounded knob of silver; it also was gilt, a daisy. Hardly knowing what she was about she unscrewed it and the potent, poignant concentrated scent of lily-of-the-valley rose up, swamping the mixed odours of the shop. She thought idiotically — The very breath of life . . . And she must refuse it.

No other breath of life penetrated into the stuffy claustrophobic atmosphere of Ten Alma Avenue as the days darkened and grew colder. The Church Bazaar was at least something to vary the monotony and although its first hours pursued the routine course, at about half past three something happened. The young man who had lived in her mind for some weeks, a curious double image, half Angela's mysterious French gentleman and half Freeman's shop assistant in a white coat, presented himself, alive and real by the muslin draped stall where Marion and Ellen were selling the things made by their own and other nimble fingers. In his top hat, dark coat, plaid trousers, silver-grey cravat, silver-grey gloves, he was indistinguishable from any other gentleman who was patronising the Bazaar. And he had — as Angela had once said — beautiful manners. He did not merely shift his hat; he removed it and bowed.

'Good afternoon, Miss Draper. Good afternoon . . .' He included Ellen in his greeting, but halted, on an inquiring note.

'Ellen, this is Mr. de Brissac. Mr. de Brissac, this is my sister, Miss Ellen Draper.'

It was as much as she could do to effect the introduction; the same weakening, overwhelming feeling swept over her and she was grateful for Ellen's presence, brisk and businesslike. Ellen was quite capable of thinking — Yes, Angela was not so far mistaken, and at the same time saying:

'I am sorry — no, I should say I am glad — we are almost sold out. There are some gloves . . .' But they had been knitted by somebody who had extraordinary ideas about the shape and size of the human hand. There was also — since everything must be enclosed and embroidered and elaborated — some cases designed to hold thimbles, little cones to place upon boiled eggs and and a few other articles whose purpose was less definable.

'I am late,' Jean de Brissac said. 'But I came to contribute, too.' By some sleight of hand he produced the green, gold-veined scent bottle which had made Marion turn dizzy, able only to repudiate.

'We,' Ellen said, 'are handiwork. Mrs. Marriot, over there, is Treasure Trove.'

36

'I see,' he said, and replaced the hat which must be removed anew in the greeting to Mrs. Marriot.

The hubbub of the morning had died down and Mrs. Marriot had a good, carrying voice. She said, 'Oh, Mr. Brisket, what a delightful little treasure! What a pity that Lady Mingay has gone. It would have been just the thing for her. But I am sure it will sell for at least ten shillings. Thank you very much.'

Ellen said, 'Yes, I see what you meant, Marion. And what Angela saw. Who would have thought that he was a shop assistant? But did not a number of most respectable people have to flee from France, very lately. He could be ... Marion, are you all right? Is your back hurting? Do sit down. We have nothing left to sell — except gloves for elephants.'

'I must just —' Marion said, and deserting Ellen she went over to Mrs. Marriot's Treasure Trove. The young man had moved away, accepting the coy invitation over a white-clothed table. It read, 'Come To Tea.'

'Mrs. Marriot, would you reserve that for me? I have so far spent nothing with you ... but Papa will be along presently. He will buy it for me.'

Mrs. Marriot did not wholeheartedly welcome this suggestion. She was reasonably sure that if she took the pretty little object out to Lady Mingay and said — I was so sure that you would like it — she would obtain not only the pound she meant to ask, but some measure of goodwill. On the other hand, the Draper girls worked faithfully and well, year after year; so did their mother; and Mr. Draper had made his usual morning round, spending freely. So she compromised, saying, 'It is a very pretty thing and rather unusual. Fifteen shillings?'

Papa arrived, as was his custom on such occasions, to collect and then distribute his morning's purchases. To accept the coy invitation and to treat the various poor women who had drifted in hoping to buy left-over buns or to pick up articles from the various stalls whose holders preferred to sell them very cheaply rather than carry them home, store them for a year and bring them out next December. As Mrs. Marriot had said in a caustic moment, what isn't sold by twelve o'clock is simply unsaleable.

So now Papa, his purchases made well before twelve o'clock, stood under the awning with its playful invitation;

and he had seven poor sycophantic women around him, stir-
ring in the sugar, slopping up the tea, gobbling the
buns — though Marion noticed, as she had done before, that
every now and again one of the women would slip something
into her canvas bag. She felt a little ashamed to attack Papa in
a most vulnerable moment, but it had to be done.

'Papa,' Marion said,'Mrs. Marriot has such a *pretty* thing
left on her stall. I long to possess it and she agreed to reserve it
for me. Until you arrived. I am afraid it will cost you fifteen
shillings.'

'Good gracious!' Mr. Draper exclaimed in mock dismay;
'Fifteen shillings! What can it be? A diamond tiara?'

'Oh no, I do not know, Papa, what it is exactly. But it is
pretty and I would like to own it.'

Mr. Draper wore a thick gold watch chain from which
hung a cylinder, also of gold, a sovereign case. It worked on a
spring; a pressure, a tilting and out into the palm of the waiting hand fell the coin — the most sought-after coin in the
world, the English sovereign, the pound sterling.

The women who had accepted Mr. Draper's invitation to
take tea with him under the awning that said 'Come To Tea',
watched while he performed the manoeuvre. Most of them on
less than fifteen shillings a week fed hungry husbands, growing children, paid rent, had boots mended.

'You girls will be the ruin of me,' Mr. Draper said jocosely.
'Buy whatever it is. And you may keep the change. And now,
Mrs. Beeton, Mrs. Mison, Mrs. Poume, another cup of tea?
Another bun? A sandwich?'

Marion took and held in her hand the pretty little thing
which had been offered her as a gift, which she had refused,
and which was now hers. And there was Jean de Brissac. He
said, 'It would seem that you were meant to have it.'

After that there was Christmas; two deadly dull dinner-
parties at Ten Alma Avenue, three, equally dull, elsewhere.
And then January. 'A happy New Year,' everybody said to
everybody else.

In the Rectory the new year brought Mr. Marriot face to
face with the question of whether it would be worth while to
continue the dwindling Musical Society.

'I think not,' his wife said positively. She was far more
worldly than her husband and, like Mr. Draper, could see the
basic weakness of that experiment. 'The truth is that what is

open to all is valued by none. To get anything really going you must have support from the middle class.' She thought with complacency of her Bazaar which had been a great success.

'I had hoped,' Mr. Marriot said wistfully, 'to bring a little pleasure and a touch of culture within the reach of all. But with only six regular attendants . . .'

Mrs. Marriot, after years of marriage, was still fond of her husband and hated to see him discouraged.

'It must be done *gradually*,' she said. 'We must form some Society which it will be regarded as a privilege to join; and then we can admit working-class people by degrees. And there is another thing to consider; seven o'clock in the evening is a most inconvenient time; it disrupts the evening meal. I am practically certain that when Mr. Draper refused to allow the girls to join it was that which he had in mind.' She herself had had almost a quarter of a century of disrupted meals, meals put forward, meals delayed, with cooks and maids smoulderingly resentful. 'Now, let me think . . . A Literary Society, perhaps. Held here in our drawing-room. Not open to all. By invitation and commencing at a quarter past eight. I think it very possible that Lady Mingay would join.'

'The enlightenment of Lady Mingay's leisure was not my object.'

'I know. But one must start somewhere. If we could make a small, thriving Society, then we could launch out, hire the Guildhall again and have Penny Readings such as dear Mr. Dickens used to give. And then we could interest the poorer people by running a competition for original poems or bits of folk-lore. That would make their inclusion seem natural. I am not trying to be a snob.'

'My dear, you have no need to *try*,' Mr. Marriot said, but he said it mildly, with a smile, and she took it with a hearty laugh.

'Just to show you,' she said, 'and to salve your conscience, I shall invite to the first meeting, that nice Mr. Brisket — he never missed a Musical, and Mr. Clegg and Miss Sharp. I will also,' she said, bravely shouldering the burden, 'serve tea at a quarter past nine.'

Mr. Marriot saw that another compromise was necessary. And so the Literary Society was born and Lady Mingay consented to join and even suggested what she thought was a more attractive name — A Literary Salon. Mr. Clegg and

Miss Sharp realised that they were specially favoured beings and showed their gratitude by doing little helpful things like moving the dining-room chairs into the drawing-room and trotting about with tea-trays. Jean de Brissac was less conscious of being honoured, but he offered to give a little talk about French novelists. Mr. Draper, unable to find any adequate reason why Marion and Ellen should refuse what amounted to a personal invitation to spend an evening in the Rectory drawing-room in most respectable company, gave his grudging consent.

The Salon opened on the second Thursday in January. Nice Mr. Brisket arrived in good time and took upon himself the duties of usher, inquiring whether people wished to sit near to or away from the fire, sometimes shifting chairs about. In the midst of shaking hands and speaking greetings designed to make this seem to be a gay social occasion, Mrs. Marriot found time to note his activities and approve them; he was behaving almost like a son of the house, she thought quite fondly. She had no son.

Jean de Brissac's interest in people's comfort and seating arrangement ceased abruptly when Marion and Ellen arrived. He led them to three chairs which occupied a space beside the china cabinet, and when they sat down, sat down himself.

His proximity prevented Marion from benefiting from what Lady Mingay assured her hearers was in no sense a lecture, simply a little informal talk about Her Majesty's genius as a writer. Mrs. Marriot had insisted that Lady Mingay as the most important lady present must be asked to give the first talk. It went a little wrong because Lady Mingay, herself a writer of some trite verse, seemed to suffer some confusion between her own work and that of her sovereign. The applause when she finished and sat down was partly sycophantic, partly polite but in even larger measure due to relief.

Jean de Brissac said, 'I am able to see a resemblance between the ladies.' He spoke solemnly and only Marion, catching just a flicker of malicious amusement in his eyes, realised that a joke was here, simply waiting for acknowledgement. She decided to acknowledge it and gave him her sudden, flashing smile. Ellen said, 'The resemblance has been much remarked,' in rather a crushing tone.

Mr. Marriot rose to thank Lady Mingay and to offer foretastes of delights to come. He realised as he faced his audience that it was, almost to a man, the same as he faced twice a day every Sunday. But it would be wrong to resent this; these were the faithful. His efforts to obey the biblical order to go into the highways and by-ways and *compel* them to come in had met with another defeat. Mrs. Marriot faced her own problem. Her budget simply did not run to providing *good* tea for some unspecified number; but Lady Mingay and a few other ladies would recognise what was called 'kitchen tea' and might take it amiss. 'The little blue-lustre teapot, please, Mr. Brisket,' she said to that helpful young man, again active and handy. Jean de Brissac, having obtained two cups of tea from the little blue-lustre teapot, carried them to Marion and Ellen and said, in a low, conspiratorial voice, 'It is the *best* tea!' Ellen missed the allusion but Marion caught it and smiled again and said, 'I always loved the Mad Hatter.'

Encouraged, he asked, 'Are you to be called for, Miss Draper?'

'Oh no. It is so short a distance.'

'May I, then, have the honour of escorting you home?'

Taking control of the situation again because Marion, ordinarily so handy with words, seemed at a loss, Ellen said:

'It is very kind of you, Mr. de Brissac, but quite unnecessary. There are two of us; the road is well-lit and other people are going our way. Indeed, Alma Avenue is well represented here.'

'I think it was a bit cheeky,' Ellen said as they pattered along the lime avenue which led from the Rectory to St. Mary's Church and then debouched into Honey Lane which after about a hundred yards branched off into Alma Avenue. 'After all, we only know him through Angela. And we have never been properly introduced.'

'I know.'

'And Papa would be very much annoyed. Mr. Freeman's shop assistant ...'

'I know.'

'If everybody from whom we ever bought anything walked us home,' Ellen said, 'it would look decidedly odd.'

'I know.'

'Why do you keep saying "I know" in that gloomy voice, Marion? Of course, I know you know. I saw, at the Bazaar, why Angela had become infatuated and you thought him unusual. But he should not presume on his looks or his manners or,' Ellen said shrewdly, 'on being the only mysterious Frenchman in a place like Bereham.'

'He did not presume. He merely offered to walk home with us.'

Ellen took some steps before she spoke again; then she said, 'And you wanted to accept the offer. You've fallen in love with him, too.'

'Yes. From the first moment I saw him. I realised that this evening.'

'Marion! Think! Mr. Taylor hit him over the head with a stick and sent Angela away. What would Papa do? Darling, this is all nonsense. He is good-looking, he has nice manners, he is well dressed; and he seems to have ingratiated himself with the Marriots. But you cannot, you must not ... In any case, I am going to have *nothing* to do with it. Angela taught me a lesson ... And now for you to go and do the very same thing. It is entirely ridiculous.'

'You are too young to understand, Ellen. Nobody in her senses would choose such a thing to happen, but when it does ... It happens and there is absolutely nothing one can do about it.'

After that they walked in silence until they were home. The front gate creaked and once they were within it, mounting the steps, both were conscious of being again within Papa's orbit and of the necessity for unity.

'I am sorry if I sounded sharp,' Ellen said.

'I am sorry if I sounded silly.'

They went in and reported that there had been between forty and fifty people present and that Lady Mingay had given a most *interesting* talk, all about Queen Victoria.

Mr. Draper looked at the black marble clock and checked it against his watch. Mrs. Marriot, tackling him personally, pleading that any venture, to be successful must appeal to the young, had mentioned tea at nine-fifteen. The serving of tea to a considerable number, and the drinking, the taking leave; yes, at least half an hour. They were back in good time and he was able to say, with sincerity, 'I am glad that you have had an entertaining evening.'

The next Thursday evening, potentially entertaining, found Ellen dreadfully torn between common sense and sisterly loyalty.

'Really, Marion, you put me in an impossible position. You know what would happen if Papa ever knew.'

'Darling, I know. But to whom else can I look for help? I'd do as much for you.'

'But, Marion, no good can come of it. And harm could. I shudder to think ...'

'Ellen *please*. I know how you feel. You are too young to understand; but one day you will. And you know that I would always stand by you.'

Ellen stood by; on that and several other Thursday evenings. Her role was passive. On leaving the Rectory she and Marion hurried along and at the end of the lime avenue did not proceed into Honey Lane but turned instead into what was known as The Old Cloister, part of the ruined Abbey out of which St. Mary's, once a mere Lady Chapel had been preserved as a parish church. It was a place generally avoided because though it was four hundred years and more since any living monk had walked there, phantom ones were said to be seen. Indeed, the sexton, a hardy old man, swore that he had seen a cowled figure glide through the ruins and go into the church at a point where there was a built-up doorway. Into this eerie place, all ruins and nettles and elderberry bushes, Ellen and Marion turned and presently the young man whom Marion now called Johnny, joined them. He and Marion then walked off and Ellen sat on a stump and waited, all her nerves on edge. She disliked the trysting-place and threatened Marion that if she and Johnny went out of earshot, leaving her with the ghosts, she would never wait again, she would go straight home, she would tell Papa ... In fact she was more frightened of Papa finding out than she was of the ghosts and was terrified that he would notice that they were ten minutes later on every subsequent Thursday than they had been on the first. So the lovers' time for the exchanging of kisses and embraces was limited by Ellen's impatience and the last clutching clasp was usually interrupted by her reminder that it was time to go. 'Marion, we must *run*. Marion, unless you come now I shall never wait for you again.'

It was all hurried and unsatisfactory, and at the same time so wonderful that for Marion life became enchanted, the hours that had dragged so tediously now spent in happy memories of last Thursday, joyful anticipations of next.

Ellen's manner became astringent. 'Really, Marion, you must pull yourself together; anyone with half an eye could see that you were in love. I wonder Papa has not observed already.' In fact Mr. Draper had observed a change, but a change for the better. It did not surprise him, he had always known that Marion would outgrow her childish sulkiness. He could imagine, for instance, how only a few months ago she would have behaved over the reassignment of bedrooms. Now she took her banishment to inferior accommodation in the right spirit, meek, cheerful, making the best of things.

For Mamma's scheme to make the little half-basement room under the stairs into a bedroom for Ada — thus saving her from all climbing — had come to nothing. 'I should be nervous, down there all by myself and everybody else so far away. I know I can't manage the top stairs any more, they're the steepest. So maybe my time has come.'

'Ada, you must not say such things,' Mamma said. 'How could we manage without you? I shall think of something.'

The solution was obvious; move Betty and Ada down, Marion and Ellen up. But there were difficulties. The young ladies of a family naturally owned more clothes than the maids; they had a wardrobe, they had a chest-of-drawers.

'And even could they be got up those steep stairs,' said Ellen, the practical one, 'there would be no room to move about. Our bed, for one thing, is bigger than theirs.'

Mamma played put and take in her mind, hampered by the fact that Papa's dressing-room was sacrosanct, and that the guest-room, though seldom used, was a necessity to any decent establishment. In her secret mind she had always hated the prim, grey, tight-lipped house with its basement kitchen, its many stairs. She had spent her happy girlhood in a great sprawling farmhouse where anything up to twenty people could sleep in moderate comfort and no matter how noisily she played the piano, it disturbed nobody. But she faced the present problem sensibly. Ada and Betty could move down into the room now occupied by Marion and Ellen. Their room, with its cupboard for clothes, would suffice for Ellen. Given a single bed it would even accommodate a chest-of-drawers. *If* Marion would not mind the semi-basement room under the steps that led up to the front door.

'It would be only for a time, Marion dear. I know that Ada cannot last for ever, but I do wish her last years to be as comfortable as possible. Would you object?'

'Of course not, Mamma. I should not be in the least nervous in the basement.'

Gratefully Mamma spoke of hanging better curtains in the

little room and the possibility that the wardrobe could be moved down.

Ellen was secretly rather pleased at the prospect of having her own room where she would not be disturbed by Marion's habit of reading in bed.

And when Marion thought of the little basement room she thought of Johnny. As she now thought of him in every connection; the first snowdrops and crocuses, the first green buds, the promise of spring in an apple-green sky and in the first, premature bird cry. She had already counted the weeks, the Thursdays until Easter when the Literary Salon would close down for the summer and it was like a foretaste of death. Now, with a room of her own she could look forward to living, not from Thursday to Thursday but from evening to evening.

Her first move was to oil the hinges on the screeching gate. Her second to absolve Ellen from further complicity. The new plan, though it promised great happiness also threatened enormous risk and Ellen must not even be aware of it. Therefore on the Thursday evening after the move was made, at the end of the lime avenue, Marion instead of swerving off into the Old Cloister, walked ahead and turned into Honey Lane. Ellen was greatly relieved, but surprised, too, and curious.

'Have you quarrelled?' she asked, almost timidly.

'No; there was no quarrel,' Marion said managing to inject the implication that although there had not been a quarrel there had been something equally final.

'Oh, I am so glad and happy, Marion. I knew all along that you would get over it, just as Angela did. And I kept thinking all the time how horrid it would be if Papa should find out and there was a terrible row over a mere infatuation.'

Now that it was over and Marion had returned to her senses Ellen was prepared to give her own opinion of Johnny and indeed of the whole affair.

'I would not deny that he has charm,' she said. Johnny had always gone out of his way to flatter and cajole her. 'But there is nothing behind it. I could see, of course, because I was not in love with him. I never felt that he was sincere. And I must confess that his style of dressing seems pretentious and not altogether suitable.'

'There have been no sumptuary laws in England for a long time,' Marion said rather coldly.

'What are sumptuary laws?'

'Laws ordering that one must dress according to one's station in life.'

After a few more steps Ellen said, 'Are you sad about it?'

'Not in the least. But I do think I would prefer not to talk about it.'

'Then we won't,' Ellen said happily. 'I will never mention the subject again.' She squeezed Marion's arm. 'I am so glad it is all over and done with and you are yourself again.'

On this as on every other ordinary evening the household at Ten Alma Avenue retired at ten o'clock. Papa made his round, locking all three doors, the front, the kitchen and the one in the conservatory, too. He looked to the window fastenings and then went upstairs, taking the keys with him. All those for whom he was responsible were now safe in their beds, well fed, well housed, well guarded.

At eleven o'clock, obeying the instructions in a long letter from Marion — a letter beginning, 'Johnny Darling, a wonderful thing has happened ...' — Jean de Brissac walked along Alma Avenue, let himself in by the now-silent gate, took the few steps over the little sloping garden and into the shadow cast by the eight steps up to the front door. The better curtains which Mamma had provided were not quite closed and a streak of light was visible as a guide. He tapped very gently on the window, a sound inaudible to any but a waiting ear. Marion then blew out the candle, parted the curtains and opened the window, which unlike the others in the house was a casement. The little room had been designed as a sleeping place for servants, unpredictable creatures, so the window was stoutly barred. It was just possible for Johnny standing at the lowest level of the little garden and straining upwards, and Marion, kneeling on the floor and craning outwards, to exchange kisses; it was possible for hand to reach for hand, it was possible to talk. There was no longer the time limit of ten minutes, or the sense of Ellen waiting; but in other ways it was less satisfactory as a meeting place than the Old Cloister and very soon Johnny whispered, 'Darling, you must let me in.' He had been quite certain that that was what Marion intended to do when she wrote of wonderful news and a room of her own down in the basement.

'I cannot. The doors are locked and the keys on Papa's dressing-table.'

'There must be other windows.'

46

There were. One in the kitchen, also barred. All the others, due to the design of the house were high above ground level. To clean them Betty needed the taller step-ladder. Also they were sash windows, and they rumbled. Equally important was that she dared not move about on the next floor with only a ceiling between her and Papa.

She relayed all this in a muted voice.

'There must be *some* way,' Johnny said. 'This is worse. I want to hold you in my arms.' She wanted to be held. She realised that she had been mistaken in thinking that this was a wonderful thing and that lovers whose bodies had known close, if inconclusive embraces, could be content with kisses and hand-clasps between bars, and with talk.

'I will find a way,' she promised recklessly, her mind veering wildly between plans for stealing the back-door key and replacing it before morning when Betty, taking up Papa's hot water, retrieved the keys and unlocked the doors, and plans for filing through the iron bars. Prisoners were said to have managed such performances.

'Tomorrow?'

'If possible, by tomorrow.'

They kissed again and he said, 'Until tomorrow, *chérie.*' She was always pleased when he used that term, so entirely his own. But after he had gone softly away she lay for a long time wondering whether, and how, she would be able to keep her promise. A forged key? Reading romantic novels had made her aware of their existence and she had some idea that wax was involved, but exactly how? She thought of stealing the key to the kitchen door; it stuck out, never used, from the moment Betty unlocked the door to the moment when Papa locked it. Take it to Rancy's, ironmongers and ask for a duplicate? Very dangerous; she was known in that shop. Mr. Rancy did a lot of work for Papa; he might casually, innocently mention the matter. Could the door be wedged in some way so that when Papa locked it it did not lock?

Betty was upstairs; Ada was making a beef-steak pudding which to be up to standard must boil, very gently, for at least six hours.

'It's that door, Miss Marion. I knew you'd notice it, sleeping down here. Rattling. I've said to Betty sometimes it's enough to drive a body mad.'

'I can see no cure for it,' Marion said. She had seen all that she needed to see. In this door, when the key turned and the tongue of the lock shot out it did not enter a socket in the door-post, it entered and was held by a kind of case of brass, properly polished, attached to the door-post by two screws, one at the top, one at the bottom. Remove one screw and swing the case upwards or downwards . . . All one needed was a screw-driver.

'Darling, go very softly round to the back. Get on to the other path. Go round and wait. There are more steps down. I will bring a candle.' She had already used the screw-driver and by the time Johnny had stolen around the house and reached the area, she had the door open.

She was ignorant of the mechanics of love; partly because at school she had never formed a friendship intimate enough to permit of the handing on of information, some wildly distorted, some speculative and superstitious, some very practical. The books she read had stopped short with a passionate kiss and the avowal of everlasting love. But the body had a knowledge of its own and in the Old Cloister, armoured in whalebone, linen, broadcloth, it *knew*; and so did Johnny's; and now in a secret place, time no longer to be considered, the night was their own.

What she had not counted upon was the effect. The shattering, the uplift, the sensual pleasure beyond the reach of the imagination. The very breath of life, hinted at in the scent of lily-of-the-valley, caught fleetingly in a chemist's shop, now expanded, filled the whole universe. For this and to this she had been born. Every sunset, every book, every line of poetry, every flower, now all one in the merging; the entry into another dimension.

When it was over she was sorry that it should have taken place in this small bedroom with the faint, pervading kitchen odour. It should have happened in some vast pink marble palace or in a green glade where wild hyacinths grew, or on one of those palm-shaded beaches where brown boys gathered shells. But there it was, it had happened here, with Papa and Mamma and Ellen, and Ada and Betty sleeping, all innocent, above stairs. And there was Johnny to be let out; the lock to be readjusted.

It was partly to fight off the sense of anti-climax that she sat down immediately and began to write to him. She wrote that she hoped that her easy yielding would not lead to any les-

48

sening of his esteem for her; she wrote that she now regarded herself as his wife; she wrote that she was the happiest woman in the world and pitied all others; she wrote that she was already longing for tomorrow evening. As thoughts occurred to her she set them down, writing quickly, eagerly and lovingly.

She was without any sense of wrong-doing. Nothing in her upbringing had led towards the Puritan conscience which would have accused her of sin. Mr. Draper was not one of these weak disciplinarians who must always make reference to God. Within his own sphere he *was* God and his will was sufficient. Church-going was as perfunctory a social duty as being correctly dressed on any occasion. Mr. Marriot's sermons were strings of gentle platitudes. Miss Ruthven had been agnostically inclined and her moral teaching had largely concerned itself with doing unto others as one would be done by and being true to oneself. So in Marion's joy there was no feeling of having sinned in a manner likely to invite punishment. She knew that the letter must be smuggled out and posted without Ellen's knowledge; but she had managed to post one earlier in the week, she could manage again. And if it were slipped into the pillar-box by eleven o'clock it would be delivered to Johnny's lodgings at about five and await him when he returned from work.

While Marion wrote Johnny walked swiftly home. He was jubilant; a not-inexperienced seducer he was able to measure the force of her response and felt that he was now sure of her. He had her now. He judged from the way in which the Draper girls were clad and guarded that Mr. Draper was a doting father; a few casual inquiries had informed him that there was no son in the family, nor even a nephew being schooled to take over the business. He did not delude himself so far as to think that a prosperous maltster would welcome a penniless shop assistant as a son-in-law; there would be protests; but if Marion stood firm and said — This is the man I love, the only man I wish to marry, the doting father would give in and very soon see the difference between Jean de Brissac and the ordinary employed man. Other people, Mrs. Marriot was one, had seen it. Jean de Brissac had great confidence in his charm, in his looks, his manners, even his clothes.

He had known from an early age that his one hope was to make an advantageous marriage; family circumstances had taught him that. His claim to be connected with the noble family of de Brissac was not without foundation, but the

49

branch to which he belonged had, for three generations, been penurious, mere peasant farmers. His grandfather and his father had both married serving girls with no dowries save physical strength and fertile wombs; but an uncle had married well and then, from the new sphere of prosperity, found a husband for one of his sisters. The old French sense of family was still active however and the young Jean was frequently confronted by the sight of his cousins, well clad, well fed, gently spoken, possessors of many enviable things. Manners and speech could be copied, clothes were occasionally handed down, on visits some of the possessions would be momentarily shared, but the real things — enough money to live without worry, a solid *bourgeois* position in life one must attain for oneself. His immediate family thought that young Jean had done very well for himself when, after a long, gruelling, unpaid apprenticeship — *un apprentissage* — he became a chemist; but he was dissatisfied, seeing clearly that without money to buy or hire a shop of his own, he was doomed to life as a hireling. He had come to London because he believed, like many untravelled Frenchmen, that England was practically classless, a place where the old systems of arranged weddings had been abandoned. This, he quickly discovered was far from true; and since in London his looks, his charm, his clothes went virtually unnoticed, he had thought that he might do better in a smaller community. So here he was in Bereham, with three failures as an adventurer behind him. One affair in London, with his employer's daughter had led to his dismissal without that essential thing, a reference; from another angry father he had only just escaped by slipping out of his jacket; in Bereham Mr. Taylor had cracked his head with a stick. So far he had had no luck at all, but he now sensed that things would be different. For one thing Marion was different; she was serious, in the French sense of the word. She had dignity, intelligence and, he thought, strength of mind. He now knew that she had a sexually passionate nature.

He read her letter over one of those sustaining but often rather indigestible 'teas' which Mrs. Fenner served up to her four young men lodgers. He was delighted to see that the letter contained nothing missish, no mawkish regrets over what had happened, none of the 'it must never happen again', stuff. She was eagerly looking forward to this evening; she looked upon herself as his wife. A few more such evenings and he would begin to move towards the next stage, a meeting with Mr. Draper so that the maltster could see for himself that Jean de Brissac was no ordinary shop assistant.

When he first mentioned this idea to Marion he was astounded by her reaction.

'It would be fatal,' she said. 'If Papa ever knew that I had spoken to you, he would be so angry. I should never see you again. And life without you now, Johnny, would be quite insupportable.'

'You think he would object to me because I am poor, and work in a shop?'

'No,' she said, truthfully. 'Because you are a man. Papa does not intend either Ellen or me to marry.'

'How can you know that?'

'Partly from what he has said when other girls become engaged or married. When Angela's engagement was announced, for instance. And on other occasions. Also, apart from that . . . After all, darling, I have lived with him for almost eighteen years. I *know* him.'

'But unless I meet him and gain his approval we shall never make any progress, *chérie*.'

'Does that matter? We have so much, darling. We must not endanger what we have.'

She was completely content with what she had. To her romantic nature even the secrecy of it all leant an added enchantment. Each time in the day when she came down to her bedroom she would glance across the kitchen and see the door to the area, looking so ordinary, and somewhere inside her something would turn over at the thought that it was not an ordinary door at all, it was the entrance through which love had come, and would come again. She had not felt a pang of envy for Angela, home again, everything forgiven and forgotten, a dark blue sapphire shining on her finger, preparations for a large fashionable wedding in June already going forward. How could Marion, with Johnny for a lover, envy anyone?

Jean de Brissac perceived that he had not been wrong in thinking that Marion had strength of mind — though he now called it stubbornness. He also perceived that if he were ever to make Mr. Draper's acquaintance it must be done without Marion's connivance. He underestimated her stated fear of and understanding of her father. Every now and again he had a dark suspicion that her reluctance to bring the whole issue to a head stemmed from her reluctance to make public the fact that she had fallen in love with a man of no estate. That she did love him, he could not possibly doubt; on the rather narrow bed installed so that the wardrobe could be accommodated in the small room, and in letter after letter he had adequate proof of her love, but in her repeated assertion, 'Papa must not know,' he saw equal proof of her reluctance to take the next, the necessary step. He decided that she must be forced to it.

On the last Thursday in May there came another of the annual landmarks in Bereham's social life, the Rectory Garden Party. Years ago Mrs. Marriot had observed that late May usually brought better weather than June. Also June was crowded with others functions; particularly weddings.

This year she was right again; it was a beautiful day; there was a crowd of people, all in gay mood. The Rectory Garden Party was a bit of a hybrid combining a social occasion with the perpetual need to raise funds for the church. There were side shows, a competitive croquet match, a Hoop-La stall, another stall upon which some of the left-over articles from the Bazaar were exposed for sale; and in a ruinous summerhouse, draped with two old curtains and a rather handsome Paisley shawl, a fortune-teller, an innovation this year. Mr. Marriot had been against it; fortune-telling smacked of black magic, of a belief in predestination, things not easily acceptable to a middle-of-the-road clergyman. But Mrs. Marriot had overridden him, saying, 'Alfred, what does it matter if it turns in an honest penny, or pound. I *know* it is all nonsense — so does everybody else. Whatever she says will be forgotten by next morning.'

Ellen and Marion took their turn in manning the Hoop-La stall. Jean de Brissac patronised it — two shillings' worth and won nothing. Marion, keeping up the pretence in front of Ellen that the whole thing was over and done with, turned aside in the little hot, canvas-enclosed space and busied herself with the mending of a toy, a model windmill which one of the hoops had injured. It was left to Ellen to say, 'Good afternoon, Mr. de Brissac,' and presently, 'Oh, bad luck!' and 'So near.'

Papa seemed to know exactly when their turn of duty was done and was there, ready to conduct them, as soon as they were relieved, to the refreshment stall, a long white-clothed table set out in the shade of the cedar tree. Here again the ambivalent nature of the Garden Party was evident. Refreshments were not sold, but between the urn and the teacups at one end and the great bowl of fruit cup at the other there was a box labelled 'Repair Fund'.

Mr. Draper had seen to it that before his daughters took up their Hoop-La duties they had had a sustaining cup of tea, so he now guided them to the fruit-cup end of the table where he was forestalled by a handsome, well-dressed young man who took the silver ladle and filled a glass and handed it to Ellen who said, 'Thank you,' in a muted voice. The young man filled a glass for Marion. Mr. Draper looked at him closely. A stranger! On these occasions Mrs. Marriot called upon all available relatives and acquaintances, but they were always introduced. This young man had not been. So Mr. Draper said, 'Thank you, I will help myself,' and, in the deep shade of the cedar tree, he and Marion and Ellen stood and sipped. Only Marion knew that Johnny had manoeuvred an opportunity for the chance, casual meeting upon which he was set; and she had failed him. Ellen suspected that Johnny Brisket was dogging Marion. She said brightly, 'Papa, let us have our fortunes told, please.'

Papa said, 'So long as you understand that it is a lot of nonsense, my dear, I have no objection. Suppose I go first. Mrs. Marriot said something about the woman being a gypsy. Let me see if she is clean and civil.'

For a gypsy she was exceptionally clean and very civil. She asked, 'By cards, by palm or by crystal, sir?' He chose cards and she shuffled them, asked him to cut, to choose. She said, 'You are, sir, a very lucky man. Very lucky. You have had troubles which you have overcome. There are other troubles ahead, but you will overcome them in the same way.' She then told him that he had excellent health and would see his eightieth birthday.

'Your next two customers are my daughters,' he said. 'I should be obliged if you would refrain from telling them anything of a sentimental nature. Or, of course, anything unpleasant.'

'You are entitled to a third cut of the cards, sir,' the woman said.

'I will not waste more of your time,' Mr. Draper said, in his most gracious way. For a gypsy she was very clean, and she was civil, and she had been warned. He went out into the sunshine and said, 'You may try her.'

'You go first, Ellen, because you are due to help with the croquet. I have nothing else to do except help Mrs. Taylor and Angela to pack up the oddments.'

Ellen chose to have her fortune told by crystal and the gypsy predicted for her a happy life. 'You'll never want,' she said. 'You'll always get your own way — in the end. There's a little sorrow, but you'll get over it and live to a ripe old age.' With that Ellen seemed quite content, somewhat to the gypsy's surprise; most young ladies wished to hear about handsome young men coming into their lives.

'For a shilling,' Ellen said, emerging from under the Paisley shawl, 'it really is very little. But all good.'

'By palm,' Marion said, offering her choice. She held out her hands and the woman who had some skill in palmistry — the cards and the crystal were garden party trimmings — said, 'Oh,' and then hesitated. Nothing of a sentimental nature, nothing unpleasant. It left so little to say, particularly of hands such as these. 'You're a very clever young lady,' she said at last. 'Yes, you have a good head on you. Health. Now there I must give you a word of warning. You must look to your health and be very careful not to overdo things. In any way.' She was, within limits, a conscientious palmist and there were other warnings which she could have given; but she had been warned herself. She looked up, met Marion's grave stare in the shrouded light and said, 'You understand me? You need to be careful *over everything.*'

'Thank you,' Marion said.

Three shillings earned in little over as many minutes; sixpence of each for the fortune-teller, sixpence for the repair fund; that was the arrangement, satisfactory to both sides. As Marion ducked under the shawl the gypsy muttered a charm, a few meaningless words, their origin lost in antiquity, something you said when you heard bad news or tried to sell linen pegs to somebody with a cold or a cough.

'It was the perfect opportunity,' Johnny said quite angrily. 'I timed it exactly and all you had to do was to greet me and effect an introduction with your papa. You behaved as though I had been a waiter.'

'Darling, please, please, do not be cross. It really was as

much as I could do to take the glass and say "thank you". You looked so handsome and I thought how perfect it would be, how happy I should have been, could I have taken your arm and spent the remainder of the afternoon in your company. Johnny, please. Perhaps it was cowardly of me, perhaps I should be ashamed, but I know Papa. Compared with him Mr. Taylor has an angelic temper.'

Not a very clever thing to say. She hastened to amend it.

'Truly Johnny, my caution is not entirely selfish. If Papa thought I was sufficiently interested in you to make an introduction, he might do *you* some damage.'

'How could he damage me?'

'He would find a way. He is ruthless. And jealous. Nobody understands. Look at this.' She reached out and took from her bedside table a copy of *Adam Bede*, leather-bound, gilt-edged, a very handsome book. 'I won — not this book, a cheaper copy, as a prize at school. I was very proud of it and *stupid* enough to say that I should always value it because Miss Ruthven had thought me worthy of it and had written my name in it. Do you know what Papa did? He said he had never read the book, so he borrowed it and spilt a cup of coffee over it. He then bought me this copy, better in every way, except for the inscription. Look. *From her loving papa.* It should read, *From her possessive papa.* And Johnny that is true. Nothing must come to us but by his gift.'

'Then what future have we? If you are so much afraid of him, or ashamed of me, to what can we look forward?'

'To the time when I am twenty-one and may marry whom I wish without asking his permission.'

Much good that would do! Four valuable years wasted.

She could see that he was hurt, diminished in his own opinion. She cast about in her mind for some restorative.

'Darling, do you like brandy?'

'Cognac? Of all the things I miss in England, cognac is foremost. In France even a working man,' he used the term in self-derision, with that eloquent twist of the mouth, 'can drink cognac occasionally.'

'This may not be very *good* brandy,' she said humbly. 'It is what Ada uses . . . but it is on this floor. Tomorrow I will take some from the sideboard . . .' That would not be difficult. From shopkeepers and workpeople Papa demanded value for money, but he was not one of those men who marked the level in the decanter or counted bottles.

She fetched, from the kitchen cupboard, and Johnny accepted, the peace offering. It even made him change the subject.

'This,' he said, 'may settle my stomach. It was again today the fat-and-lean pork which does not agree with me.'

He was inclined to talk about his stomach. Perhaps because he was French.

She watched him sipping.

'Is it all right?'

'It is not good. Nor is it bad,' he said. Inside herself, in her heart, in her head a more intoxicating brew fermented and presently she said:

'Johnny. I know that my behaviour this afternoon has made you doubt the sincerity of my love. There you are mistaken. Listen, I love you so very much that I am prepared to run away and go with you anywhere, somewhere where Papa could not find us, and marry you. Once we were married he could do nothing.'

Of all the dim-witted ideas!

'*Chérie*, it is unthinkable. It would be to condemn you to a life of poverty.'

'I would not mind being poor, darling. If we were together I should enjoy it.'

'You have never been poor. Never in your life have you spent a day not knowing where your next meal would be or where in the night you would sleep. I have had that experience and I assure you it is nothing to enjoy. On what I earn — even if I found another job immediately — the two of us would be very poor.'

'But *I* could work, Johnny. And I would. In London I should be free to work. I would do anything. I would scrub steps.' Her face was alight with eagerness.

'London is a place where for every job, even the scrubbing of steps, there are four people ready to cut each other's throats. And for one bed there are four people willing to do the same.'

'Some other place then, darling.'

He said sombrely, 'For the poor all places are alike. No, no, my Marion, for us the only hope is to act as you should have acted this afternoon. Allow your father to know me and let him see that you love me. Unless you are ashamed of loving a chemist's assistant.'

'Johnny, you know that that is not true. How can I convince you? I swear that if this afternoon I could have said — Papa, this is the Marquis de Brissac — it would have made no difference. No difference at all. If we wait for his consent we shall never be married.'

She and Ellen had compared notes on their fortunes and it was significant that marriage was mentioned in neither.

Unappeased, Johnny left without any love-making. In fact, for her it should not have been possible tonight. But she was two days late this month. Not that two days was anything to worry about.

Among the June weddings was Angela's. Marion and Ellen had seen little of her lately. Her fiancé's family was large and scattered about the west of England from Westmorland to Wiltshire; she had made visits to them all. She had also stayed with her rich godmother who lived in London and was providing her with a lavish trousseau.

Ellen was to be one of the six bridesmaids. It was her second time to serve in that capacity. Marion, just an inch too tall, had never been a bridesmaid. Mamma and Marion were both to have new dresses, very fine, Mamma's dove-grey satin, Marion's garnet-coloured silk, banded with velvet. And for her eighteenth birthday Papa gave her a pair of garnet earrings. 'I know,' he said complacently, 'that it is said that most men are colour-blind. I am not. I carried the colour in my eye pretty well, I think.'

'They are very beautiful, Papa. And a perfect match. Thank you very much.'

He then wished her many happy returns of the day.

Wearing the splendid dress and the matching ear-rings Marion stood and sat and knelt and heard Mr. Marriot's gentle parsonic voice say 'for the procreation of children' in such a way that it could not offend any lady in the congregation who affected to dissociate cause and result. Now envy was there, not of the paraphernalia of marriage, of marriage itself; the giving and taking of the simple gold ring which meant all the difference in the world; for it was now over a month. Behind and within the seams which tapered into the elegant waist-line of the new dress a process had started, a process which, short of a miracle, could not be halted and must culminate in such shame that just to think about it made her tremble and sweat. Several mornings lately as she was dressing and the scent of the breakfast bacon reached her she had been overcome by nausea and been obliged to scurry through the kitchen to the water-closet in the area — the other one being a flight and a half of stairs away. She wondered if Ada and Betty had noticed, thought it strange. There was the washing. The Draper laundry was collected each Monday by a gnarled old woman with a little cart drawn by a gnarled old donkey. It was returned on Thursday. The old woman was hardly like to fret about certain omissions, but Betty who unpacked the clean clothes and put them to air might well have noticed.

Kneeling for the last time she prayed. *God help me. Let me come on or let Johnny marry me. Please, God, I could not face the disgrace.* She prayed with great earnestness but without much faith. She had never been pious and it seemed a little dishonourable to turn to God simply because one was in trouble. In trouble! That was the phrase used for girls in her state. In trouble. The organ boomed and Mamma gave a little shiver. Then they trooped out into the sunshine.

That night she gave Johnny the brandy which was now a regular offering. She kept it in a bottle plainly labelled, 'Dr. Martin's Hair Tonic'. The label also mentioned the long list of things the stuff was good for; dry hair, greasy hair, falling hair, fading hair, dandruff, alopecia. The bottle was replenished from the cooking brandy — 'I reckon we need a new bottle,' Ada would say; or from the cellarette in the sideboard. 'Getting low,' Mr. Draper would think. She watched while Johnny drank, hoping the liquor would provoke an acceptive mood. He asked a few questions about the wedding and she answered him rather absentmindedly, thinking about what she must presently say.

'Darling, I know I have said this several times and that the idea finds no favour with you. But now ... Johnny it is urgent. We must get married. You see ... I am going to have a baby.'

He asked the ritual, banal question, 'Are you *sure*?'

'Quite sure. I'm more than a month overdue. I'm sick in the morning. I'm sure. And, oh, Johnny, the relief of being able to speak of it ...' She began to cry, leaning against his shoulder and he made some perfunctory gestures of comfort while his mind span.

Any respectable man, and Mr. Draper was nothing if not respectable, confronted with a pregnant daughter would prefer marriage to scandal. Any man in his right senses would prefer a shop assistant son-in-law to a grandchild born illegitimately.

'This needs thinking about,' he said.

'I have thought. Day and night, since I was sure I have thought of little else. Darling, in just over three weeks time we go on holiday to Yarmouth. Now that opens the way for us. Banns must be called on three Sundays and one of those about to be married must live in the parish.' She had obtained this information from a book called *An Encyclopaedia of Knowledge* which had also been terse and lucid on the subject of pregnancy. 'If you went to Yarmouth on your next half day and found a little church and gave some boarding-house as your address ... Do you see? At Yarmouth Ellen and I are allowed to bathe. Papa also bathes, but from a different part of the beach. It would be quite easy for me to make the usual excuse not to bathe. Then I could slip away and we should be married and nobody, not even Papa, could do anything.'

Except disown and disinherit you, you foolish girl.

A pregnant, penniless wife, presently a baby. A bleak prospect.

'I do not think that this is the right way to go about things.'

'Can you think of a better?'

'I can think of nothing worse. There is now, or soon will be the child to think of. Three of us, Marion, to live on a guinea a week. Decent places take only single men — and in London charge fifteen shillings a week. We should end in a slum, probably sharing a bedroom, crawling with bugs. In the yard there would be one tap or one pump, one privy serving anything up to thirty people. I know, Marion, I *know*. I have experience. Would you wish your child — our child — to be born in such conditions?'

'There is no alternative.'

'There is. Your father must be faced with the truth. You say he is a very possessive man. It is possible that he would feel possessive towards his grandchild; wish it to be legitimate, to be properly brought up. With you, *chérie*, he may be angry;

with me, very angry indeed. But not with the child. There will be some unpleasantness and then all will be well.'

'You say that because you do not *know* him. I do. Sooner than tell him the truth I would kill myself. I would sooner die than face Papa in such a situation. Johnny, unless you go to Yarmouth and make arrangements for us to be married, I will drown myself.'

'Darling, that is wild talk. But wait ... Something has occurred to me. I also have a plan. Listen ...' It was positive inspiration and he outlined it in detail. He was angry when Marion said, 'It would not work. Papa would give you ten shillings, perhaps.'

The last words were typical of something in her that he deplored. A harsh realism suddenly cropping up through the romantic unworldliness, disconcerting as a pebble in mashed potato. It jarred.

'Well,' he said, 'will you try it?'

'If I must, I suppose I must. But, darling, I know my way would be better. I know. Please, Johnny, try my way.' She said, 'Please, Johnny,' much as she had earlier said, 'Please, God,' without much hope. Men were not open to reason, or persuasion.

Jean de Brissac's vanity persuaded him that before the testing moment came Mr. Draper should know that he was not the fellow to be dismissed with ten shillings.

So on the next Sunday morning, impeccably dressed, he took up his position outside the church door. It was a fine morning, so Mamma had come to church and had suffered from the organ. She and Ellen walked out ahead of Marion and Papa. Johnny did not greet Ellen, but as Marion came level with him he swept off his hat and said, 'Good morning, Miss Draper.' It was a shock; he had not warned her of this plan and the session of nausea had been very severe that morning. She just managed to say in a low, stilted voice, 'Good morning, Mr. de Brissac.' Papa raised his hat the stipulated half inch and then said, in an audible, rather truculent voice, 'Who *is* that young man?'

Ellen was alert; she was now certain that Johnny was dogging poor Marion, and since Marion gave no answer to the question Ellen looked back over her shoulder and said with a disarming lightness. 'Someone with whom we became acquainted at the Literary Salon, Papa. Mrs. Marriot could never get his name right. She called him Mr. Brisket.

Mr. Draper received this information with a silence that might or might not be ominous. When, half-way along Honey Lane Ellen said, 'Oh, that purple clematis is in flower. I always associate it with the holiday,' and received no reply both girls knew that the silence was ominous. So did Mamma who, as soon as home was reached, did her vanishing trick, so quickly and quietly that no one could say whether she had made for the stairs or the drawing-room. The girls were prepared to vanish too, but Mr. Draper, hanging his hat upon the stand, said, 'Wait,' and turned into the dining-room. The table was set and Betty, coming and going, had not always closed the door at the head of the kitchen stairs. There was a faint but definite odour of roast chicken and green peas with mint. Let me not be sick! Please, God!

'You may pour my sherry, Ellen.' Ellen removed her gloves and performed this service. 'Now,' Papa said, taking the glass, 'who is that very forward young man? I noticed and disapproved of his manner at the garden party last month.'

He is my love; my husband in all but name; the father of my child. My *stupid* love who must always know best.

'As Ellen said, Papa; he attended Mrs. Marriot's Literary Salon.'

'And does that justify his familiarity?'

'Papa, he merely wished us good morning.'

Ellen could see that Marion looked pale. She always looked *pale*, but there was a difference; the same difference as there was between ordinary full-cream milk and skim. Bravely she moved to the defence.

'You must not take exception to his manner, Papa. He is French. They have different ways.'

'And what else do you know about him,' Mr. Draper said, turning his penetrating stare upon his younger daughter.

'Only that he assists Mr. Freeman in his shop, Papa.'

Typical, typical. Like master, like man. That rabid, nonconformist liberal would employ a foreigner, a dressed-up jackanapes. It was in fact worse, far worse than he had thought. At the garden party Mr. Draper had half-recognised the enemy — young, personable ... And it was true that had Ellen said that the potential enemy were a well-connected young man he would still have been annoyed. But a shop assistant!

'A shop assistant!' he said in a voice of infinite scorn. 'And since when, I wonder, have shop assistants, impersonating gentlemen, been accustomed to greeting young ladies *by name*?'

I must not be like Judas; I must not betray my lord; at least not wholly.

'Papa, he is a rather unusual shop assistant. He is a gentleman and a man of education,' Marion said.

Ellen said, loyally, 'Yes indeed, Papa. His talk to us about the French novelists was generally agreed to be the best we had heard. I did not understand a word, of course, but those who did had nothing but praise.'

'Arrant nonsense,' Mr. Draper said. 'A dressed-up popinjay. Encouraged by Mrs. Marriot with all her Jack's-as-good-as-his-master-if-not-better notions. This is what comes ... What is the world coming to? If he ever accosts either of you by name in future you are not to reply. Say nothing, look straight ahead. Well-mannered men of that class know their place. They remove their caps and they should be acknowledged. But upstarts ... "Good morning, Miss Draper!" indeed, they must be firmly kept in place. And there is another thing. Whatever idiocy the Marriots intend to perpetrate next autumn, you will have no part in.'

I shall not. I shall be married to Johnny and far away; or I shall be dead.

The curious thing was that Mr. Draper had what he called 'a nose'. He was a practical man and not given to fancies. But more than once, ten, a dozen times he had refused to give credit to firms which seemed sound enough, firms with nothing wrong with them upon which one could put a finger. Then, when the crash came he was not one of the creditors who must take a shilling in the pound. Even over so small a thing as a faulty horse, dosed and tortured into giving a good performance, his nose served him. 'No, it's not what I want,' he would say. And it was the same with samples of barley. And now, as his daughters went off to remove their hats and he drank his sherry, while his mind informed him that the situation might easily have been more embarrassing — a young man backed by Lady Mingay even, some offshoots of the Taylor-Everett family, Mrs. Marriot's nephew — his nose recognised in its blind, instinctive way some threat from the chemist's assistant. It was vague, it was undefined, but it said quite clearly — Watch out for that young man.

'Darling, that was a foolish thing to do.'

'Because once again you failed me, Marion. If you had only said my name, introduced us, I had the words ready. I watched him all through the sermon. It bored him. I had a suitable comment, something that would have arrested his attention and made an appeal.'

'Johnny, could you have heard him. Merely because you *greeted* us. Ellen and I had *such* a scolding! Darling, you do not understand ... But there is time yet. We could be married in the *second* week of the holiday ... If you would only do as I say. Darling, I know that your plan ... It might work with *some* fathers. With Papa it will not. Please, Johnny, please, if we are ever going to be married, if this child is to be born in wedlock, there is only one way. My way. I do not mind being poor. Somehow we could manage. I have a few things, of no great value but they would fetch something. Johnny, if it came to the worst we could buy a barrow, sell flowers or fruit or fish ... Darling, if you would only realise that there is nothing to hope for from Papa and if your plan fails, as it will, as it must ... Johnny, I cannot bear it ... I simply cannot bear it.' They were sitting side by side on the bed and she turned away, towards the pillow end and wept violently, her sobs muffled, her clenched hands beating on the bed rails.

She knew that he was wrong.

He knew that she was wrong.

She was frantic.

He was adamant.

The annual holiday at Yarmouth was, like everything else in the Draper household, a matter of routine. The Drapers never stayed in a hotel — open to all and sundry — but in a boarding-house kept by a Mrs. Radley who had a house, Sea View, overlooking the South Beach. Her best apartments, two bedrooms and a dining-room-parlour, facing the sea, were booked from year to year for exactly the same fortnight, chosen so that Mr. Draper might be fortified for his busiest season when the barley was harvested.

It would have been foolish to pretend that Mrs. Radley's beds were as comfortable as those at home or that her food was in any way comparable to that served by Ada, but the holiday was the only real interruption in the year's routine and it was valued accordingly. Preparation for it began well in advance. Trunks and valises were brought down from the box-room and set to yawn in the sunshine. The word holiday found its way into almost every conversation. A new hat, a new dress, new shoes, a new parasol for the holiday; this to be done before the holiday, this to be deferred until after the holiday; this not to be contemplated even, because of the holiday. Had the Draper family been planning to emigrate there could not have been more stir and bustle. On one dreadful occasion there had been so much stir and bustle that nobody had remembered to cancel Papa's newspapers. He had thought of it as soon as he was in the train and had grumbled all the way to Norwich, where, changing trains, he had been able to send a telegram. Such an oversight was unlikely to happen again.

Nothing else was likely to happen and everyone knew it. Life at Ten Alma Avenue was simply lifted up and set down in Sea View; but there would be the sea, the sea air, the sea sky stretching infinite towards the east; a change of scene. For Mamma no piano and nothing to take its place; though there was always the hope, shared by Ellen and Marion, that Mrs. Radley's apartments which did not face the sea might be taken by a family of whom Papa could bring himself to approve. It had happened; admittedly only twice within Marion's memory, but it might happen again.

Ellen and Mamma talked about and prepared for the holiday in the usual way; Marion, feeling slightly unwell, but terrified of seeming different, pretended.

Ladies who wished to bathe used what were called bathing machines, conveyances not unlike caravans but set lower, on smaller wheels. Each had a door and a pair of shafts at either end. A lady entered from the landward side, fully dressed. The old woman who owned the machine cried 'Hup' to the horse, hitched to the seaward end, and it advanced into the sea, knowing exactly where to halt — when the water was a shade more than belly deep. The lady then emerged through the front door and slipped modestly into the sea, wearing her bathing costume. This was made of thick navy-blue serge and consisted of a pair of drawers reaching half-way down the shin and kind of tunic extending from collar-bone to knee, and of elbow length. One could have little white frills at neck and elbow and at the ends of the drawer-legs, but to do so was considered to be very dashing and daring; to abandon the regulation navy blue and choose instead grey, or buff or even cream, was to be almost abandoned.

In the water the ladies enjoyed, for the only time in their lives, freedom of movement; no corsets, no clinging skirts. Elderly ladies, advised to bathe for their health, remained staid, bobbing and plunging conscientiously; younger ones, made lively by the informality of the circumstances, frisked like porpoises, splashed one another, laughed and emitted screams of mock terror. While they enjoyed themselves the old woman unhitched her horse and harnessed it again at the other ride, ready for the short return journey that would convert a sea nymph into a sedate lady, fit for the public eye.

The Drapers had arrived on Saturday, too late to bathe. On Sunday there was no bathing. Mr. Draper had taken stock of the family on the other side of the house and decided that they were not to be known. Very common indeed; the sort of people to whom one might say Good day if one came face to face with them in the doorway, but certainly would not offer any encouragement, such as a remark about the weather.

This was disappointing; but on Monday at the bathing place, Ellen quickly found a friend, a girl named Florence, very gay and dashing; her bathing costume was cream-coloured and her manner what Papa, should ever he meet her, would call 'pert'. They were mutually attracted and frolicked and laughed together, leaving Marion to her thoughts. Marion seemed not to mind; indeed on the first day she said, 'I am taller than you. I must go out further to submerge my shoulders.'

She was still undecided. Go Johnny's way which had perhaps one chance in a thousand of being successful; or take her own?

'You're a bit venturesome, young lady,' said the old woman who owned the machine they patronised. 'It's a sandy beach and sand can shift. You could find yourself out of your depth in no time at all.'

Undecided on Monday; on Tuesday; on Wednesday. It was fine weather; the holiday atmosphere, with in their case nothing but the holiday atmosphere to sustain it, was infective. She was eighteen. Life was – or at least could be, so good. Trust Johnny and take the one in a thousand chance? Go your own way?

No decision could be for ever deferred. Thursday came. Another beautiful day.

The actual area where the bathing machines operated and the ladies went in and out was roped off, but the bit of rough pathway, ambitiously called the Promenade, was free to all. A few louts, residents or day-trippers who could not afford to patronise the offered entertainments or the places of refreshment at the other end of the beach, would gather and stare, hoping for some revelation, a momentary glance of a female figure, clad in wet, clinging serge. At a time when a female ankle, exposed by the lifting of a skirt to avoid a puddle, was something upon which lascivious eyes could feast, the ladies' bathing place was an attraction. Real ladies ignored the watchers, and their calls and their whistles. Florence counted them. 'Six today,' she would say.

Florence was fortunate. When she came to bathe, a carriage, two sleek horses and man in a cockaded hat brought her, deposited her and waited. Ellen and Marion were fortunate too; Mrs. Radley's house overlooked the South Beach and they had only to cross the stretch of sand and marram grass, the path that pretended to be a promenade, and they were home. Others were less lucky; fully dressed they had to walk past the louts who chanted, 'I sawyer; I sawyer in your drawerser. Your drawers dropped, your belly flopped. I sawyer.'

'Oh look,' Florence said on this Thursday morning. 'A different-looking vulture!' Ellen looked and recognised Johnny Brisket. She was surprised to see him there, among those rude, ill-dressed, ill-behaved louts. He looked completely out of place. He wore a natty suit, light tan in colour, trimmed with braid of a darker shade and a white straw boater hat with a bi-coloured ribbon.

She waded and splashed her way to Marion and said, 'Look! Fancy Johnny Brisket with those louts!'

'Fancy,' Marion said, not even looking. 'Ellen dear, your chin is practically awash. Go back.'

Now, now was the moment; the decision no longer to be deferred. Johnny's plan could never work. She had known it from the first and been a fool to agree. In a sharp, self-re-

66

vealing moment she saw that to the natural instinct of self-preservation, in her case had been added that something more, the intent of the gravid female to protect ... She had allowed herself to be talked round, but she had never been certain of anything but her own power to avoid the issue. And that was still hers.

She turned and walked deliberately into the glittering sea. She lost her footing, was lifted, buoyed up, rolled over, smacked down. I am going to die; I have done with it all ... She had thought of water as a soft thing, something to be yielded to, a blessed, obliterating embrace. In fact it was hard ...

The old woman having taken the horse to the rear of the machine had come back to sit on the front shaft and smoke her little black pipe. The place where Marion had gone down was too far out to be under the casual supervision which she exercised over her bathing ladies. Johnny stood by the barrier, waiting for the waving arms, the screams for help that had been pre-arranged.

It was Ellen who screamed. She would have gone out to where Marion was rolling over and over, now visible, now submerged, but Florence caught and held her and joined in the screaming.

Johnny jumped the barrier and ran into the sea. He had said to Marion, 'Never for a moment will you be in danger. I swim like a fish.' He could swim, after a fashion, but in effecting the life-saving exercise which was to bring Papa to his knees from gratitude Johnny had counted upon a living, conscious collaborator, not a limp inert corpse.

The old woman, moving without haste, but with every movement certain and economic, unhitched her horse, clambered astride and turned him into the sea. 'Hup,' she said; and when he halted at the usual level, just over belly deep, she said 'Hup' again. She snatched Marion up and laid her across the horse. 'Catch hold of his tail, if you can,' she said to Johnny. She allowed no time for this act, nor did she look back to see if it had been performed. She owed a certain duty to her bathing ladies; none to a stranger.

'She's dead! Oh, Marion, Marion,' Ellen said.

'Give us a chance,' the old woman said. Marion lay face downwards across the horse's withers and the old woman beat her across the back. Anger as well as a desire to resuscitate weighted the blows. I warned you. Headstrong. Getting

67

bathing a bad name. Thump. Thump. Thump! The seawater was expelled in spurts, like vomiting.

'She'll do,' the old woman said, hearing the gasping intake of air. Marion's hair hung straight and limp, reaching almost to the ground. Water streamed from it, and this water was reddened.

'Oh, but she's hurt,' Ellen wailed.

'You're up at Sea View, ain't you? Run on ahead. Tell them to get a bed ready. And send for the doctor.' Ellen sped away. The old woman said 'Hup' again and the horse moved forward. Some people followed. 'There's nothing to stare at,' the old woman said sourly, but they still came on.

Mr. Draper had already taken his bathe: invigorated by it and a brisk rub down, he took his *Times* on the verandah outside the sitting-room and was about to settle down when some slight commotion drew his attention. He looked out and saw Ellen, in her bathing costume, soaked and clinging — as bad as naked, not even a towel, as he said afterwards — running towards the house. Behind her came the plodding old horse, two other shameless females, one in a pale costume looking even more naked than Ellen, and a group of the Peeping Toms. In the one immediately alongside the horse Mr. Draper, even in that moment of shock, recognised a fellow-townsman. That impertinent shop assistant.

Mr. Draper remained in control of himself and of the situation.

'It's Marion,' Ellen gasped. 'She's hurt. Doctor!'

'Find yourself a wrap,' Papa said, before snapping out his orders. The maid to run for the nearest doctor; the odd-job man to help him in getting Marion upstairs. 'On the sofa; no need to soak the bed,' he said with great presence of mind. To Mamma who had come white-faced out of one of her mysterious retreats and to Ellen, now decently covered by a dressing-gown, he said, 'Dry her off and get her into a nightdress.' This, he thought angrily, was the result of Doctor Barlow's drivelling talk about the value of sea-bathing as a restorative of health in the summer when Ellen had suffered a series of sore throats and showed signs of being delicate. He'd actually spoken of 'Doctor Yarmouth'. Well, there'd be no more of that!

He went down prepared to deal sternly with the riff-raff. Mrs. Radley had forestalled him and there remained only the old woman, anxious to exonerate herself, and Johnny waiting for the fructification of his plan. 'Stay on the verandah, then,' Mrs. Radley said. 'One body dripping about is one too many. And get that horse off the flowerbed.' The old woman's skirts were soaked, but they were seldom completely dry and she suffered no discomfort. Johnny was beginning to shiver and his face wore the dirty look of a naturally dark complexion turned pale.

'Now,' Mr. Draper said. 'I understand you wish to see me.'

'Yes, sir,' the old woman said. 'I don't want you to go thinking it was my fault or giving bathing a bad name. I always warn my ladies. Twice this week I warned that young lady, but she's a bit headstrong. And I keep a sharp look-out. I'd have had her safe sooner but for interference.' She gave Johnny a scathing look of contempt. 'People think they can swim. Interfering!'

'I had the privilege of rescuing the young lady,' Johnny said.

'Rescue. All you did was screech "Marion", waste of breath. And get in the way. Had to be rescued yourself. Drag on the horse, you were.'

'But for me she would again have hit her head on the groyne.' That was true. Under the gently rippling surface there had been a strong drift towards the groyne and half his efforts had been directed to keeping himself and Marion clear of the stone. Neither of his hearers was prepared to give him any credit.

'You'd both be drowned now, but for me and old Trot here.'

Johnny had now attained his wish, a face-to-face encounter with Mr. Draper, in circumstances favourable to himself. But the plan which had begun to go wrong when Marion failed to give the signal, continued to misfire. Not a word or look of gratitude, no handshake, no slap on the shoulder. Apart from one flicking glance which took in everything, Mr. Draper had paid him no attention at all.

'Well, so long as you know,' the old woman said. With amazing agility she scrambled astride her horse again and turned him beachwards. In her job time was money.

'Wait,' Mr. Draper said. The whole episode had angered him extremely, but the old woman, turning against the young jackanapes against whom his nose had warned him, had ingratiated herself. He worked his sovereign case. Click, click,

click! Three gleaming gold sovereigns lay in his palm and were transferred to her horny, salt-encrusted hand.

'Well, sir,' she said. 'Thank you indeed. There was no call ... I wasn't looking to be paid ...'

Even to her he had expressed no obligation but she noticed the omission only in a roundabout way. There were a lot of gentlemen who'd have been more lavish in thanks and less generous with their money.

'And now,' Mr. Draper said, before Johnny could speak, 'we must be fair, must we not? Whatever you did or did not do, you appear to have ruined a very fine suit.' His glance, his tone showed exactly what he thought of summer suits trimmed with braid. 'You come from Bereham, do you not? Then I suggest you go to Ager's in the Buttermarket and tell him to supply you with another suit and charge it to me. Up to three pounds.' It was a calculated insult. Ager's did not make suits for gentlemen; it was the place from which Johnny's fellow-lodgers, all working men, bought their horrible best suits.

Johnny told himself, and fully believed, that he could have said something even then which would have convinced Mr. Draper of his difference, but he was unlucky again, for the doctor, who lived close by, came up, all in a flurry, carrying his bag.

Johnny lay on the firm warm sand and allowed his clothes to dry on him. The ridiculous rules that governed the issue of a cheap day return ticket compelled him to wait in Yarmouth till six o'clock. He lay and drank the cup of humiliation to the dregs. He had failed entirely; he had made a very poor showing; he had been dead unlucky. He could see now why Marion, poor darling, held her father in such awe. A horrible, inhuman man, a veritable ogre. And she had been right in predicting the outcome of the exploit — he will give you half a sovereign. Absolutely right, for the most expensive suit Ager could supply would cost fifty shillings at the very outside.

Though the sun and the sand were warm and his clothes were drying, he shivered again. He had suffered a shock as well as a humiliation. He had, like Ellen, believed that Marion was dead. In his hands she had felt like a corpse, across the horse she had lain like a corpse. And thinking her dead he had realised not only that all his chance of an advantageous marriage had vanished, but that he had lost someone who had loved him and whom he, as nearly as his nature would allow, had loved. He lay and remembered how she had offered to marry him and be poor; and then how she had begged and beseeched him to marry her because of the baby. He saw, as clearly as he would ever do, that he had treated her badly and that even in her most desperate moment — terrified, and rightly so, of that dreadful father — she had never once reproached him; never once said — You got me into this, you must get me out!

By three o'clock he was thoroughly dry; he had breakfasted at half past seven and on the six o'clock train he would be back in Bereham long after the meal that Mrs. Fenner called tea would be over and cleared away. A man must eat. So he got up, brushed the sand from his clothes and tried to smooth out the worst of the creases. He had no hat and no man with the slightest claim to respectability went about hatless. He went back to the bathing area, deserted now, with the tide at its lowest and there was his hat. It had been cast up, sodden, but it also had dried in the sun, and apart from the fact that in the ribbon the colours had run, it was undamaged. He put it on his head, not knowing that it was at a less jaunty angle than usual and went in search of something to stay his stomach which, left empty for too long, or fed the wrong things, was always a trouble, with a pain as though a rat were trapped there and trying to gnaw its way out.

As he approached the more frequented area of the town he came upon the various places where honest pennies were turned by services to such day-trippers as himself. Some were stalls, some were merely stands on a corner. All were manned by old women, sisters of the old woman, of all the old women who ran the bathing machines. Yarmouth herring, cockles and mussels, cups of tea, pigs' trotters, shrimps, jellied eels, sandwiches. He stopped by a corner stand where one of the old woman's sisters – but wearing a big white apron — sold tea and sandwiches. And flowers. In a bucket below the rickety little table that held the provender, there were bunches of Sweet William, red, white, pink and striped. Johnny paused there, bought himself a cup of tea and a sandwich which purported to be ham but was in fact the fat-and-lean pork which his stomach rebelled against. Even the mustard could not conceal that fact, plentifully as it had been applied. Johnny removed the meat and dropped it on the ground. A lean, watchful cat with six kittens to support, pounced upon this

71

unusual offering — most people only dropped crusts, and all too few of those. Johnny ate the thick, sparsely buttered bread which made the rest of the sandwich and sipped, cautiously at the stewed dark tea. The rat in his stomach turned its attention to this provender and Johnny began to feel better. 'And I'll have a bunch of these,' he said, pointing to the flowers.

While the old woman lifted them from the bucket and shook off the slime which announced that the flowers were no longer fresh, Johnny tore the corner from the sheet of paper that served as table-cloth. On it, using a well-painted gate as desk, he wrote, 'I wish you a speedy recovery. J.' At Sea View he went to the back door, hating it, but not wishing to risk another encounter with Mr. Draper. Not yet! The day would come when the score would be made even. But not today.

The little maid who had run for the doctor answered the door.

'How is Miss Draper?' Johnny asked.

'She's got the concussion.' She said the word proudly.

'She is still unconscious?'

'She's asleep like. But they expect her to wake up any minute now.'

'If you give her these . . . when she wakes.'

'All right. That's the potatoes boiling over.'

Over the whole of Sea View a thunderous atmosphere brooded. It was not merely that there was, under a shared roof, someone who had almost drowned and now, snatched from Death's jaws, lay unconscious in the second best bed-room. Mr. Draper's displeasure was making itself felt. The common, not-to-be-known little honeymoon couple felt it. They had gone straight out and bought a bunch of hothouse grapes.

'Much too kind,' Mr. Draper said, now even putting out a hand to receive the offering. 'I am afraid that it will be some time before my daughter will be in a state to appreciate your kindness. I really think it would be better if you enjoyed them yourselves.'

Enjoying them the bride said, 'But it was rude.'

The groom said, 'I'd say sensible. I mean, after all . . .'

Mrs. Radley came in for her share of condemnation. 'I am so sorry about Miss Marion, sir.'

'If I remember rightly, Mrs. Radley, you recommended

that particular bathing place. I suspect that it shelves sharply. I see no other way to account for the accident. I am of the opinion that bathing should be restricted to the further end.'

And she had been planning to expand, to build on, to have not two but four sets of apartments, all occupied by people who liked to be within such easy reach of the bathing machines.

But these little snubs and rebukes were merely froth. The real target of this rage lay elsewhere, protected for the moment by unconsciousness.

Ellen and Mamma took turns at watching by the bedside. Mamma was admirable, but Ellen, silly child, cried and cried. On the one occasion when Mr. Draper tried to get to grips with Ellen, she had sobbed so loudly that the couple across the hall had come out, 'Is she dead? Is she dead?'

The water was hard, not soft, but afterwards it washed up into enchanted lands, full of things that she had never seen, but had imagined, waterfalls, glassily smooth and musical, palm-fringed beaches, forests full of flowers and forests hushed with snow. Usually her progress from scene to scene was unimpeded but sometimes there was need for effort and a voice urging her, 'Marion, please! Marion, try!' The voice sounded like Ellen's, but Ellen was not there. She was completely alone, yet not in the least lonely.

Then she was in the dark and someone was crying. Dark because her eyes were closed. She opened them. The light was not bright, but painful, so she closed them again and then in a series of brief squints saw Mrs. Radley's second-best bedroom; and by the window Ellen crying. But I had done with all this. This is not where I should be. Desperately she willed herself back to the place where she had been alone and untroubled; but that was useless and something must be done about Ellen's weeping.

'What is the matter, dear?'

'Oh! Oh, Marion. My dearest, dearest sister ...' Ellen ran to the bed, checked herself in the very act of throwing her arms around Marion and instead took her hands very gently, and very gently put her warm wet face down to administer a

73

butterfly kiss. For a moment she was quite incoherent, saying what a long time, saying how worried, saying how shocking. Then she said, 'How do you feel?'

'My head hurts.' There was another pain, too; the kind one learned never to complain about.

'You hit it on one of those horrid groynes.' She quickly added what, in Marion's place, she would have wished to hear. 'The mark will not show. It is under your hair. Dearest, perhaps you should not talk. I must tell them, too.' Mamma would be relieved; about Papa she was not certain, he had shown no anxiety, nothing but anger, as though Marion had done something more than usually annoying.

'Where are they?'

'Having dinner. It is Friday now. You have been unconscious for a day and a half.'

'Ellen, what happened?' She meant what happened *after*.

'I think you fainted. I think you should not have bathed yesterday.'

What did that mean? Exposure? Disgrace?

'You came on. As we brought you back to the house.' Again she said what she would have wished to hear. 'Nobody noticed.'

Oh. Out of that trap! Free. Her own woman again. The terror lifted.

'And then? Ellen, sit on the bed. Tell me everything.'

'I think we should not talk too much . . .' But Ellen who had rarely been for long out of favour had suffered in the last day and a half, and welcomed a chance to talk. 'Well, I went back to Florence, then I turned and you had vanished and I saw you going over and over in the water, so I screamed and then . . .' She gave an exact account of the happenings.

'Did Papa see Johnny?'

'Truly, dear, all that can wait. I must tell them. And you must have something to eat, or at least to drink.'

'I will not take a sip until you have told me everything.' Whatever it was, she could bear it. Even if Papa had struck Johnny it would only serve him right for being so stupid and stubborn.

'Yes. Johnny and the old woman stood on the verandah quarrelling about who had saved you. Johnny Brisket said he had — and as I told you, he did try, but he muffed it. Papa gave the old woman three pounds and told Johnny to go to Ager's and get himself a new suit, to that value.'

Marion startled Ellen by laughing, not very loudly, but for quite a long time.

'Well,' Ellen said a bit dubiously, 'now that you no longer like him, I suppose ...' A few thoughts about love flitted through her innocent mind. Look at Angela, crazy about Johnny Brisket, engaged the next day almost to another man; Marion, crazy about Johnny Brisket and then all at once not caring at all, and laughing to hear how he had been insulted. Sent to Ager's! 'What is less amusing is the way Papa has taken it all. And Johnny made it worse. He brought a bunch of flowers early last evening. That girl, Rosie, didn't give a very good description, but there was a scrap of paper in the middle of the bunch. It said, "I wish you a speedy recovery, J.", and Papa wanted to know who knew you were ill. Marion, on the spur of the moment I couldn't think of anyone except that other woman we bathe with — she did come, with Florence up to the house; or the old woman who keeps the bathing machine. Papa said neither one would have written in such familiar terms, or sent flowers so nearly dead. They were almost dead. Sweet Williams.'

'They would be,' Marion said.

Every single thing he had ever given her had been dead; killed by greed, selfishness, pig-headedness. Even the baby was dead. When she thought how she had begged and besought him to marry her and give the baby a name ... No, he must know best.

'Papa,' Ellen said, using Papa's own phrase, 'is very displeased.'

Marion lay and contemplated Papa's displeasure without a tremor.

'He'll get over it,' she said.

'I am in disgrace for not wrapping myself in a towel. I'm never to bathe again. He saw Florence in her cream costume and said she was fast and I am never to speak to her again. But,' Ellen said, bravely and with truth, 'I do not mind, now that you are back with me. Until I thought you were dead, dearest, I did not ... at least not fully ... know how much I loved you.'

'Dear Ellen. I love you too.' She had done with them all, except Ellen, innocent, loyal Ellen.

Once Miss Ruthven had quoted Dr. Johnson's remark that the prospect of being hanged concentrated a man's mind. 'I wish I could threaten this whole class with hanging,' she had said. The prospect of death might concentrate the mind; facing death, taking the steps necessary to drown oneself did more than concentrate, it changed. Sir, the sage might have said, suicide gives a man a sense of proportion.

'Florence called this morning — luckily while Papa was bathing,' Ellen said. 'She wished to know how you were. I was obliged to tell her that I was not allowed to bathe again. Then she gave me this, as a keepsake.' She showed Marion a small gold locket, shaped like a heart, set with seed pearls and turquoises, slung on a thin gold chain. 'I can never wear it, can I? And I feel I should give her something, but Papa might notice.'

'Give her my garnet ear-rings.'

'But he would certainly notice them — I mean that you were not wearing them.'

'Whether Florence has them or not I shall never wear them again.' Nor the garnet dress that she had worn for Angela's wedding. Nor the street wear in which she had entered Freeman's shop and worn to the Literary Salon. There were a dozen things she would never wear again; never do again; never think again, never feel again.

'Well, if you are quite sure. Do you not like them? But how should I get them to her?'

'You could post them.'

'It sounds absurd,' Ellen said, 'but I do not even know her surname, or her address.'

It was, in fact what Papa had called it, a silly girlish fancy of which Ellen should be ashamed.

'The doctor said I might take a short walk tomorrow. It is a short walk to the bathing beach. And it is like the Library, Ellen, Papa has not forbidden me to speak to Florence . . .'

He had in fact not addressed her directly since the accident. While she lay abed he had never paid her a visit, sent a message or an inquiry. And when, shakily she had ventured down to the family table he had ignored her entirely except to say, 'Pass your sister the salt', or 'Marion has no bread'.

Back home it was different. They returned on Saturday to a house which had been thoroughly cleaned and scoured during their absence and to a supper which put Mrs. Radley's dinners to shame. Immediately afterwards Mamma had fled to her piano. Through every holiday she had suffered the deprivation and this holiday had been exceptionally trying.

'You stay here. I want to talk to you,' Mr. Draper said, when the girls, murmuring about unpacking, would have made their escape. 'Now, I intend to get to the bottom of this and I will not be put off with evasions. A young man, of whose conduct I have already had cause to complain was among the oafs at that bathing place. Was that by pre-arrangement?'

'I was never more surprised in my life,' Ellen said. 'I told you, Papa.'

'I heard your account, Ellen. I wish to know what Marion has to say.'

'I can offer no explanation, Papa. Except that it was Thursday when day-trips are available and a few people who cannot afford to watch the puppet and Pierrot shows do tend to congregate.'

'That is not a satisfactory answer. As he made his ineffectual attempt at rescue he screeched — that was the old machine attendant's word, "Marion". Can you account for this use of your Christian name?'

'In a moment of panic, perhaps. He knew my name. Mrs. Marriot used it often enough; her Salon was very informal. And I was, by all accounts, about to drown. I think it would have seemed more extraordinary if he at that moment had said, "Miss Draper".'

'Are you attempting to start an argument?' That was one of his tricks. He reasoned; other people argued.

'No, Papa. I am trying to explain.'

'Actually, it might not have been him,' Ellen said. 'I was screaming all the time and I may have used Marion's name. In fact I am sure I did. There was so . . .'

'That will do, Ellen. Unless you wish to confess that you also sent the flowers, with an intimate-sounding message, signed J.'

Sarcastic facetiousness was another weapon, and against Ellen it served. She changed colour.

'Well?' Papa asked, looking at Marion.

'I never even saw the flowers, Papa.'

He had said that he wanted no evasions, and evasions was all he was getting.

'There is altogether too much coincidence about this affair,' he said. 'First,' he laid the forefinger of his right hand in the palm of his left, 'the Garden Party. That young man did all he could to draw your attention. I observed his manner though I said nothing then. Second,' he laid another finger alongside the first, 'the incident outside the church door. And now this. He was not merely in Yarmouth but at the bathing station which you patronised — incidentally the least accessible — at a time when you were bathing, waiting, I suspect, for you to emerge. A rendezvous? Was it?'

'No, Papa.'

Ellen had an uncomfortable feeling that Papa knew more than he had yet revealed. Guilty memories of those spring evenings in the Old Cloister made her inside quiver. If they had once been seen and a whisper started, it would go the rounds, slowly perhaps but with deadly certainty.

'When did you last see the fellow?'

'Outside the church when his manner gave you such offence. He may have been at church on subsequent Sundays. If so I did not notice him.'

'Then how do you account for a bunch of wilting flowers? And the message?'

'Is there any evidence to connect them with him?'

What had got into the girl. To answer a question with another question was perilously like answering back.

'Ellen saw him,' Mr. Draper said, knowing that this was untrue, but he knew the worth of shock tactics.

'Excuse me, Papa, I did not. Rosie handed me the flowers. I did not see them delivered.'

'Then I was mistaken. I am still far from satisfied.' His look of disapproval included them both. 'I need hardly point out that this has been a disastrous holiday. Ellen takes up with a thoroughly fast, immodest female and behaves hysterically over what was after all a simple mishap. You, Marion, brought about the accident by ignoring instructions. Your mamma was too much worried to benefit by the change. And as for me . . .' He did not describe his own pitiable state.

'I am sorry, Papa,' Ellen said.

'And I was punished for my rashness.' Marion put her hand to her head where the wound, healing nicely and bristly with the regrowth over the shaven patch, still throbbed.

Papa saw that he was making no headway at all. The thought — They are united against me, formed in his mind.

'I am displeased with you both. Go and unpack,' he said.

He saw that he had been far too lenient. Allowing them to have any part in Mrs. Marriot's runagate schemes — where all this had started. Allowing them to bathe. He tried to think of any other liberty which had been allowed and could now be curtailed, but he could think of none at the moment. Nor could he bring himself to believe that his infallible nose had misled him. Discontentedly he settled down to his cigar and a perusal of the weekly journals which awaited him.

At the point where one flight of stairs went up and one down, Ellen said softly, 'At one point I was really afraid ... Marion, you look quite exhausted. I will come and unpack for you.'

'I should be grateful. My head still thumps when I stoop.'

In the dining-room Mr. Draper brooded. He knew what he would do about the chemist's assistant. He wished he could see an equally simple way of driving a wedge between Ellen and Marion. Ellen was fundamentally docile, yielding, dutiful. Marion had never been wholly satisfactory and now he sensed a change for the worse, difficult to define, but there, like a bad odour.

Presently he rose, went into the hall and opened the drawing-room door. In the unlighted room Mamma was playing passionately. He said, 'My dear, that is enough of that infernal din.' She lifted her hands instantly and in the sudden silence he could hear, drifting up the stairs, the sound of girlish laughter, some words, more laughter.

He was bound to go downstairs to lock the kitchen door. This evening he went more quietly than usual, intent, indeed upon eavesdropping. The door of Marion's little room stood open; it was like looking at a stage. Marion lolled on the bed. The trunk yawned. Ellen had one of Marion's hats on her head. 'But it is true,' she said. 'What suits you never suits me. I look like Mrs. Andrews.' Mrs. Andrews had a face like a horse and a tongue like a viper, Ellen said, and it was a creditable imitation, 'I wouldn't say this to just anyone, but I heard it on the best authority. That elder Miss Draper fell in the sea because she was inebriated at the time. Like Father, like daughter, I always say.'

They both laughed. Giggled. Had he hoped, or feared to overhear something relevant to what he still thought of as a mystery; had he wanted, or dreaded to learn that the laughter arose from the fact that they had followed him? He went to the door and said, 'Ellen. I thought I told you to go and unpack.' It was a rebuke, but genial.

'Mine won't take me five minutes, Papa. I came to help Marion, because of her head.'

'To help is one thing; to do it all quite another. Unless you exercise care, my dear, you will end as your sister's serving-girl. A common fate with younger sisters, I believe. You must not allow Marion to impose upon you and turn you into a Cinderella.'

Mrs. Andrews at her most venomous could not compete with Mr. Draper.

'I have just finished, Papa. And I did *offer*.'

'Marion has always been thought clever. Come along.'

That, he thought, turning away was the line to take — until he thought of something better.

Ellen followed him out. As she did so she put her hand behind her back and waggled her fingers in a gesture that was both conspiratorial and derisive. Papa was not to know it, but by his behaviour towards poor Marion who had almost died and then, miraculously come back, he had lost ground with Ellen.

Marion undressed, put on her nightgown and robe and lay on the bed, awaiting Johnny's tap. It was sure to come; he knew that the holiday lasted exactly a fortnight.

She had made no plans at all, how she would act, what she would say depended upon so many things, most of all the effect of his physical presence. She had chosen to die rather than play his silly futile game and her mind was capable of regarding him as a fool who would not listen to reason, and as a weakling who had failed her in her hour of greatest need. About her mind she knew; about her body she was less sure. It would be an interesting test. She was too young and inexperienced to realise that the test had already been made.

He tapped.

She said, 'Hullo, Johnny.'

'Darling,' he said. 'Darling. It has been a lifetime. Marion, I knew nothing, heard nothing, I have been in Purgatory.'

It was all right. His voice had lost the power to stir the marrow of her bones.

'*Chérie*, let me in. There is so much to say.'

'Something has been done to the door while we were away.'

'Kiss me, then. Kiss me through the bars. As in old times.'

He stretched up, she crouched. Their lips met; the old raging hunger was less than a summer thunderstorm remembered in mid-winter and even so only remembered for the damage it did.

'I cannot stay in this position,' she said, withdrawing. 'To stoop hurts my head.'

'Ah yes; your poor head. How is it, darling?'

'Better, but not yet well.'

'When I saw . . .' He spoke at some length of his feelings on that calamitous day, recapturing as he spoke some of the genuine emotion that he had felt and which in some way he had enjoyed, proof that he was not simply mercenary, a fortune-hunter. 'And then your father,' he said. 'He is a monster, a man of no feeling. I did not know. I did not believe . . . Darling, I have done so much thinking. The plan failed . . .'

Yes, because it was idiotic and I was an idiot ever to consider it for an instant.

'I told you how it would be.'

'*Chérie*, I know. You were right. I was wrong. I see now that he will never consent. We must marry as you planned.'

It would happen like this! When I begged and implored, when I was half crazy with fear . . . When you and only you could help me, would you lift a finger? No, all you could do was mount a masquerade, and even that you mismanaged. Swim like a fish, and once your feet left land, glad to clutch at an old horse's tail. You wanted some of Papa's money; and you got it. Three pounds' worth of credit with the cheapest tailor in the town.

'Darling, are you angry with me?'

Not angry; finished.

'You have no need to marry me now. What with being knocked on the head, or nearly drowned — I lost the baby.'

He said, 'Oh,' not knowing quite how to take this piece of news. To express the relief he felt might offend her; women were curious creatures; the prospect of having a baby might be appalling, the loss of it nevertheless a grief. Perhaps that accounted for her strange, off-hand manner. She was usually lavish with endearments. 'And you are sad about it?'

'If you had done as I asked, Johnny. If you had made the

arrangements. If we had been married, I should have felt the loss very much. In the circumstances it would be idle to pretend.'

No doubt about it, she was angry with him. But he knew he had only to get his hands on her, be able to kiss her properly and all would be as before.

'There will be another — after we are married.' He managed to inject a good deal of sexuality into that sentence. She remained unresponsive. 'Because we are going to be married, my darling. In *your* way. I wish to talk to you about it. But not like this. Will you have mastered the new door by tomorrow?'

'No. I shall have no opportunity. Papa will be home all day. Besides it would not be safe. I am still regarded as an invalid, looked in upon from time to time. Papa and Ellen had only just gone when you knocked.'

'Then when shall I be able to see you — properly.' There was that note again.

'Perhaps in a week.'

'But we have already been apart for a fortnight.' She knew that she should have told him the truth, but she knew he would argue and after the journey, the scene with Papa and the discovery that her body was now as indifferent to Johnny as her mind had been for a week, she lacked the physical strength. She would write to him. Tell him not to come again. A letter could not be argued with. 'I have so much to tell you. I have investigated a thing called a Special Licence. And the joke is that your papa will pay for it.'

'Another plan?' The weariness in her voice was unaffected. 'I really am too tired even to talk any more.'

'Poor darling, of course.'

It was probably exhaustion which made her seem so different. She seemed unlike herself because, as people said, she was not herself. People were always coming into the shop seeking some remedy because they did not feel like themselves. Very considerately he said, 'Do not stoop again. Give me your hand.' He kissed it very lingeringly, back, front, on the wrist.

Going home he thought again, with complacency, of his deal with Ager. First he had explained the situation, setting five, not three pounds as the limit. This did not astound Mr. Ager, a gentleman like Mr. Draper would naturally think in such terms. Then Johnny said that the summer now more than half over, he did not need a suit this year; so would Mr. Ager oblige him by letting him have the five pounds and charging Mr. Draper with that amount. The tailor minded very much indeed. It was the equivalent of lending five pounds with no interest; and think of the book work involved. Humiliating himself — for Marion's sake — Johnny suggested that he would be willing to take four. That made more sense and three pounds ten made even better. So the deal was made. And the buff-and-tan suit was as good as new after Mrs. Fenner had worked on it with a damp cloth and a flat-iron. Not that three pounds ten was much of a nest-egg; but it would pay for the Special Licence, and the fares to London.

The bell on the door jangled. Mr. Draper stepped into Mr. Freeman's shop, noted the mahogany and ground-glass enclosure behind which the dispensing was done, the shining orderliness of the shelves, the absence of muddle.

It was just after nine o'clock on Monday morning, and the owner of the shop, not the assistant was on duty.

'Good morning, Freeman. I want a shaving brush. The best you have.'

Mr. Freeman was not exactly surprised to see Mr. Draper in his shop. The mills of God ground slowly, but they ground exceedingly small. Industry and enterprise were, in the long run, rewarded, and Baxter was definitely on the decline.

Mr. Freeman busied himself. 'All pure badger bristles,' he said, laying one brush after another on the counter. 'Only the handles vary; wood ten shillings, bone fifteen, solid ivory twenty-five.'

'I think this will do,' Mr. Draper said, indicating the ivory-handled one.

'And you couldn't find a better brush wherever you looked,' Mr. Freeman said, faintly resenting the implication that his best was hardly good enough. 'You could have a silver-plated handle, but no better brush.'

'I'll take it.'

He put a sovereign and two half-crowns on the counter. Mr. Freeman busied himself making the neat little parcel, white paper, red sealing-wax. 'I can have it delivered if you wish.'

'By that impertinent young man of yours?'

Mr. Freeman's errand-boy was twelve, employed because his mother cleaned the Baptist chapel. He was stupid, humble and afflicted with a cleft palate. How could he ever have been, how could even Mr. Draper say that he had ever been, impertinent?

'Bobby?' Mr. Freeman said, taken aback. 'You can't mean Bobby.'

'I do not know how many people you employ, Mr. Freeman. But this I do know. Baxter's business is on the decline and quite a number of people would transfer their custom to you, but for the fact that one of your assistants is, as I said, inclined to be impertinent.'

'I have only one assistant . . . French by origin. Is it possible that French politeness could have been misunderstood? In what way has he offended? I would call him to give an account of himself, but he is not well. Something that his landlady provides on Sunday upsets his stomach . . . this is not the first time he has been late on Monday. He makes up the time, of course. Did he offend you in any way, Mr. Draper?'

'Only indirectly. But enough to make me think again over a move I was contemplating — the transferance of my custom to you, Mr. Freeman.' He paused to allow time for Mr. Freeman to do some mental arithmetic. 'One hesitates to expose one's womenfolk to insult. Tales get around, you know.'

'If you'll excuse me asking — Have you got the right tale, Mr. Draper? I can hardly see de Brissac acting insultingly to a lady. There must be some mistake. What did he do? Or say?'

'I do not propose to go into detail. What I can say is that if you want to catch Baxter's slipping trade, you'd do well to get rid of the fellow.'

In almost any shop in Bereham this would have been sufficient; and even Mr. Freeman was tempted. He knew about the ban and would have been glad to see it lifted. But his nonconformity reared up, he was not going to be bullied. He also remembered that lately even Mrs. Marriot, the rector's wife, had begun to use his shop.

'I am very sorry, very sorry indeed that my assistant should, in some way have given you offence. I have never had any other complaint; I'd say he was popular rather than otherwise. And I could hardly dismiss a man, satisfactory in every way, on such flimsy grounds.'

Mr. Draper picked up his little parcel.

Flimsy?

Flimsy! The custom of about fifty families, besides his own. But nothing was every gained by allowing temper to show. He said 'Good day' civilly enough, and stepped out into the sunshine, making for Baxter's, halting to study its dismal façade. It needed paint. The pleasant bowed window displayed no single item of merchandise; just the flagons of coloured water, very dusty; Freeman's shone like jewels; the rest of the window covered with dingy, dusty, fine wire mesh on which the words, once written in gold, 'J. Baxter. Chymist', were still faintly discernible. Dating back to the time, Mr. Draper reflected, when some ancestor of the present John Baxter had not been able to spell the name of his own trade. He went in and to the young man behind the counter said:

'I want a shaving brush. A good one. Badger bristles.'

The boy made some show of willingness to search; but the best shaving brush in this shop was of hog-bristle. 'The best hog though, sir. Russian.'

Mr. Draper then said, 'Is your master about?'

'He's in the back, sir. Just finishing his breakfast. I'll call him. But that, sir, really is the best brush we have.'

'I don't doubt it,' Mr. Draper said, almost genially. 'Don't bother. I'll go through.' He was not, naturally, on social terms with a shopkeeper, but he was an old and valued customer, and both of them worshipped at St. Mary's.

The interview was not prolonged. Mr. Draper went straight to the point, ignoring any hurt he might cause by his criticism, his use of phrases like 'slipping downhill', 'lagging behind'. Mr. Baxter said simply that financial straits were responsible and that family responsibilities were responsible for the financial straits. His eldest, a daughter, was a widow with two children — 'Her husband's folks give them a home, but she has no spending money except what I send her.' His eldest boy — very clever — was at Cambridge, his second in Edinburgh, his youngest at the Grammar School. 'It all takes money, Mr. Draper. I'm often hard put to it to pay my bills, leave alone go in for renovations and such.'

Mr. Draper did not criticise or deplore this paternal concern and ambition. His own father had made sacrifices in order to give him a good education. He said, 'It was a good business once, and could be again. And it stands on one of the best sites in the town. Have you ever thought of raising a mortgage?'

'Often enough — and I may be driven to it. And then I shall have the interest to meet, as well as the bills.'

'Not if no interest were charged.'

'And who'd take a mortgage without asking interest?'

'I might,' Mr. Draper said. 'On certain conditions, of course.'

(This act of spite, decided upon in the course of a short walk, was eventually to prove one of his most profitable investments. Four years later a firm of wholesale chemists sent out their spies who, like Mr. Draper, knew a good site when they saw one and reported that for so thriving a business, for premises so recently brought up to date, the price would be high. And although Mr. Draper had received no penny of interest, he had a document, carefully drawn up by Angela Taylor's father, which established him as the virtual owner of the place.)

Mr. Draper went home in a glum mood that Monday. All through the day when his mind had not been occupied by other concerns, he had brooded over Freeman's lack of co-operation — he looked on it now as defiance. True, he had set revenge on the trail, but it would be some time before the results were seen. Moreover, ruining Freeman, as he hoped to do, would not immediately get rid of that young man.

Ill-humour did not spoil his appetite. He ate a plateful of one of Ada's 'summer' soups, a crystal clear consommé, and then carved the cold joint, giving himself the pinkest, juiciest slices because he knew that women, always contrary, preferred their meat overdone. Then he looked about and said, 'Where is the chutney?'

Chutney and mustard pickle were usually served with cold beef, brought to table in heavy cut glass jars.

'I'll fetch it, Papa,' Ellen said, pushing her chair back.

'You will ring the bell and then sit down.'

Betty came in, a little breathless and flustered.

'You rang, sir?'

'If you will look about the table you may see *why*.'

Betty looked, clapped her hand to her mouth and said:

'Oh. The chutney. Sorry, sir.' She vanished.

'That girl is becoming slap-dash,' the master of the house said, gladly seizing upon this trivial excuse to exercise his sense of grievance.

Mamma emerged with — in the circumstances — some

degree of heroism and said, 'It was my fault. I should have noticed when I looked over the table.'

'We do keep a maid,' Papa said.

'I know. But she has rather much to do these days. Ada is so incapacitated.'

Papa, still awaiting the arrival of the chutney, refusing to start without it, pounced upon this chance to be unpleasant.

'If Ada can no longer pull her weight, she must go.'

Mamma blanched and shrivelled. She regretted saying anything. Really, only silence was safe. But Ada and her piano were the two things that had never failed her. She felt bound to protest.

'Ada still cooks well. It is just that she is no longer very active and so all the running about falls on Betty. And Ada has no home. Where could she go?'

'To the Poor House. What do you think we pay rates for?'

Mamma made a little whimpering sound.

Marion said, 'To send Ada to the Poor House would be like sending a faithful old horse to the knacker's yard.'

Betty panted in, 'I'm sorry I was so long, sir. I had to open a fresh jar.'

'And now that it has arrived am I supposed to dig it out with my fingers?'

Betty, in her flurry, had forgotten the spoon.

Marion said, 'That is all right, Betty. There are spoons here.' She rose and went to the sideboard and opened the drawer where, nested and shrouded in baize the 'best silver' lay. It was fashionably heavy and ornate, used only when they entertained.

Papa looked at the spoon, brought into service on an ordinary day, and felt an impulse to repudiate it. But Betty, sly creature, had scuttled away. To ring the bell, recall her and send her for one of the plain, very old, worn-thin-by-long-use-and-polishing spoons, would further delay his meal. So he dug into the chutney — Ada's own special concoction; Ada would give a recipe to anyone who asked for it, but she always seemed to withhold some vital thing. Having helped himself he passed the jar along and proceeded to eat in silence. His hunger was presently assuaged; his sense of injury was not and presently he turned to Marion and said, very smoothly, 'Did my ears deceive me, or did I hear you say to that careless girl, "That is all right, Betty"?'

'Yes, Papa. That is what I said. I meant that there was no need for you to wait any longer. A spoon was here.'

'About Ada, also, you made a remark?'

'Yes, Papa. I remarked that to send Ada . . .'

'I heard. What has come over you, Marion, I am at a loss to say. I have borne a great deal one way and another, but disruption of my household I cannot and will not tolerate. I am of the opinion that the blow on your head had more serious results than were evident. I feel that you are not fully responsible and that a stay at Heatherton would be advisable.'

The horrible word 'Heatherton' exploded in the quiet room.

Ellen said, 'Oh no, Papa, please. Not there!' and even Mamma looked distressed.

'And what, may I ask, do you know about Heatherton?'

'A lot,' Ellen said incautiously. 'Mr. Taylor had something to do with that case. A great many things were said then that couldn't be put in the papers because of libel.'

Mr. Draper remembered the case. An old man, a medical, not mental patient had changed his will and left three thousand pounds to the woman who owned and ran the place — Miss Rose. The family had contested the will. There had been talk of undue influence, of coercion, of downright intimidation. Miss Rose had emerged triumphant and in possession of her legacy, but with a curiously parti-coloured reputation. There was no lack of ex-patients ready to vouch that Miss Rose had been consistently kind to them or patients confided to her care. Other people had said other things and Miss Rose herself, asked if she had ever struck a patient, replied, 'Of course I have. And shall again, I am afraid. It is the most effective way of dealing with incipient hysteria in the mentally unstable. But Mr. Woodhouse was not in that category at all. He was in the terminal stage of carcinoma and in need of nursing.'

Locally, after that, Heatherton had come to be regarded as a place to be avoided and nowadays those under Miss Rose's roof tended to come from distant parts of the country.

'If a statement is likely to be libellous when printed, it can hardly be accepted as Gospel,' Mr. Draper said. 'If Marion goes to Heatherton determined to behave herself and to get better, she will have nothing to fear. Ring the bell, Ellen, we are ready for the pudding.' Ellen, beginning to cry, did as she was told. 'And if you propose to make an exhibition of your-self, go to your room. Enough tears were shed at Yarmouth to suffice for a year.'

With Ellen gone and the pudding served, Mr. Draper looked at Marion who had sat throughout as though the talk concerned some other person. At that moment a really abject apology, a promise of better behaviour in future, might have saved her. Mr. Draper might, between accepting the apology and the promise, have had a few cogent things to say about playing upon Ellen's emotions and allowing her to become too dependent. But Marion for a time said nothing and when she did speak what she said confirmed his self-inculcated suspicion that she was not in her right mind.

'It will be further expense for you, Papa. It would be cheaper to let me go back to school and then on to St. Hilda's.'

'Back to school, at eighteen! How absurd. You appear to have taken leave of your senses — and to have lost your memory. I must remind you that I positively forbade you ever to broach that subject again. As for expense, you can hardly have failed to observe that I never consider expense when it comes to providing the best for you all.' As he said this he looked from his sullen, unresponsive daughter to his wife who managed a nod of the head and a rearrangement of her features, too slight to be called a smile. It was true; disapproving as he did of the kind of music that appealed to her, Jonathan had provided her with the very best grand piano . . .

At the end of that dismal meal Mr. Draper went to his study and hesitated between a forthright, 'Dear Miss Rose', and 'Dear Matron'. It was a title to which Miss Rose was entitled, for before an eccentric old uncle had left her his large country house, with contents, but not a penny for its unkeep. Miss Rose had been matron at St. James, one of London's famous hospitals. Finally he compromised with 'Dear Madam'. That letter, completed, he wrote another, be-ginning, 'Dear Doctor Barlow . . .' He wrote that one in the comfortable assurance that had he been about to suggest that Marion was suffering from rabies, Doctor Barlow was unlikely to contradict. He was not only the Drapers' family doctor, he was the pivot of a very progressive insurance scheme, devised by Mr. Draper himself. For years all but the feckless few of the Maltings' employees had contributed twopence a week to the scheme; to each twopence Mr. Draper added a halfpenny. The scheme was of benefit to all; to the workmen who received medical attention that they could not otherwise have afforded; to Mr. Draper because men properly treated and not left to home-made remedies based largely on superstition, recovered more quickly and more thoroughly; to the doctor who received a small but certain income, and who had by his manner and rather drastic treatments taught the Maltings' men — and their wives not to come running to him with trivial ailments; not to disturb him at meal-times, not to wake him from sleep. Doctor Barlow would readily agree that in a house with so many stairs, and only one maid active, with a vaguely ailing mother, a sister so easily provoked to tears, there was no place for a young woman who, though the wound on her head was healing well, 'was not herself'. Was in need of care and attention.

Yet, in his own fashion, the old man had integrity. After examining Marion, he said, 'I would suggest the medical, not the other side, where sorry sights and sounds might retard rather than aid recovery.'

'I propose to leave that to Miss Rose.' Mr. Draper poured sherry. 'The truth is, Marion's condition is variable. This evening you saw little wrong with her. Is that not so?'

'The wound is healing well. Her manner seemed composed.'

'Yet last evening, believe it or not, she was pleading with me to send her back to school! — She has had her eighteenth birthday!'

'I see,' Doctor Barlow said, sipping his sherry.

'It is very short notice,' Mamma said, 'but I have no doubt that Ada will rise to the occasion.'

A dinner-party, arranged with almost dizzying haste, for Friday, and this was Wednesday, would surely show Ada at her best. Mamma was anxious to rehabilitate Ada, infirm as she was becoming. Artichoke soup, lobster mousse. Grouse; no, too early; duck; Ada's special Tipsy Cake.

'It is rather short notice,' Mr. Draper agreed. 'It so happened that Mr. Taylor — who has just done a useful job for me — expressed a wish to meet Mr. Horridge. Hoping for a new client, of course. Not that it will come to anything, Horridge, I have no doubt has his own man of business, probably in London. But I made the gesture, hurriedly because the Taylors start their holiday next week. And we owe the Andrews hospitality.'

'Ada will manage.'

There was altogether too much emphasis upon Ada. It smacked of reproof. As though Ada, whom he regarded as expendable, was in fact indispensible.

He said, quite affably, 'Ada's efforts will be adequate, I do not doubt. But there is more to entertaining than the food. Betty needs stricter supervision. You know, my dear, you are inclined, when at the piano, to lose all thought of time and mundane things. I think that as a precaution, I shall lock it until after the party.'

Mamma accepted loss of her piano as stoically as Marion accepted banishment to Heatherton. Ellen wept enough for all. She wept as she said, 'Dearest, I am sure you have only to apologise and it would not be too late even now.' Miss Rose had written to say that she could accommodate Miss Draper on Monday. 'I cannot bear to think of you in that horrid place. Promise me you won't let it drive you crazy. Angela said lots of people, not a bit mad to start with, did go mad through being locked up with people who were, and treated like them. And Miss Rose is so bad-tempered they say.'

'I am not exactly unaccustomed to ill-humour.'

'It has been bad lately,' Ellen admitted. 'You won't be away long, will you? I honestly don't think I could bear this house without you. It was bad enough when I was young.' She remembered the two years when Marion was at school and she was not. 'I just hope and pray that Papa will forget that silly idea that a young lady should not go out alone. Without you, without Angela and Mamma so inactive . . .' She drooped at the prospect. Then she mopped her eyes and her soft little face took on an obstinate expression. 'Anyway, of one thing I am determined. You are going to have dinner with us tomorrow.'

'Ellen, please. I do not mind in the least. If you speak of it you'll get into trouble, too. It will in any case be a very dull party.'

'There will be a new face. Mr. Horridge sounds exciting.

Imagine just walking about in Africa and picking up gold.'

'Who said he did?'

'Angela. Mr. Taylor said he is very rich indeed. He made himself into a company or something.'

Ellen went about persuading Papa to change his mind about allowing Marion to be present at a party with a certain amount of subtlety. A sidelong attack.

'I wish,' she said, 'that Marion felt well enough to face company for just a little while.'

'In her present state Marion is not fit for company,' Mr. Draper said.

'But the Andrews are invited.' A *non sequitur* if ever there was one.

'And what,' he asked testily, 'has that got to do with it?'

'*You* have no idea, Papa, what Mrs. Andrews' tongue is like. She restrains herself in front of gentlemen. But I *know* that if she does not see Marion tomorrow and then hears that she is going to ... that place, by Saturday she will be saying that Marion was chained to the bed-post. Or something worse.'

'Ridiculous! People go to Heatherton to be nursed after breaking a leg.'

'Anyone Mrs. Andrews knew who did that she would say he broke it kicking his wife.'

Mr. Draper gave one of his rare laughs.

'Then perhaps Marion should be present. On the strict understanding that she is not to be surly or jump about doing Betty's work. And something must be done about that bald patch. She is convalescent but there is no need to be unsightly.'

'I will see to it, Papa.'

The best dinner service had been taken out and washed, not merely dusted; the best silver had been rubbed with a chamois leather, the best glasses repolished. Two extra leaves in the dining-table, now spread with the best damask cloth which bore within its starched white-and-silver surface a design of pheasants; napkins of the same damask had been made into water-lilies. In the centre of the table an epergne sprouted, at various layers, white roses, white carnations and trails of asparagus fern. Exercising an unusual supervision, Mrs. Draper was sure that all was in order.

And also in the drawing-room. The door to the little conservatory was open and that lent a feeling of space, the pot plants on the slatted shelves gave colour. On the table at the other end, sherry and Madeira, suitable glasses to the forefront of the vast silver tray, and to the rear of it the blue-hued syphon, the whisky, the tumblers from which the gentlemen would drink before leaving. On the closed piano was what was beginning to be called an arrangement of flowers. Against the black, polished surface the flowers, mainly white, in a white bowl looked well, but Mrs. Draper looked at them with disapproval. Nothing should stand upon a piano. But the piano, locked, used as a stand for flowers, shared her mental withdrawal. Impossible, this evening to play those stupid, sickly, sentimental little tinkling tunes. And thank God for that! She went upstairs to dress.

In the basement kitchen Ada pulled the soup aside and stooped down, painfully, to look into the oven to see how the ducks were doing. The lobster mousse, her own special secret, lobster being a tough thing and few people knowing how to reduce it to creamy smoothness without loss of flavour, and the Tipsy Cake, there again her own, stood ready on the dresser.

The ducks were doing nicely; but straightening up from the oven Ada said, 'I don't know, Betty girl. I somehow feel that this'll be the last party I shall see to. I'm getting past it, and it comes hard on you.'

'When you go, I go,' Betty said. 'And there's that blasted bell.'

Ellen said, 'Heavens, that'll be the Andrews. Darling, it is the best I can do — and though I say so, not bad.'

She had pulled Marion's hair — so plentiful on one side, mere bristles on the other, up to a kind of coronet on top of her head, the end of the tail brought over to conceal the shaven spot and the scar. A little action with the curling tongs assured that the falling tail curved inwards. 'I think it is rather becoming,' Ellen said. She was aware that she was not very clever — but her hands were.

Betty said, 'Mr. and Mrs. Andrews,' and thought, what a lot of rot. They know each other. It was a kind of game, designed to keep idle footmen employed. 'Mr. Horridge. Mr. and Mrs. Taylor.'

Inside the drawing-room Mr. Draper took over. He named

his daughters in a peculiarly casual way. 'Mr. Horridge,' he said; 'My daughter Marion, my daughter Ellen.'

Later he would have something to say to them both. A fringe, a Piccadilly fringe! The very badge of a prostitute, except that the Princess of Wales ... Not that that was any recommendation. Mr. Draper had nothing against Alexandra but he disapproved strongly of the Prince of Wales' goings on ...

But, as usual, he controlled himself. 'Sherry or Madeira?' He was at his best when dispensing hospitality.

Mr. Horridge, subject of this hospitality, found himself slightly confused. In the year and a half that he had spent in Norfolk, he had gone through a peculiar social mill, the upper grindstone plain avarice, the lower simple snobbery. He had denied that he was related to Sir Charles Horridge of Swaffham, or to Dean Horridge of Asham. 'No. Never heard of them in my life. Nor them of me.' Disappointing; but at least the man was honest. And presentable. And rich.

Mr. Horridge knew the drill. But in this comparatively modest house — no stables, he had been obliged to leave his horse and gig at the livery place, in Honey Lane — there was a difference; Mr. Draper was certainly not trotting out his fillies. He introduced them by name, rather as a dog owner might say, 'This is Rover. This is Fluff.' And the girls, after giving him the briefest acknowledgement had gone off to join the older women at the far end of the room. Probably both spoken for. They were a good-looking pair; one very pretty in the ordinary way; the other one most unusual. A beauty!

It took Mr. Horridge several minutes, several peeps to learn that neither Ellen nor Marion wore the outward tokens of betrothal. He found himself hoping that in Marion's case this was true evidence. The more he looked, the more he liked. He was not a romantic man and he was past his fortieth birthday, but he found himself thinking — There is a face I could live with; something secret, mysterious about it.

Mr. Draper intercepted one of Mr. Horridge's looks and for once his instinct failed him entirely. No wonder the man stared. The hair-style was deplorable; and why on earth was she wearing that shabby old green frock? Heaven knew she had a wardrobe crammed with newer, more sumptuous ones.

Mr. Horridge would have liked to step over and speak, first to all the ladies and then to Marion in particular; but he had lived in Norfolk long enough to know that, except with parents who had designs on him, this was the usual pre-dinner form, men in a clump pretending not to be talking business, but actually doing so, women in another clump discussing whatever it was women talked about. He hoped that he would find himself beside Marion at table.

He did not; he was seated between his hostess and Mrs. Andrews; he wasn't even directly opposite the face he wished to study. He could, however, hear her voice which pleased him as much as her appearance. It was soft and she did not, as most young women did, try to lend animation by over-emphasis. Nor did she laugh. Once or twice she smiled. When she did so it made more change than on a more-generally lively face and Mr. Horridge found himself wishing that he had been the one to bring about this transformation.

None of the old tricks were played at this table. Nobody drew attention to how beautifully Marion — or Ellen — had done the flowers, folded the table-napkins, supervised the preparation of the excellent meal. No mention was made of the girls' interests, good works, talents or foibles.

Mr. Horridge found his hostess difficult to talk to. To each of his remarks she murmured some sterile agreement upon which the subject died; and she offered no comment of her own. Occasionally, especially when the maid was changing plates, she looked a little anxious and preoccupied. Fortunately his other neighbour was garrulous and inquisitive. She asked again the question he had answered so many times about his relationship to the eminent Horridges. 'Yet it is not a common name,' she said. 'It's common enough where I come from,' he said. He did not say where that was. His reticence was not — as Mrs. Andrews suspected — due to desire to conceal his origins, it was simply that the Cumberland village which he had left at the age of fourteen held no interest for him and he could not imagine it being of interest to anyone else.

At one point Mrs. Andrews addressed Marion directly, leaning across the flowers. 'Marion, dear, remember I am counting upon your help next Thursday with my croquet party.'

The fascinating, inscrutable face turned; the low clear voice said:

'I am sorry, Mrs. Andrews, I should have let you know. I shall not be here. On Monday I am going to Heatherton.'

The word evoked a curious silence, broken by Mr. Draper.

'Marion is still far from fully recovered. Doctor Barlow advised a convalescent period in the Nursing Home.'

'I am sorry,' Mrs. Andrews said. She then turned to Mr. Horridge and said, 'Marion had a terrible accident.' She gave him what details she knew, adding in a lower voice, 'I should hardly have thought Heatherton . . . but I suppose Mr. Draper knows best.'

Mr. Horridge would hardly have thought Heatherton, either. It adjoined his own estate, Sorley Park, and most of his staff was related either directly or by some involved process of intermarriage, with most of Miss Rose's. Still, servants' gossip was not to be trusted.

He remembered that the Drapers kept no carriage; so he addressed himself to Mrs. Draper, offering, should she wish to visit her daughter, the use of his carriage and pair.

Mrs. Draper applied one of her conversation stoppers. 'How very kind,' she remarked, neither accepting nor refusing the offer.

The ladies withdrew; the gentlemen remained to drink Mr. Draper's first-class port and to resume the business-tinged conversation. Back in the drawing-room Mr. Horridge was disappointed to see Marion seated on a sofa between Mrs. Taylor and Mrs. Andrews. The sofa was so placed that it was impossible for him to go behind it and lean over its back. Nor could he approach it from the front because exactly opposite her daughter Mrs. Draper sat in a low chair, with a table and the coffee tray before her. Mr. Horridge must content himself with staring; and although through the rather boring evening he did not manage to exchange a word with the girl he admired so much, he knew by the end of it that he was in love. He had always avoided matrimony because of its threatened tedium; the same face, the same voice three hundred and sixty-five days in a year; but here was a face, he was certain, that one could look at for ever, and still not know it all. He thought rather naïvely, that just as his physical wanderings had ended and he had settled down, so his emotional journeyings were over.

A sign of encroaching old age? He thought, dolefully — Of course, I'm almost twice her age. He thought she was over twenty; twenty-two perhaps.

The evening was enlivened by one curious small incident.

Mr. Andrews said gallantly, 'I hope you are going to give us some music, Mrs. Draper. Of all the delights that hospitality under this roof offers, your playing is the greatest.'

Taking her assent for granted, he went to throw open the piano. It was locked. There was nothing extraordinary about that. What was unusual was that Marion and Ellen exchanged a long eloquent look, while Mrs. Draper behaved as though the piano had nothing to do with her. She sat staring down at her hands.

'Ellen, my dear. The key. It is on my dressing-chest.'

Ellen sped from the room as though she had been propelled. Mr. Andrews assured Mr. Horridge that Mrs. Draper's playing was positively of concert standard; a piece of information that was received with indifference since music to him was noise, varying only in loudness. However, when the piano was opened and Mrs. Draper began to play, her competence and dedication were obvious. She played without printed music and with her eyes half closed. She played the kind of music popular in drawing-rooms, not very loud, drifting from one tune to another. And then suddenly she changed her style and seemed almost to attack the piano. It was very loud music indeed, with something about it of passion and power. Mr. Draper rose, crossed to where she sat and spoke into her ear. She struck three crashing chords and stopped. 'I dislike loud music,' Mr. Draper said.

The guests hastened to congratulate Mrs. Draper upon her performance. Mr. Horridge hoped that either Mrs. Taylor or Mrs. Andrews would now be asked to play, or to sing. Then he thought that with so gifted a mother one of the girls would sing. But when Mrs. Draper resumed her seat the room became static again and presently, with the arrival of the Taylors' carriage the party began to disperse.

'One would have thought,' Papa said in his most cutting voice, 'that one of you could have remembered the key. Three of you about here all day long with absolutely nothing to do; yet what I happen to overlook is neglected.'

Mamma and Ellen said the only thing there was to say, 'I am sorry.' Mr. Draper noticed that Marion did not speak. 'You, I suppose take no blame for the oversight?'

'I never considered it necessary to lock the piano.'

A daft answer if ever there was one.

'I have never known a more unsatisfactory evening. I told

you, Ellen, to do something about your sister's hair. I meant an improvement, not a vulgar imitation of your chance-come-by friend. And why are you,' his attention shifted, 'wearing that old dress? If your object was to shame me, you succeeded admirably. You have ear-rings, bracelets, a locket and chain, and you look like a pauper. As for you, my dear,' he could use the term like a smack in the face, 'you know how much I detest that kind of noise. One would have thought you had gone mad.'

'I am very sorry. I momentarily forgot that company was present.'

'And the meal was not what it should have been. Roast potatoes with duck, in itself a greasy dish. Is Ada now too infirm to mash a potato? And the girl breathing so hard. I was mortified. And not helped, Ellen, by hearing you give to Mr. Taylor a quite unnecessary detailed account of Marion's accident. Blood is not a subject for dinner-table talk — especially when eating Tipsy Cake.'

Marion felt an almost overwhelming desire to laugh, thinking of the strawberry jam oozing out between the layers of sherry-soaked sponge cake.

'But he asked me, Papa,' Ellen said. She began to cry. She had done her best with Marion's hair; had urged unavailingly, the wearing of some ornaments. And it could have been such a lovely party. Ellen's standards were not high; to look pretty, to have a nice meal — and despite what Papa said it had been a nice meal, fully appreciated — and to have everybody happy and amiable was enough for her. So she wept because what should have been pleasant was not. And because of the music ... Whenever Mamma played in that particular way something in Ellen responded. She had herself wished to learn to play the piano and was sure she could have done — not so well as Mamma, but well enough. Papa, however, had decided otherwise, 'One pianist in a family is enough,' and Mamma had given no support. But when Mamma played real music, Ellen often stopped and listened; tonight the sudden breaking off had jerked her nerves.

'Go to bed. You are overtired. Go along, Marion can manage to unhook herself for once. She will have no maid at Heatherton.'

Over Marion, ever since Monday, Heatherton had cast its shadow. But she had lived through the time of terror and felt that she was hardened to anything, even the company of drooling lunatics. Going to Heatherton would rid her of Johnny and it might offer her a chance of escape, since the precautions taken would be such as were effective for those infirm of mind or body. Which I am not!

But there was Ellen, sent away, crying, and there, a minute after was Papa locking the piano again, saying, 'When you wish to play, agreeably . . .'

Marion remembered that twice, monumentally selfish, she had tried to escape. Once through marriage to Johnny; once through death in the water. Oh no, another time too, through Miss Ruthven.

I thought only of myself.

I did not think of them.

I have been as selfish, as self-centred as *he* is.

Different now. I will save us all.

Ellen shall have parties so different from this.

Mamma shall play the piano, as she likes all day, all night; go to concerts . . .

If it works.

She had written to Johnny, telling him that it was over, that her feelings had changed and she no longer loved him. She had added that arguing about it would be useless, and in fact impossible, since she was going away, probably for a long time. She intended the letter to be posted on Saturday morning so that it would reach him by the late post. He would imagine that she had already gone. Or if, hopefully, he came along after all, she would not reply to his tapping.

She had planned to ask Ellen to post it, telling her that it was merely a civil note to thank him for the flowers.

Now she tore the letter into shreds and dropped them into the kitchen fire where a few red embers still glowed. Let Johnny come tomorrow, as arranged, and be made use of.

She was half undressed when Johnny tapped at the window. Coming so unexpectedly the sound made her jump, but she hurried to the window and greeted him with a good imitation of her old warmth.

'Why, Johnny, what a surprise. I did not expect you until tomorrow.' She sounded as though the surprise pleased her.

'I could wait no longer. Can you let me in?'

'Soon. Papa may be moving about. We are late tonight. We have had a party.'

'I know. I saw the lights. I have been walking up and down.'

His coming on Friday seemed providential, if one could use the word in such a connection. Silence fell on the house and presently she used the screw-driver which she had thought never to use again.

Tonight her behaviour confirmed his belief that her odd manner on the previous Saturday was due to fatigue. Except for the fact that there was no actual love-making, they seemed now to be back on the terms which had existed before she was pregnant and had begun to nag about marriage.

She gave him some brandy. He told her about his arrangement with Ager; what he had discovered about Special Licences. It was he who now urged a runaway marriage, the sooner the better.

'It cannot be next week, Johnny. I have to go to Heatherton.'

The word had its usual effect. 'What? Oh no. Not that abominable place. This I will not permit.' He looked wildly round the little room. 'You must dress, darling, get a few things together and come away with me. Now.'

'Johnny, the last train has gone. What about all your belongings?'

'Tomorrow, then. You must not go to that place. In a shop one hears things and if you knew as much about it as I do . . .'

She pretended to hesitate. 'No. I think that would be unwise. For one thing Papa has convinced himself, and Doctor Barlow, that I am not quite right in the head. I should not merely be a runaway daughter, I should be a lunatic at large. He would be justified in asking police aid in finding us.'

'We could cover our tracks.' He was now as eager as he had been reluctant.

'There is another thing, too. I want to find out about my money.'

'What money?'

'A legacy my grandmother left me. It might come to me when I am twenty-one, or on marriage. I do not know; but I mean to find out.'

'How much?'

'About five thousand pounds.' Lies came easily now.

'And you never even *told* me.'

She said with just the right touch of lightness, 'I had no wish to be married for my money! Now that you *have* asked me, I felt I could mention it. Have a little more brandy.'

He sat and sipped happily. This put a completely different face upon things. Even if they had to wait until Marion was of age, the poverty would be bearable, since there would be a limit to it. In fact it might be possible to borrow money immediately on the strength of such expectations.

'You are a strange girl,' he said, giving her a hug with his free arm. 'Perhaps that is why I love you so much.'

Now.

She studied the backs of her hands and said, 'It is a curious thing; my face never tans, but my hands are like a gypsy's.' Then, as though the thought had just occurred, 'Johnny, you could get me some pure white arsenic, could you not?'

The theory that arsenic was the best whitener for skin was a popular one, and the request for it in its pure form was not remarkable if it were to be used as a cosmetic. In order that the dangerous stuff should not be confused with salt or fine sugar it was often adulterated with soot or indigo or other colouring matter.

'I suppose I could,' he said cautiously. 'It would not be easy. Mr. Freeman is fussy about checking the contents of the poison cupboard against the poison book.'

'Is arsenic a poison? We never knew that. We used it at school, regularly. It never hurt anyone.'

'How did you obtain it?'

'We soaked fly-papers. But that is so messy. The sticky stuff soaked off, too. And it could not be done secretly, so then we were teased about being vain. I thought that if you would get some for me I could sit and soak my hands at Heatherton. It would be something to do. But of course, if you cannot,' she managed a casual voice, a casual shrug, 'think no more of it.'

He accepted the challenge. 'Of course I can. And I will. But you must promise to be very careful. It is, you see, very different from soaking fly-papers. Of them you could soak a dozen and not have a very lethal solution. When you have soaked your hands you must wash them thoroughly before touching your eyes or your mouth, or taking any food. And another thing, darling. If your hands should develop a rash, or even become reddened, you must stop using the stuff at once.'

'I promise, I promise, I vow and declare. What a fuss about nothing!'

Johnny walked home by his usual way, up Alma Avenue, into Honey Lane. The brandy had calmed his stomach, and although he knew that the relief was only temporary and that he would probably feel worse in the morning, he felt better. In spirit he was jubilant. Five thousand pounds! What a secretive girl she was — and should he not be grateful for it? And then, just outside Jarvey's livery stables, smelling of manure and horse sweat and the old cracked leather of the hireling vehicles, he stopped abruptly, let out a small exclamation and began to breathe more rapidly. It was not for her hands that Marion wanted arsenic. It was not a mere five thousand pounds that she wanted to find out about.

The idea, the suspicion slid into his mind, disrupting all thought for one stunning second, and then beginning to burgeon.

He remembered things she had said. 'I should be a lunatic at large. He would be justified in asking police aid in finding us.' Wherever she was, while her father lived, she would fear him. And who could wonder?

He walked on, slowly, debating with himself what to do, whether to do anything at all. Between being a callous self-seeker and accessory-before-the-act in murder there was a long step which he was half unwilling to take. There was also the risk which he was wholly unwilling to run. Yet, against his repugnance stood the memory of his humiliation at Mr. Draper's hands. Nothing was too bad for that horrible man; not even death by arsenical poisoning, the very negation of all dignity. Financial considerations weighed, too. If Mr. Draper persisted with his idea that Marion was out of her mind — and what else could his sending her to Heatherton imply? — would she be allowed to control her legacy, even when she attained it? The choice seemed to lie between running away and being hunted down by a ruthless and vindictive man, and being poor, or doing this thing, staying in Bereham, inheriting at least half of Mr. Draper's estate and — the only man in the family — gaining control of the business. Precisely what he had aimed at; and what he would have been happy to achieve in a harmless, amiable way. In fact Mr. Draper, were this fate to overtake him, had only himself to blame.

But if anything should go wrong — *You work in a chemist's shop!* Instantly suspect. Against that set Mr. Freeman's Baptist scrupulosity over the Poison Book. All things recognised as poisons were kept together in a cupboard, always locked, and on its bottom shelf lay the book. Nothing, not the smallest quantity of rat-or weed-killer, left that cupboard without being noted, dated and signed for. Country people bought most rat poison and many of them were illiterate. Against their purchases, their names were written by whoever served them and then they were required to make their mark. Fresh supplies were always listed and from time to time Mr. Freeman checked, counting, weighing, and then punctiliously writing, 'Checked and found correct. Sam Freeman.' Such entries were always dated.

But in the shop there were many harmless substances which, put into, well-mixed with the contents of the tightly stoppered, plainly labelled jar could masquerade under anything but the most stringent chemical analysis.

One must remember, too, that there was no known connection between the maltster's sheltered daughter and the chemist's assistant. Well, at least, Ellen knew; but Ellen had now for many months been completely deceived, and in the event of disaster — he knew Ellen well enough to be certain — Ellen would be so eager to say that Marion never would, Marion positively could not, Marion never went into a shop without her ... Ellen was not stupid. And Marion was extremely intelligent. So why should anything go wrong? Of all murders by poison, that by arsenic was the most likely to succeed, the victim's symptoms so closely resembled enteritis. How many deaths had the Marquise de Brinvilliers inflicted before she was even suspected? This would be only one. In hot late-summer weather ... A man highly esteemed.

What could go wrong?

And, at the very back of his mind was the certainty, solid and reliable as rock, that if the worst happened, if things went most badly wrong, Marion would never utter a word that would incriminate him.

She'd die first.

She'd die.

And I ... I should be back where I started. With a year of youth, of charm, of effort, of hope wasted; and all to do again, in another place, with another girl.

'Oh, Johnny,' Marion said on the next evening, taking the little package. 'You did not manage much.'

'Enough to kill a regiment.'

'This? The size of a matchbox!' And she handed it as though it were a matchbox, laying it aside among the clutter on the top of the chest-of-drawers.

'Enough to kill several men, anyway. I told you yesterday darling. In its unadulterated form ... You will be careful. Careful how you use it?'

'I shall be very careful. Look, I will put it in my jewel case, safe under lock and key. Until I get to Heatherton.' She laid it alongside all the things Papa had given her.

Abruptly, and for no reason that he could have put into words, he became sure that in his overnight thoughts he had wronged her. Altogether too gentle, too kind. Such a thought would never occur to her. Nor to him when he was completely sober.

He said, '*Chérie*, whatever you do, do not provoke Miss Rose. She is said to have a villainous temper. And you will write to me?'

Some of her later letters, insistent and pleading, had pleased him little; but that was all over and done with now, and he would welcome a letter in the old, fond style. She had not written to him since her accident.

'I cannot promise, Johnny. The care and attention may include a supervision of correspondence. I must spy out the land, first.'

Behind her calm face the thought flashed — The next letter I write to you, Johnny Brisket, will surprise you very much!

'It will be another sojourn in the desert, beloved.'

And who is to blame for that? There was an oasis. I tried to steer you towards it, but you must go your own headstrong way. We could have been in London now, married; the child quickening within me. She put that thought away; that kind of thinking served no useful purpose. What was fantastic to reflect upon was the fact that had Johnny listened to her pleadings, fallen in with her plan, she would probably have gone on, on her life's end, believing that she loved him.

Ellen cried so much at the prospect of parting that Mr. Draper knew he had been correct in thinking that the bond between them was undesirably, unhealthily close. He spoke severely, 'Ellen, my dear, you really must make some effort at self-control. It may aid you if I say that for every time you cry — and I shall know by your eyes — Marion will spend an extra day at Heatherton.'

That was such an effective threat that when the moment of parting came, Ellen did not shed a tear. Mr. Draper went out to supervise the placing of Marion's trunk on the hired cab, and in the hall the two girls embraced. 'I shall soon be back,' Marion said. 'I shall behave impeccably and convince even Miss Rose that there is nothing wrong with me at all.'

But, Ellen thought, if Angela Taylor's stories were to be believed, Heatherton was full of people with whom there was nothing, or nothing very much wrong.

'I shall write to you every day, without fail,' she said. 'And if you are not home after a week, I shall manage somehow to come and see you.'

'I shall be all right, dearest. Just wait and see. And above all do not annoy Papa by seeming to mind.'

Out from Bereham the road they took was familiar, the road gladly taken towards Asham and Miss Ruthven's school. Then, at the crossroads they turned left instead of right and the trees thickened. They rode in silence. Mr. Draper was still annoyed with his daughter and disinclined to make a conversational effort; Marion, more like him than she would have admitted, was unwilling to venture the first, the seemingly sycophantic word.

'Here we are,' Mr. Draper said at last as the cab drew up on a wide space of well-raked gravel in front of a flat-faced, red-brick house, not unlike the dolls' house which had once been Mamma's and which Marion and Ellen had cherished until Mrs. Marriot had said that her granddaughter wanted a dolls' house and she must try to contrive it somehow. It was quite impossible to say — 'Have ours!' — but it was possible to offer the dolls' house, rather apologetically because it had no real value, to the Treasure Trove stall at the next Bazaar.

Now, here it was, the fanlighted door, two windows on either side; five on the next floor, neat, symmetrical. On each side of the house was a wall, built of the same red brick; the one on the left softened by a growth of tea-roses, sprawling up from the garden within, the one on the right broken by a carriage entrance, double doors, well painted and at this moment firmly closed.

'Never known it open, sir,' said their driver in response to Mr. Draper's suggestion that he should alight and open the gates. 'Been here, on and off a lot of times. Never known it open, sir.'

'Oh, very well,' Mr. Draper said. 'Come along, Marion.' He went to the door and gave a vigorous tug at the bell-pull, a bar ending in a kind of iron pineapple. Its response could be heard, muted by distance.

'I said what time we should be arriving,' Mr. Draper said irritably. The door had a knocker, too. A lion's head with a ring in its mouth. He lifted and plied it vigorously. And even then nobody came running. When the door opened it was defensively, not with apologies for delay. The man who opened it wore a sleeved waistcoat, the sleeves black, the rest of it striped, yellow and black, like a wasp. He had a hard-bitten face.

'Yes?' he said.

'I am Mr. Draper. Miss Rose is — or should be — expecting me.'

'Draper. S'right,' the man said, opening the door a little wider. As he entered Mr. Draper half turned and said, 'Coker, bring in the luggage.' He then added, because he was not pleased by his reception, an order which was to have re-percussions; though it was simple enough. He said, 'Give him a hand,' to the wasp-waistcoated man.

Miss Rose, just at the turn of the graceful staircase, heard a man, standing in *her* hall, giving *her* servant orders.

She said, 'Very well, Stubbs, if Mr. Draper's driver cannot manage, help him.'

With the single word, *driver*, she had put Mr. Draper in his place. Gentlemen had coachmen.

Up to that moment she had had no feelings about Mr. Draper or his daughter. Marion was a case; Mr. Draper a father arranging for a case to be taken care of. No details, of course, but then most people were too stupid to state things clearly, or if not stupid, reluctant. Now, standing on the bottom stair, thin, very upright, very trim in dark blue alpaca, stiff white starched collar, stiff white starched cuffs and a little fluted cap on her dark hair, Miss Rose took stock. She had heard the bell; she had heard the knocker. Impatient; masterful. And sleek. Well fed, well dressed, not bad looking. The very image of the kind of dominant male under whom Miss Rose had in her day suffered. And from whom she had escaped.

She came down the last stair and extended her hand.

'Good afternoon, Mr. Draper. Of course I was expecting you. You are a few minutes early. Miss Draper . . .' Her hand was thin, dry, hard. 'If you will come this way . . .' She went to a door at the rear of the hall and stood aside, ushering them in.

The dolls' house front, formal and conventional, was deceptive. The room was long and rather low, opening at its far end not upon the Alma Avenue conservatory but straight into the garden. And the room was stripped and stark. No velvet, no fringe, no touch of the fashionable colours, dark brown and crimson. No wallpaper even. No carpet. The walls were white, painted or whitewashed, the floor honey-coloured boards with a rug here and there. There were a few chairs and a sofa, covered with a kind of calico, brown and green leaves on a white background, and the fireplace was almost indecently naked. Marble; children with no clothes, playing with lambs.

Just right, Mr. Draper thought — a week here will bring Marion to her senses.

Just right, Marion thought, the most beautiful room I ever saw in my life. And one wall, all shelves, full of books.

'Please sit down,' Miss Rose said. She took her own seat behind a beautiful, clear-lined writing-table, near the window, so placed that she faced the room. 'Your letter told me very little, Mr. Draper.'

'I told you that my daughter had sustained an accident and needed care and attention. You replied that you had room for her. Perhaps she could be shown to her room. Now.'

'What is the point,' Miss Rose began. She then saw his point and said, pleasantly, 'Perhaps, Miss Draper, you would like to sit in the garden for a few minutes.'

She stood up and opened the french window behind her table; Marion said, 'Thank you,' as she passed and smiled. The smile, Miss Rose observed, made a great difference to her face.

'By telling me so little, Mr. Draper,' said Miss Rose, returning to the attack, 'you left me uncertain as to where to place her. Of necessity I must make some distinction between my medical patients and those with mental afflictions. What kind of care, what kind of attention does she need?'

'I think you must decide,' Mr. Draper said. 'As you see, she is in apparent good health; the wound on her head has healed. But some damage was done. She is not herself. A change in personality is as near as I can describe it. What I am bound to bear in mind is that my wife is far from strong, and my younger daughter is very sensitive. They have been much distressed by what I can only call domestic scenes. Doctor Barlow, our family physician, advised a period of convalescence here.'

That was, in itself, astonishing, since the scandal Miss Rose had had few local patients, and none from Doctor Barlow.

'This is all rather vague, Mr. Draper. Is Miss Draper forgetful? Melancholy? Hysterical?'

'It would be equally true to say no; or yes all on occasion. I have no doubt that she will exercise more self-control here than in the bosom of her family.' He sensed that Miss Rose did not like him much; he knew that she was not impressed by him. Not that the opinion of a woman who could live in a room like this was worth a fig. No taste at all. But he produced a small sigh, calculated to protect him from further questions. 'The accident ruined our holiday, and since then things have been very trying.'

'I can see,' Miss Rose said crisply, 'that I shall be obliged to form my own judgment.'

'That would be best.'

Miss Rose also possessed a sensitive mental nose which now informed her that here was some mystery. Such reticence could only be preserved for purposes of concealment. Never mind, whatever it was she would know as soon as she had the girl to herself. It was just on four o'clock but she did not offer him tea. 'If you can tell me anything else that would be useful ... No? Then we must not keep your driver waiting, must we?' She stood up.

Mr. Draper said, 'My daughter needs a firm hand.'

Miss Rose thought — I should have imagined you quite capable of applying it! But she said, 'You may depend upon me to take the best possible care of her.' Then, because he was turning towards the door into the hall, she said, with just a flash of mischief, 'You wish to say goodbye to her.'

The leave-taking, she observed was noticeably lacking in warmth. The father went through the motions of kissing his daughter on the brow and said, 'I hope you will soon be better.' The daughter made no pretence of returning the kiss. She said, 'Thank you, Papa.' She remained where she was, not accompanying him to the door to see him off, and Miss Rose, glancing back, saw her staring after him with an expression so intensely sad and at the same time so cynical that, hardened as she was, she felt a slight sense of shock.

'And now,' she said, coming back and ringing the bell, 'we will have tea.'

'That will be delightful,' Marion said, sitting down at one end of the sofa in the easy manner of one making a social call. 'You have a very beautiful room,' she added, looking round and thinking that when she was free to make choices and decisions, this was how she would decorate and furnish.

'Most people think it distressingly bare. But I dislike clutter.'

Across the tea-tray, placed on an elegant rosewood table, they took stock of one another. The girl looked well enough Miss Rose reflected, rightly judging that such a complexion would always be pale. And her manner was so normal that every now and then Miss Rose was obliged to remind herself that even quite severely deranged people had seasons of sense. In repose her face had a melancholy look, at odds with its youth and beauty. It was a look which pain could inflict.

'I understand that you had an accident, Miss Draper. But I know no details.'

'I fell in the sea at Yarmouth and hit my head on a groyne.' I chose death; and death rejected me.

'Your head gives you pain?'

'Not now, except sometimes when I stoop, as I did just now to smell your wonderful lilies. I have never seen anything like them.'

Evasive? There were some blows on the head which could lead to fits not easily distinguishable from epilepsy. And since fits were regarded as in some way shameful that might explain.

'They are quite rare, I believe. The bulbs were sent to me by a grateful patient who had some connections with the Far East. Miss Draper, I am sorry to persist — over the tea-table, too. But if I am to help I must know. Do you suffer from dizzy spells?'

'Oh no.' Not as a result of the blow, anyway.

'From impulses that seem uncontrollable?'

'Oh no.' Once I did; the impulse to love, and look where that ended. 'I am in good health, Miss Rose, and shall give you little trouble. It was just that my mamma and my sister are inclined to worry, and Papa thought ... I suppose in the ordinary way I should have gone to visit a relative, but as it happens we have none.'

'A change is often a good thing,' Miss Rose said, wondering what Mr. Draper had meant by domestic scenes.

Marion had been thinking that Miss Rose looked utterly unlike the ogre of the rumours. In fact her face with its sallow skin, wide-nostrilled nose and eyes that were lively, wary and sorrowful, was singularly like that of the organ-grinder's monkey for whom Marion had once felt sorry. Even her voice seemed to belie the legend of the scolding virago, nagging a sick man into leaving her money; it was a low-pitched voice, velvety.

'You have such a lovely lot of books, Miss Rose.'

'You enjoy reading?'

'It is my chief joy.' A very positive and very unusual statement from a girl of eighteen, nineteen?

'And who is your favourite author?' The answer might be enlightening. By their books thou shalt know them.

'That would be impossible to say. Except,' the smile that made so much difference showed again, 'the author of the book I happen to be reading at the moment.'

'Once,' Miss Rose said, 'when my real life was immensely unsatisfactory, I took refuge in Ouida.'

That was deliberate bait; naturally responded to, it should evoke a matching confidence and reveal what was wrong here.

Marion said, 'Yes; that I can well understand. May I look at them?'

'Please do. The bottom shelf contains medical works — very dull reading, but I try to keep abreast. Some of the others, the leather-bound ones are the remains of my uncle's library. His library I was obliged to put to other purposes — I mean the actual room, but of the books I saved what I could. The novels are my own.'

'Would you allow me to borrow one?'

'But of course. Take anything you like.'

And yet, vastly experienced in the ways of people not quite right in the head, Miss Rose watched, alert, as Marion went to the shelves. The demented were infinitely cunning. If the girl had taken the heaviest book and turned, brandishing it, maniacally, Miss Rose would not have been surprised. Nor helpless . . .

Marion handled the books with love. 'I remember this. On a very cold, drizzly day it took me into the sunshine.' An illustrated edition! I am glad I never saw it before, it is not in the least as I imagined.' Finally she said, 'I'll have this, if I may; a Rhoda Broughton that never came my way. *Not Wisely But Too Well.*' And did not the five simple words sum up, explain, condemn all love?

Miss Rose made one of her instant decisions.

'If it is agreeable to *you*, Miss Draper, it would be convenient for *me* if you took your meals here. With me. On this side I have three medical patients, all bedridden; on the other side, things are, of necessity, run on more institutionalised lines.'

'I should like that, very much. And, Miss Rose, while I am here, anything I can do. To help, I mean.' Humbly she reviewed her domestic skills, very scanty. Papa had never held, as he said, with keeping a dog and barking himself, or allowing his kin to bark. Marion and Ellen had merely made their own beds, hung up their own clothes, kept their rooms tidy. 'I can lay a table,' Marion said, 'and do flowers. And I am a careful shopper.'

The monkeyish planes of Miss Rose's face shifted.

'I am afraid shopping is out of the question. I was obliged to make a rule, the result of a painful experience. A patient, elderly, but making a good recovery, overestimated his strength and walked down into Sorley, to the Post Office, and died there. Since then ... But if I make exceptions it is confusing for the staff. I should be most grateful for help with the flowers, as you see ... ' She indicated the single dark-red rose on the writing-table. 'I have no time,' she said. 'And if you would read to poor old Colonel Fraser. He finds *The Times* so difficult to handle now, lying flat on his back. He would be so grateful.'

'I will do anything,' Marion said offering to the future a promissory note never likely to be exacted.

The trim black-and-white parlourmaid who had brought in the tea-tray came to remove it. Miss Rose, said, 'Clarke, Miss Draper will have the Blue room. Will you ask Stubbs to carry up her trunk?'

Mr. Draper was a creature of habit. Just as he went through the performance, every evening, of choosing one cigar from a number of others, absolutely identical, so, every evening, before pouring from it he lifted the heavy cut glass decanter that held his claret and inspected it against the light. A gesture almost automatic and quite meaningless; he had never, over the years found anything wrong. And how could there be; he dealt with, chose, decanted his wine.

But on this Monday evening, as he performed the ritual gesture he saw that something was wrong. Sediment? It was nothing, many a man would have ignored it, but Mr. Draper was already discontented with his domestic arrangements; old Ada towards whom his wife evinced a sort of sentimental attachment, Betty who breathed so hard. He had never in his life washed a decanter, or seen one washed, but that faint cloudiness at the very bottom, disturbed and rising into little peaks and subsiding, was evident proof that the decanter had not been properly dealt with.

When Betty came to remove the meat plates and bring the pudding he said, 'Take that away. Empty it and clean it properly.'

At Ten Alma Avenue the servants ate well. Mr. Draper was not, and never had been, Ada said, the easiest man to deal with, but at least he was not mean. Up to a point that was true. Mr. Draper had his pride and he believed that if he could afford to employ servants he could afford to feed them properly. Never once had there come to Ten Alma Avenue one of those two-tiered deliveries, sole for the family, herring for the staff; sirloin for family, shin for the servants. Where business was concerned, the price at which labour could be bought, the product of that labour sold, Mr. Draper was sharp and shrewd; if you could get a good man for ten shillings a week, why pay more? But Ada and Betty had always fed well. They had not, naturally, been given wine.

Removing the decanter from the tray Betty said, 'Look at this! I reckon he must be a bit upset about Miss Marion. Couldn't drink it. Said to chuck it away.'

With a gesture unconsciously similar to Mr. Draper's Ada held the decanter to the light. 'You shook it up a bit,' she said, seeing the cloudiness at the bottom. 'But it'll settle. Time the dishes are done. You sure he said chuck it away?'

'I may not breathe right,' Betty said. 'But I can hear.'

So when the dishes were done and the pan of oatmeal porridge maturing away on the back of the stove where the fire was dying, dying, Ada and Betty sat down to enjoy an unusual treat; the red wine, the master's wine. They sipped and swallowed; both disappointed, neither anxious to say the first derogatory word.

'It may be something you have to get used to,' Ada said, sipping again.

'Like curry,' Betty said. And she sipped again.

Ada took another mouthful and gave up. 'I dunno,' she said. 'All the fuss about how it should be carried, how it should be poured. Nothing more than sour old plum juice if you ask me.'

'Not a patch on my old granny's elderberry,' Betty agreed.

'If it'd been fit to drink he'd have drunk it,' Ada said. 'We should've known.' Known that life never gave anything. No lucky dips. 'Chuck it down the sink,' she said, 'and put a good handful of salt into the decanter and leave it to soak.'

Upstairs, in the dining-room Mrs. Draper chose her moment ill.

'Mr. Horridge who was here on Friday, very kindly offered to send his carriage for Ellen and me so that we could visit Marion.'

She very seldom volunteered a statement and regretted this one as soon as it was made.

'When *I* consider a visit is due, it will be made,' Mr. Draper said. 'And *not* in Mr. Horridge's carriage. I may not keep a carriage but I have so far not been obliged to borrow one. I consider such an offer from a virtual stranger most impertinent. Ellen, after supper, you will pen a note to Mr. Horridge, refusing his offer civilly but coolly.'

'Yes, Papa. And if I post it this evening he will receive it tomorrow.'

Behind that simple and innocent statement there was cunning. She had already written a hurried little letter to Marion, thinking that it would be nice for her to have a letter on her first morning at Heatherton. She had, however lacked the courage to suggest going out alone to post it for fear that Papa might be led to issue a general order against her ever going out alone. So she had intended to ask Betty just to pop out to the pillar-box; and by the time Betty had cleared away and washed up the box might well be cleared. And now, with a sentence slipped in; not a question, a statement which had not been contradicted, she had gained ground. Marion's letter would go into the box with Mr. Horridge's, and if in the future, Papa questioned the propriety of her venturing out from the house unaccompanied, in daylight, she could always say, 'But, Papa . . .' and remind him that she had gone to post alone, after dark. It might not work, but it should.

At Heatherton Marion looked at her watch. The Blue Room was pleasant, pretty and uncluttered; no skirts on the dressing-table, no valance on the bed; blue curtains, blue bed-spread, blue rugs. There was an easy-chair and an upright one, a table at which one could write. Marion had unpacked, hung and laid her clothes away, washed, changed her dress, and just dipped into *Not Wisely But Too Well*. Her real attention was, however, focused on the watch. Not Papa's gift. It had belonged to Angela, a pretty trinket, blue-enamelled, hanging from a pin in the form of a true-lovers' knot. Angela's rich and doting grandmother had sent her another for her birthday, gold, intricately chased: and Angela had said, 'I can't wear two. You have this, Marion.' Papa had been dis-pleased. 'I intended to give you a watch for Christmas,' he said, eyeing the pretty thing with scorn. 'But since Angela has forestalled me and you appear to be satisfied with her cast-off, I must think of something else, must I not?' That was the Christmas when he had given her the gold bracelet.

The little watch kept good time. Now, at Ten Alma Avenue, Papa, Mamma and Ellen would be sitting down to supper. Miss Rose had said, 'I dine at eight, but if it suits you come down earlier. I am usually here ten minutes before the meal.'

The crucial minutes ticked away. We shall all be free. Mamma shall play the piano as much, and in what manner she likes; Ellen may marry whom she chooses, and I, I shall be the most free of all, bound to nothing, to nobody; no material thing and no person shall ever hold me in thrall again.

Ten minutes to eight. It was over now.

She went down to the pretty room where another table had been opened out and rather elaborately laid for two. A bowl of roses between silver candlesticks, a lacy cloth, napkins folded into mitres. And on the table in the window embrasure a silver tray, a cut glass decanter ... decanter, decanter. Do not weaken. It is done now; we shall all be free. And alongside this momentous thought ran the superficial one – This is certainly not what Papa visualised when he said *Heatherton* in that menacing way.

Miss Rose came in. She had discarded her matron's uniform and wore a curious garment made of dark-green silk, full-skirted, long-sleeved, with cuffs and lapels of velvet. Too rich-looking to be called a dressing-gown, but certainly not a frock. A hybrid. The skirt rustled, very feminine; the lapels struck a masculine note. High heels tapped on the honey-coloured boards as she went to the table where the sherry waited. She said, 'I have just made what I hope is my penultimate round. Do you like sherry, Miss Draper?'

A drink for ladies, but not every day. Parties only.

'I like it very much.'

'I told Colonel Fraser that somebody pretty and young was going to read to him tomorrow. It did for him more than medicine could do. He was most intrigued,' Miss Rose said.

Tomorrow.

'The glasses are very small,' Miss Rose said when they were emptied. She refilled them. Wine loosened tongues, and ever since tea, making her round of her establishment, shedding her uniform, she had become more and more curious to know why a girl apparently in good health, apparently in full possession of her senses should have been sent here. By domestic scenes did Mr. Draper mean quarrels? Daughter with mother, sister with sister, this daughter with father?

At the end of a delicious and leisurely meal — clear soup, fillet of sole, lamb cutlets, fresh fruit and white wine, Miss Rose was no wiser. On the contrary, it was she who was telling Marion something she had never told anyone before.

'It sounds absurd,' she said, 'but I fell in love with the house. I had never seen it before; I had never seen the uncle who left it to me. I came down for the sole purpose of seeing what was saleable, and to make arrangements for disposing of the house. He had left me no money for its upkeep, you see. It was June, early June. The first roses were in flower and the cuckoo was calling. Something came over me, though I am a very practical person. Both house and garden were neglected and I realised that it would cost money to get the place into trim. In London I had a good job, as jobs go. But I just stood there and thought — This is *my* place, we'll sink or swim together. It was very uphill work at first, but I have never for a moment regretted that decision.'

'I can understand that,' Marion said.

At the end of the meal Miss Rose made an unusual concession.

'There is a quite comfortable chair in your room, Miss Draper; but if you prefer to sit here you will not disturb me. I have some correspondence to attend to.'

A few relatives of people on the other, the idiot side, liked to receive fairly regular reports; 'in excellent physical health,' 'no change in mental condition', 'appears to be quite happy'. From time to time as she composed these comforting, occasionally untruthful phrases Miss Rose looked across to where Marion sat, seemingly absorbed in her book. The colour of her hair and her dress matched those of the sofa's cover and she herself fitted in with the room's austere elegance. The reason for her being here was still a mystery but Miss Rose found herself hoping that she would have such charming company for quite a long time.

Ellen's cool, civil little note, with more of regret in it than she realised or than Papa would have approved, was delivered into Mr. Horridge's hand at eight o'clock next morning. Her letter to Marion was forced to wait a little. With very few exceptions Miss Rose read all in-coming and out-going mail. Much information could be gained, much trouble avoided by this censorship. Letters were steamed open, handled delicately and resealed with a flick of white of egg. Ellen wrote that she already missed Marion terribly and found it difficult not to cry. 'But I must try not to, you know how my eyes stay red for hours and you know what Papa said. When I think of you in that *horrid* place, with that *dreadful* woman . . . ' Such a sentence did not ruffle Miss Rose at all; it was mild compared with some she had read. One old woman, on the idiot side, a Mrs. Selton, wrote a letter every day; she was, in fact only quiet and untroublesome when writing long screeds describing in libellous terms the conditions of her incarceration and appealing for help. She wrote to every relative she possessed — except her son and her daughter-in-law — and to every friend she had ever known. She wrote to the police, to

Chief Constables, Members of Parliament, the Prime Minister, to Queen Victoria. All her letters said the same thing — there is only one truth — 'I am not mad. I am shut away because I would not allow Reginald to play ducks and drakes with the business or Vera to take over the bedroom in which I had slept for thirty-one years. Get me out of here, please get me out.' Rational enough, so far; but when she began to describe the conditions under which she lived dementia showed through. Compared with Heatherton the torture chamber of the Inquisition was a pleasure garden; a patient suffering from rabies had bitten her; she had been without food for forty-eight hours ... Who wanted to read such stuff? Indeed, Miss Rose no longer bothered; she knew Mrs. Selton's writing now and burned the letters unread.

In future she would know Ellen Draper's writing, too, a girlish, unformed but quite firm sloping back-hand. But she would read them unless or until she had solved this now fascinating mystery. Why was Mr. Draper, a man not even in the carriage class, willing to pay the not-negligible sum of fifty shillings a week in order to have this beautiful, amiable, companionable girl out of his house. Ellen's letter had ended, 'I send you all the love in the world, dearest, and so does Mamma.' Did that sound like domestic scenes?

To this letter Ellen had added a hasty post-script.

'After supper. Mamma said at table that Mr. Horridge who was here on Friday had offered the use of his carriage should we want to visit you. Papa said I must write to Mr. Horridge and refuse and if I am quick I can post this at the same time. I did want you to have a letter on your first morning. Love again. E.'

Mr. Horridge and Miss Rose were neighbours; only a strip of pasture lay between the spinney and the little stream that formed the boundary of Sorley Park and the high brick wall of Heatherton's kitchen garden. But they had never met. Miss Rose nowadays seldom set foot outside her own domain where she was paramount, and being paramount, happy. However, without ever having set eyes on the man, Miss Rose bore him a grudge. By marriage and intermarriage, widows with children marrying widowers with children, almost every member of the working class in Sorley was related to all the rest. Most of them were Clarkes, the rest were Hubbards. Mr. Horridge, said to be a millionaire, and with no wife to provide the needed good sense, paid his servitors wages well above average and this led to discontent. To mutterings, 'Up Sorley Park I'd get two shillings a week more.' 'In that case, Elsie, you must go to Sorley Park. I am the last woman in the world to wish a girl to stay in a place at six shillings a week when she could earn eight. When do you propose to go?'

When? Not until second-cousin Flo, up at Sorley dropped dead, or got married, the one prospect far in the future, the other case of never-never.

'I was only saying, Madam . . .'

It was only saying, but it did crop up often enough to irk Miss Rose who was therefore not kindly disposed towards her neighbour.

Mr. Horridge read his letter and brooded over it all day. Damn it, he had been anxious to do things properly, in a gentlemanly way. And this was a knock on the nose. His nose had taken so many knocks in the past that it was not unduly sensitive. But he had seen Marion, wished to see her again, had devised a plan by which he might see her, and been defeated. But not for long. What could not be in one way, must be tried in another.

One of his gardeners seemed to spend all his time coddling carnations. Sheltered by glass from the weather, fed, watered, debudded they made a splendid show. 'Clarke,' Mr. Horridge said, 'cut a dozen red and a dozen white and put a bit of fern stuff with them. Make a bunch and bring it up to the house.'

'Yes, sir. Asparagus fern'd look nice with them. But Hubbard don't like the asparagus touched.'

'If he wants to grouse, he can grouse to me.'

'Yes, sir.'

Two dozen exceptionally fine carnations and rather more asparagus fern than was strictly necessary made a large bunch. Carrying it awkwardly, but with tender care, Mr. Horridge took the short cut through the spinney, over the single-planked bridge that spanned the dwindling stream, across the bit of pasture, out by the gate into the road and then, only a few steps, to Heatherton's front door. There he rang the bell and it was promptly answered.

'I want to see Miss Draper.'

'If you will wait here, sir, I will inform Miss Rose.'

'I want to see Miss Draper.'

Stubbs vanished, was gone but a very short time, came back and ushered Mr. Horridge into the living-room where the scent of freshly cut lavender hung. Miss Rose sat at her writing-table and finished adding a column of figures before she looked up. When she did she thought how clumsy, even sheepish, he looked. The promptitude of his call, his uneasy air, the over-lavish bunch of flowers gave her the answer to the question which had been puzzling her.

A rich man, but old and far from handsome; a suitor a father would favour, a girl reject. Mother and sister probably supporting the girl. Domestic scenes. And the solution not unsubtle. Let propinquity and loneliness do their work. In a horrid place like Heatherton a kind and attentive neighbour would look less old, less unhandsome.

Ha! Miss Rose thought, but Mr. Draper was reckoning without me!

'Mr. Horridge,' she said, extending her hand. 'I am Miss Rose.' In order to shake hands he had to juggle with his bouquet which suddenly seemed as large as a wheatsheaf. His hands and feet were enormous, too.

'Is Miss Draper expecting you?'

'No. Well, at least ... I thought ... You see I dined with Mr. Draper on Friday and something was said ... So I thought ... a few flowers ... ask how she was.'

'I see,' Miss Rose said, in no very encouraging manner. 'If you will sit down, Mr. Horridge.' She rang the bell which was answered not by Clarke who had a half day off every other Tuesday but by Sarah, her understudy.

Very distinctly, as though speaking to someone slightly deaf, Miss Rose said, 'Sarah, Miss Draper is reading to Colonel Fraser. Tell her that Mr. Horridge is here, in my room. *If she wishes to see him.*'

Clarke, reliable girl, would have delivered the message verbatim but by the time Sarah had climbed the stairs and gone along the corridor and entered the room with its faintly sick odour, she had lost all but the gist of it. 'There's a gentleman to see you, Miss.'

It was now five o'clock in the afternoon and all day Marion had been expecting a telegram. In any untoward circumstances Mamma and Ellen would naturally turn to her. Now she thought — But of course: Mr. Taylor, family friend, family lawyer, kind; he had come to break the news gently and to escort her home.

'Thank you, Sarah. Colonel Fraser, I am sorry to leave you so abruptly. If possible I will come back and finish that article. If not, I hope you sleep well.'

Now, surprise, shock, grief.

There was surprise, and it was genuine.

'Mr. Horridge!' she exclaimed as, still clutching the flowers he jumped to his feet. 'What a delightful surprise.' Even at such a moment training told and the agreeable adjective came readily even as her mind fell back on the thought that very occasionally Papa did not take claret. Monday might have been one of those occasions.

'. . . a few flowers,' Mr. Horridge said, thrusting the bunch at her.

'How very kind. What superb blooms. Do sit down.'

She sat down herself and for a second buried her face in the flowers. The red ones smelt of cloves.

'Being so near; just next door,' Mr. Horridge said. He was now having trouble not only with his hands and feet but with his voice as well, sounding as though he were fourteen again, alternately squeaking and growling.

He stared at her; lovelier even than he had thought her on Friday; and sitting there, quite close to him, her lap full of his flowers.

'I hope you're feeling better,' he said. The worst was over now, his voice, the middle register back in use.

'Oh yes, thank you; much better.' She smiled. Another rule governing polite behaviour was that no one should be excluded from a conversation. 'Miss Rose, are they not magnificent?'

'Mr. Horridge's carnations are quite famous.'

'I don't take much credit for them. Clarke sees to them. And the green stuff is Hubbard's. Clarke was half scared to cut it, but I . . . well, I thought it'd look better.'

Quite suddenly, and for no reason that she could put a finger on, Miss Rose found herself liking him. She was not fond of men as a rule — just a few with the arrogance beaten out of them by age, ill-health or adverse circumstances; to them she was capable of being kind, with a kindness strongly flavoured with patronage, with triumph. So why she should feel tolerance, even a kind of pity, towards a man of about forty, in robust health, said to be a millionaire, she just did not know. Except that, clumsy, fumbling, mumbling, gaping at Miss Draper with such obvious adoration, he seemed pitiable, de-manned.

'I still have a few things to do,' she said, and went away, leaving them together. Miss Draper could handle him. But the theory which had seemed to be the solution of the mystery had fallen down. Miss Draper had been surprised, but pleased.

Surprised — because Sarah obviously had not conveyed the message properly. So one of the things to do was to administer a rebuke. 'I am afraid you will never make a *proper* parlourmaid, Sarah, unless you try much harder.' Another was to organise *two* vases for the flowers. Red and white together were a sure sign of death. A silly old superstition, but so often right that it could hardly be disregarded.

As soon as they were alone together Mr. Horridge said in a hurried, quiet voice, 'Are you all right here?'

'Quite all right.'

'I did wonder. You hear such tales you know . . . I was a bit worried. And I'd offered your mother my carriage, and then this morning I had a letter from your sister. So that was no good.'

'I know. It was a most kind and generous offer and I am sure Mamma and Ellen were very sorry not to avail themselves of it. But I expect that Papa did not wish to impose.' No word that gave so much as a hint of enmity between herself and Papa must ever pass her lips.

In thinking him awkward, socially inept, almost pitiable, Miss Rose had been in error. Momentarily he had been a little off-balance, but he had recovered now, knowing what he wanted and going straight for it.

'What do you find to do all day?'

'I have read a good deal . . .'

Mr. Horridge had never in his life read a book for pleasure.

'You like reading?'

'Almost more than anything . . .' *Now*, with that other source of pleasure drained away, love drowned in a salt sea wave.

Mr. Horridge's mind leaped forward; he would give her books; big, thick ones, bound in leather, with gilt edges.

'And today I cut the lavender.' She moved a hand to indicate the place where the lavender lay, spread out on news-paper. Mr. Horridge knew that never in his life had he seen such a graceful gesture. 'And I have read aloud to Colonel Fraser. He is so ill, and so brave. Still interested in the news — especially anything of a military nature. Unfortunately the only thing of that kind which I could find was an obituary ... I did rather wonder ... but he took it admirably. He said, "So old Fred's dead. I've beaten him at last. A live Colonel is better than a dead Brigadier." I thought that so brave.'

And who wouldn't be brave, or pretend to be, with you watching him with those beautiful eyes?

Resolutely he took the next step. 'What I was wondering was whether you'd care to take a drive. As I told your mother, there the horses stand, eating their heads off.' In fact a single man had little use for a carriage; but a carriage and pair had been part of his dream, a thing a gentleman should have; just as he should have a silver inkstand, though most of his writing was done with an indelible pencil, well-licked; just as he should have a silver teapot, though he never took tea.

Marion swiftly considered this invitation. Tuesday, spent in waiting for news from home, had dragged; the little watch consulted again and again. Would Wednesday be equally tedious? A drive would help.

There was another thought too, full of horrid suspicion. Had Johnny failed her yet again? Fobbed her off with some-thing that looked like ... She had never seen the genuine article.

Over the flowers she looked at Mr. Horridge, willing her expression to pleasure and gratitude while her mind gave itself to heartless calculation. She knew that adoring-spaniel look, she had herself directed it towards Johnny across the church, across Mrs. Marriot's drawing-room. A visit at the first possible moment; all these flowers; an invitation to take a drive.

If it could be done it would mean that, with one road to freedom blocked, another would open.

She said, 'I should enjoy a drive more than anything in the world, Mr. Horridge. But I am here as a patient and Miss Rose has explained the rule, for which she has good reason. Patients are not allowed to go out alone.'

'But you wouldn't be alone. You'd be with me.' Still, there were, he knew, other rules to be observed and he was willing to pay them lip-service so long as it suited him. 'I'll ask her, too. Though ... Well, I'm grateful to her for treating you kindly, but there's something about her. It's her eyes I think. Knowing. A bit like a monkey's.'

'How very strange, Mr. Horridge. I thought so too. As though she knew something she could not communicate. There was an organ-grinder once who had a monkey. I never thought it looked well-fed, so one day instead of giving him twopence I bought bananas for the monkey. That did not please him at all. So then I had to borrow threepence from Ellen and give it to him to put things right.'

Tender-hearted, too, he thought dotingly. He had a soft streak himself where animals and children were concerned. And a few women. Outside this limited range he could be extremely ruthless.

The talk about twopence and threepence sounded like a memory of childhood. Like all people newly in love he was anxious to know about, to have some share in, the beloved's past.

'That was when you were small,' he said, trying to imagine her so.

'Oh no. I was grown up. About two years ago.'

That struck an odd note. She was the daughter of a man who if not rich by Mr. Horridge's standards, appeared to be comfortably off. Giving away twopence; borrowing threepence. Kept short of spending money? With this thought in mind he looked her over in a different way. He was not sufficiently informed to know that the green silk dress was out of fashion, but it was worn. And she wore no ornament unless that trumpery little watch could be regarded as such. He began to have grandiose thoughts about silks and satins and gleaming furs, about diamonds, pearls, emeralds. Missing nothing he noticed that her ears had been pierced though she wore no ear-rings.

Mr. Horridge's attitude towards money was simple; it was something you had to have because without it you were nothing. He had spent years in that state; born poor, minimally educated, and enduring more than necessary hardship because he never could bring himself to settle for the meagre rewards and modest comforts of thrift and industry. Hungry, thirsty, hopeful, despairing, bloody well near dead at times, he had followed the will-o'-the-wisp of wealth in abundance, suddenly acquired. When it came he felt that he had always known ... or, at least, if that was too fanciful a thought, he had at least always known what he would do with it when it came. Supperless, without a roof over his head or a penny in his pocket, he had often edged himself into sleep by planning what he would do, if ... And then, in Africa, in a hot hole, a suburb of Hell, a place called the de Kaap valley, where one man's claim to the gold-rich soil so closely encroached upon another that mere walking was a hazard, he had struck it rich. And he had kept his head. Not for him the wild excesses that so quickly reduced men to beggary again. For him Sorley Park, the life of, the appurtenances of an English country gentleman. The irony of it was that Fortune, after cold-shouldering him for so long, having once smiled, continued to do so. Every investment he ever made prospered, and the estate itself, a potential drain, proved to be yet another source of income.

But there was a limit to what a man of good sense could spend upon himself. With a wife ... If he could just be lucky here, too.

'I'm sorry, Mr. Horridge. The truth is, while I am here things go smoothly but the moment I leave the place some crisis crops up. I took a convalescent patient to London and a silly old man walked out and died in the Post Office.' It occurred to neither of her hearers to wonder why the silly old man had chosen that moment, or why it was so imperative that he should reach the Post Office. 'And another time I went to Norwich and Mrs. Selton set fire to her bed. So you see, it is impossible for me to act as chaperone.'

She was actually leaving the way clear for Marion to make her own decision.

Marion said, 'What a pity. I should have enjoyed ...'

'Well,' Mr. Horridge said. 'That can be got over. My house-keeper, Mrs. Clarke, is very fond of an outing.'

Mr. Horridge's Mrs. Clarke was an aunt to Miss Rose's Clarke. A highly respectable widow.

'I shall look forward to it,' Marion said.

'I'll call for you at three o'clock.'

Still some hours left of Tuesday; all tomorrow morning. This appointment I may not keep ... To make up for his possible disappointment, she took leave of him with a little extra warmth and Mr. Horridge went home, his feet and hands the right size, a positively youthful exuberance in his heart.

Sarah brought in the two vases and Miss Rose explained the superstition. She arranged the white flowers, Marion the red.

'I suppose Mr. Horridge is an old family friend?'

'Oh no. Papa has known him for some time, I believe, but he dined with us for the first time on Friday.'

'And fell in love at first sight, poor man.'

'Did you really receive that impression, Miss Rose?' She looked up, innocent, candid. Even Miss Rose, herself an adept at deception was deceived and felt, for a second or two, that the remark had been out of place, in bad taste.

'Well,' she said, half retracting, half justifying, 'to call so soon, with such flowers . . .'

Yes! Johnny started off by offering me that pretty scent bottle. And with that thought came another, to be stated with truth.

'I rather think that Mr. Horridge is a kind man.' And kind was the one thing Johnny had never been; flattering, a good lover, exciting but demanding. Never kind.

Miss Rose thought — What a strange impenetrable girl! But she did not, oddly, resent the frustration of her curiosity. Most women talked far too much and on the subject of men could be positively indecent in their confidences. Slipping the last white flower into place she said, 'I suppose your papa would approve of your encouraging him?'

'I know exactly how Papa feels,' Marion said with conviction. She looked at her watch. Six o'clock. At Ten Alma Avenue supper was served at seven, on the dot. An hour to go. And between now and three o'clock tomorrow afternoon, ample time for that telegram — 'Come home; sending cab.' Or for Mr. Taylor — 'My dear Marion, you must be brave.'

She said, 'Miss Rose, you must have some of these. Would you like the white or the red?'

'You must choose. They were brought for you.'

'You settle, Miss Rose. Left hand, right hand. And I'll choose. Ready? I'll say left.'

'Then the red ones are yours,' Miss Rose said untruthfully. The red were scented.

And behind the monkey eyes which knew more than they could communicate the uncommunicable thought reared — I wish . . .

Miss Rose was not averse to marriage: for other people. The man was not born to whom she herself would have

125

wished to be married, but for girls brought up to do nothing of any purpose or value, marriage was not only desirable, it was a necessity. And there was, after all, something to be said for a man past his first youth; his wild oats were sown, possibly harvested. Sorley Park and all that went with it were not to be sniffed at. Perhaps, best of all was the man's obvious infatuation, Marion's coolness. It could give her an initial advantage which, carefully handled, might last.

Wednesday and a letter from Ellen. 'Dearest, I am writing this at the kitchen table, of all places. Both Ada and Betty are indisposed; a surfeit of plums. Need I say more???? So I am cook. Mrs. Taylor called this morning and said that she had had a letter from Angela, hinting that she was in an interesting condition. You always said she was *hasty*, did you not? Darling, thank you, thank you for your letter saying how kind Miss Rose was, how much she had been maleened. That does not look right but you will know. I do hope and pray you will soon be home. I promise you, I have not cried *once*.'

Mrs. Clarke's fondness for a drive was not to be pandered to. The model chaperone, in a black bonnet and short cape trimmed with jet beads, she rode, on Wednesday afternoon, down the lime avenue, almost a mile, and to the front of Heatherton, that mysterious place where her niece Sophie worked and, questioned always said, 'I don't know anything about the other side. I never go there.'

Mr. Horridge got out of the carriage and rang the bell while Drake the coachman turned the carriage round. Miss Draper was ready and came out; looking young, looking pretty. Oh, Mrs. Clarke thought, so that's what he's up to! Bound to come. But young enough to be his daughter. No fool like an old fool; look at him grinning. And God knows she's lucky. Good master, good husband. And from Mrs. Clarke's point of view far better the young, inexperienced girl than the widow, accustomed to running a household, upon whom he *might* have picked.

So, amiable and submissive, Mrs. Clarke left the carriage at the gates of Sorley Park and went, flat-footed, up the avenue, under the limes, prepared to supervise the tea that Mr. Horridge had ordered. 'Fit for a lady,' he had said in his blunt way. He knew about afternoon tea, having suffered on several occasions. Tiny sandwiches, about the size of a postage stamp, fragile slices of cake, crumbling at a touch. Ladies, taking tea, removed only one glove, eating had to be made easy for them. Gentlemen had a harder time, jumping up, handing cups and the silly little snippets. He wanted his tea to be correct, but comfortable too; on a good solid table, spread with a cloth that had never yet been used. And the silver tea service, bought not for shape or size, but by the ounce.

'And now, Miss Draper, where would you like to go?'

'Oh, anywhere. Just to drive, Mr. Horridge, is a pleasure. And all this countryside is new to me.'

(Once, long, long ago, before Mamma gave up and took refuge in silence, before Marion was tamed, Mamma had said, 'Marion, I cannot go against Papa. I owe him so much. But for him I should have been giving music lessons at threepence an hour.' A remark not much noticed at the time except that upon whatever the debatable matter was, Mamma was not prepared to take a stand. Now it came back, cogent, not to be disregarded. Men liked to be powerful; the Prince had married Cinderella; King Cophetua had married the Beggar Maid; Mr. Rochester had married Jane Eyre. If, when she returned to Heatherton, there was no news from Alma Avenue, she would know that her plan to free them all had failed and must try to free herself through Mr. Horridge. Therefore she must flatter him, let him seem powerful.)

'I always reckon Biddleford Common is pretty. Especially when the heather's out. Drake, we'll go by Clopley and home by Asham.'

'Oh, then I am not so far off the beaten track as I thought,' Marion said. 'I went to school at Asham.' She remembered her last visit there; the bitter disappointment; the late arrival at Angela's home. Everything had in fact started on that afternoon. Less than a year ago. Behind the Stoic calm of her face something moved, discernible only to the eye of love.

'You were unhappy there?'

'Oh no. Quite the contrary. I was happier there than . . . I was very happy there.'

'I expect you were clever.'

Cleverness in females was not admired.

'No. I liked reading and could remember, so some things

came easily to me. What beautiful horses you have, Mr. Horridge.'

Presently she said that she had never ridden in such a comfortable carriage. And that was true. It was only the deliberate, conscious effort to please that made her feel a humbug.

Soon, however, she forgot the need to pose. He was very easy to be with and out of him there flowed, even when he was silent, something that she had never met with before, but recognised instinctively, his assurance to her that whatever she said, whatever she did would be pleasing to him for no other reason than that she said it, she did it. It was something she had never experienced before, even in the best days with Johnny. Because she had loved and he had been the beloved. Was it always like that? One to love, one to accept and exploit? If so, how sad.

Mr. Horridge had thoughts of his own. Everybody said better have measles when you're young, it's worse in later life. Maybe love was like measles. But he wasn't old. Older, but not old. And she was younger, but not silly young. She didn't gesture, or exclaim or emphasise some words, or give sidelong glances. Several young ladies, some of good family, had worked on him and he thought he knew all the tricks. His confidence in his good judgment held, and joined hands with his confidence in his luck.

When, at the end of the drive, he said, 'I hope you'll take a cup of tea with me,' she agreed readily. She removed both her gloves, she said, 'Would you like me to pour?' took up the silver teapot as though it belonged to her — as it did already so far as he was concerned. She ate four of the little sandwiches and two slices of cake. She was real. And now besides being in love with her, he was at ease with her.

Of his house she said, forgetting that girls should not be knowledgeable, 'It's Elizabethan, is it not? Oh dear, it is so difficult to decide. Heatherton is Georgian and up to this moment I thought it was the most beautiful house I had ever been in. Now I am not so sure. The panelling is so cosy; in winter, with a fire in that vast fireplace, the walls must give back the glow.'

'Would you like to see it?' He would have the fire lighted on this warm, late summer afternoon. He would have set the whole house ablaze.

'Oh no. It would be very wasteful and I can imagine it.

Besides, Miss Rose will be wondering what has happened to me. She did not know that you were going to give me that delicious tea as well as that delightful drive.'

And the cold things that had been dredged up out of the sea said — And what is wrong with that? It was a delightful drive. It was a delicious tea.

'I'd like to show you over the house. And the maze. Did you know I had a maze? I reckon you know what that is.'

'I think I read somewhere that it was a device for giving people the maximum of exercise in the minimum of space ... when it wasn't very safe to walk out, or the roads were bad. Or something.' You tell me.

'It was a bit overgrown when I bought the place. But I had it cleared and clipped. Would you like to look at it? Perhaps tomorrow?'

'I should like that very much.' If no message, no messenger awaited her return to Heatherton, then she must work fast.

Neither of them, in fact, had any time to lose. Over forty, coming late to love and by now accustomed to having what he wanted when he wanted it, Mr. Horridge was not inclined to dalliance. And Marion, serving a sentence of undetermined length at Heatherton, knew that she might be recalled at any moment. She had, maybe, made a mistake in writing — trying to comfort Ellen — that Miss Rose was most kind, Heatherton a very agreeable place. Yes, that was a mistake. Papa would ... But would Papa will anything again?

'I really must get back,' she said.

Unwillingly he rose and said, 'The carriage is waiting.'

'Could we not walk back, Mr. Horridge? You walked last evening, you said.'

Further proof that she was real and unspoiled.

'I'll get a stick,' he said, remembering certain patches of nettles. This afternoon whenever he reached such a patch he went ahead, slashing them flat — in his mind slaying dragons. When they came to the little bridge he said, 'Careful now,' and jumped down into the muddy little stream, reaching up and holding her elbow. His hand was hard and strong and steady. Dependable. Safe on the other side she did not make any immediate move to release herself, but seemed to lean against him, laughing a little. 'Rather like walking a tight-rope, Mr. Horridge.'

Tomorrow, he thought, he must do something about this Mr. Horridge business. It was all very well for young men, waiting to establish themselves, waiting for promotion, waiting to inherit, to toy about, dancing attendance on a girl for a year before asking permission to call her by her Christian name, prefaced by 'Miss'. He had no time to waste. He'd take that fence tomorrow. He had another to deal with now.

Crossing the bit of pasture he said, 'Tomorrow, before going through the maze, would you care to take another drive?'

'I should like that very much indeed.'

He had enjoyed sitting beside her in the carriage; but there was Drake, well within earshot; and his own rôle was passive.

'How about the gig?'

A pretty confession. 'I have never ridden in a gig, Mr. Horridge.' A touch of feminine timidity. 'I always think they look rather dangerous. So high and so fast.'

'You'd be safe with me.'

Safe with me, my pretty one; safe and cherished as long as I live; safe after. But why think of that? He came of a long-lived family. At the age of ninety his great grandfather had been capable of giving a boy a sound thrashing; his grandfather had lived to be eighty and died through a drunken fall on an icy path. His father, seventy if a day, was still working his fell farm in Cumberland, man enough to refuse to take a penny from the son he had never forgiven for leaving the holding as soon as he was big enough to be useful. (From time to time this old man still known as Young Josh, to distinguish him from *his* grandfather, had curious little strokes of luck which he innocently attributed to the God who had promised that the righteous should never be forsaken, nor their seed beg their bread. A true promise. Even that bad boy, Edward, who resembled his grandfather more than his great-grandfather or father, was not begging his bread, though the money with which he bought it had been made in dubious ways.)

'Then I shall look forward to a new experience,' Marion said.

'I'll call for you. Shall we say two o'clock? That cob of mine can cover the ground. We could go further afield. Can you think of anywhere you'd like to go?' Then as she hesitated, he said, 'How about running into Bereham and making a surprise visit?'

He felt her arm go rigid.

'Oh no, Mr. Horridge. That would never do! Mamma and

Ellen are just becoming used to my absence, it would unsettle them. And Papa ... Papa would think I was not taking my convalescence seriously. Riding about in gigs.'

It was a pity; he had an urgent desire to establish himself with her family; to be accepted as a suitor. And he had entirely overlooked the fact that she had come out of, and was going back to, a Nursing Home.

'I keep forgetting,' he said. 'You look so well, you seem so well ... Maybe, after all, we'd better stick to the carriage.'

'Oh no. The gig, please.'

'The gig it shall be. And there's nobody you'd care to look in on? Somebody who wouldn't be upset?'

He wanted to be seen with her, if only for half an hour.

It was a little shaming not to be able to name a single friend.

'I know what I would dearly love to do. I would like to visit my old schoolmistress, Miss Ruthven, and I would like — oh dear, you will think me most presumptuous ...'

'I could never think badly of you, Miss Marion; not if I sat down and gave my mind to it.'

There, he'd said it. She neither blushed nor bridled; the sky did not fall down.

'What would you like?' Tell me, I'll do it, I'll get it. Anything that human flesh and blood, anything that money ...

'I would like to take her a few of your lovely carnations. It is almost a year since I saw her, and then she seemed a trifle ... dispirited. I came away quite saddened. I know she loves flowers, but she also believes in exercise for girls — even cricket. So she has no garden.'

'She shall have a bunch,' Mr. Horridge said. As he opened the gate between the pasture and the road there came to him, coldly and from far away, the memory of a Negro proverb. *Look out when you getting all you want: fattening hogs ain't in luck.* Swinging the gate open he tapped it three times. Just a precaution.

'My dear Marion,' Miss Ruthven said, rising from behind the table spread with schedules of work and time tables for the new term, soon to commence. 'What a delightful surprise!'

Hair perceptibly greyer, face thinner, posture less assertive.

'May I present Mr. Horridge? Miss Ruthven. Mr. Horridge

very kindly drove me here. And these are from his garden.' Marion presented the huge bunch of carnations. Without greenery. (Hubbard had said to Clarke, 'If you're going to cut it to go with bloody flowers, no sense in me trying to do right by it.' And he had taken a scythe and spitefully laid all the fern low.)

'They are beautiful,' Miss Ruthven said. She looked out of the window. A glossy, well-fed horse, a shining gig. Well, she had been right, in a way. In another way wrong; it was a thought that sometimes came to her in the night, in those hopeless hours between three and five; what of Marion Draper? I failed her. But, in his own good time Mr. Draper had produced a suitor. Not in his first youth and not hand-some in the way that Marion Draper, a novel addict, would have hoped for. But he looked kind and reliable, and quite besotted.

By repute Mr. Horridge was not unknown to Miss Ruth-ven. She was not a church-goer, but Dean Horridge, no bigot, was a friend of hers. They shared some interests, all academic. And he had mentioned Mr. Horridge of Sorley Park who un-fortunately denied all kinship.

She thought she must say a word or two to inform Mr. Hor-ridge that he was not getting merely a pretty face, a graceful figure, an amiable disposition.

'Marion was one of the best, if not the best — and I rather think she was — pupil I ever had.'

'So I reckoned. She says she was happy here. Dunces don't say that about their schools, Ma'am.'

That was shrewd.

'And how is Ellen? And your Mamma?'

'Both very well. Actually, Miss Ruthven, I am not at home now. I had a very slight accident but Papa took it seriously and I am at Heatherton. If one is not very ill life in a Nursing Home can be dull. I am fortunate in having Mr. Horridge so near. And so very kind.'

'I'm the fortunate one.' Mr. Horridge said; and Miss Ruth-ven, regarding him knew that if he had a tail he would have been wagging it.

Marion Draper, given a different father — or no father at all, might have done, might have become, might have been. Useless thinking. We must be practical; and the truth was the girl looked better, happier than she had ten months — how time flew! — ten months ago. And that reminded her.

'Marion, do you remember your last visit to me?'

Only too well. My first attempt at escape. Thrown back. Then Johnny; then the sea; then patricide. And now Mr. Horridge.

'I mentioned Louise Hayward who was then having a rather trying time. Since then I have better news. It seems that the bullying old clergyman had a curate who obtained a living some three months ago and immediately asked Louise to marry him.'

'I am so glad for Louise,' Marion said. About herself she offered no information but Miss Ruthven was sure of one thing; Mr. Draper was not the man to allow his daughter to ride about the countryside in a gig with a man whose intentions were not serious. And if only Marion would take off her gloves one could see, and if appropriate offer good wishes and congratulations.

For that was what it boiled down to, Miss Ruthven admitted to herself unwillingly; you did your best to emancipate them, make them see themselves as people, with their own rights, responsibilities and capabilities. And you ended like the most die-hard mamma, simply grateful that a man had been hooked.

Early as it was, she offered tea, and Marion — a good wife already — looked questioningly at her Mr. Horridge who said, 'Not if we're going to see that maze in the light.'

Miss Ruthven went with them to the door. She noted, with approval how Mr. Horridge handed Marion into the gig, tucked the light woollen rug about her knees. She noted also, with deeper confidence, his behaviour towards the horse. No jerking of the reins, no whip. Mr. Horridge said, 'Come up, Stormer,' and the amber-coloured horse responded.

On the cluttered desk, above the syllabuses and the time-tables the beautiful flowers lay. Nice to be remembered, Miss Ruthven thought. But, starting out, full of hope and vigour, she had thought to be remembered in other ways, for different reasons. The very flowers smelt of failure . . .

'Perhaps you can see, Mr. Horridge, why we were all — almost all — so fond of her. Though I must admit that today she seemed a little preoccupied. I saw a timetable; and they are very difficult to arrange. I know. In my last term I helped — at least I drew the frame, that is I drew the lines.'

He said, 'This thing about names is a bit lopsided. Last

night I jumped the gun a bit. I called you Miss Marion. You didn't seem to mind. Did you mind?'

'Not at all. I thought it friendly.'

'Then do you think you could manage to call me Edward? That's my name. And for men there isn't any half-way house, is there?'

'Let me see,' she said. 'Thank you, Edward, for driving me, and for providing the flowers. Quite painless! Edward is a very nice name indeed, and I shall enjoy using it — if you will call me Marion.'

Before tea he showed her the maze, the garden, the greenhouses; after tea he led her all over the house. There were rooms that he had not bothered to furnish and in one of these they shared, without speaking, a thought. Mr. Horridge's took the form of being glad that he had met her when he had something to offer. The young wives of poor young men aged early, worn down by cooking and washing and childbearing without proper attention. She, if she accepted him, should have the best. Marion thought that if only he would ask her quickly, how very different the next pregnancy would be.

Leaving her, laden with choice fruit and more flowers at Heatherton's door, he apologised, almost abjectly, for the fact that he would be unable to take her driving next day. 'I've got to get to Leicester,' he said, 'a shareholders' meeting. I'd skip it but something's coming up that I want to be in on. But if you'd come out on Saturday. Will you, Marion?'

'Of course. I shall look forward to it. And thank you, Edward, for a lovely afternoon.'

'Maybe on Saturday you could have lunch with me.'

'I should like that very much.'

'I'm sorry about tomorrow. But it really is rather important.'

'But of course you must attend to business affairs, Edward. You can't devote all your time to entertaining me.'

He almost said it then; but despite the need for haste he wanted to do the thing properly, speak to her father, ask for her hand.

'I'll be along, then, at eleven. I'm looking forward to it already.'

It would be a week tomorrow since they first met. They had made exceptionally rapid progress and Mr. Horridge was satisfied. Marion was becoming a little frightened. Plainly Papa was still alive and well, and if he had read the letter, intended for Ellen's eyes alone, he would now know that Heatherton was not — for her — the punitive place that he had intended. She might be recalled at any minute. Back into purdah.

Outrageous schemes ran through her mind. Miss Rose, Miss Rose, lend me five pounds to pay my fare to London and keep me until I can get a job scrubbing steps; I cannot, I will not go back to Alma Avenue. Miss Rose, Miss Rose do you know anyone who would employ a maid called Mary Smith and not ask where she came from?

Miss Rose would then know what she had tried so hard to pry out, why Marion was at Heatherton at all. And straight over to the other side. A lunatic girl anxious to run away from a good home.

About the other side, Marion knew a little. More than most people in fact because at the end of the corridor, near Colonel Fraser's room there was a window of thick frosted glass against which on Tuesday morning a butterfly was beating futile wings. She saw it when she came out from reading about the deceased Brigadier. She tried to open the lower half of the window, but it was stuck fast. She tried the top and it gave. She guided the butterfly out and it fluttered away into the sunshine. Her eyes followed its flight, and then, because she was that extra inch tall — the inch that had prevented her ever being a bridesmaid — she could see into the yard which was divided from the ordinary garden by a high brick wall. She saw nothing to justify the nasty stories. A woman with an idiot face sat in a wheelchair, a vegetable growth exposed to the sun. A young man, thin and haggard stood in a corner tearing newspaper into shreds, into little pieces which he tossed into the air and then, with urgency, gathered up again and put into a bucket. Tear a strip, tear that, throw the pieces into the air, gather them. Again and again. The two were fixtures, the one in the chair, the other by his bucket. Between them a girl of about Ellen's age, in fact not unlike Ellen except that her hair hung loose, walked up and down, cuddling a doll, kissing it occasionally. Then, out of the open door, just visible, came a woman, very trim and neat, dressed for an outing. An attendant, Marion thought, taking a last look round before going off duty. But she walked about, aimlessly and then suddenly, unprovoked, began hitting the young man about the head with her velvet reticule. He emitted several shrill screams, but did not even put up his hands to defend himself. And then Miss Rose came out, took the neat woman by the elbow and led her back indoors. Nothing horrific really, but the thought of being doomed to live with such people was appalling. She would not ask Miss Rose to aid her escape. She must hang on and hope that Mr. Horridge spoke out. He was in love with her she knew, but unconventional as he was, unconventional as she had been, he would hardly think it seemly to propose to someone he had known so short a time. Oh, if only Papa were like other fathers!

Friday lagged. She read to Colonel Fraser, now perceptibly weaker. Once as she read, he closed his eyes and she thought he was asleep. She stopped reading and was prepared to go quietly away when he said, 'I am not asleep. Read on, my dear, of you can spare the time. This is lonely country.'

She wrote to Ellen, a non-committal letter which, seen by Papa, would not spur him into instant action.

And she knew that she should write to Johnny. The letter that would surprise him with the information that it was all over and that she never wanted to see him again. Then it occurred to her that her position would be infinitely stronger, and Johnny more likely to accept her decision if she could mention 'somebody else'. So she deferred that letter, thinking that on Saturday she must do something, or say something that would provoke Mr. Horridge into declaring himself. And then, she realised, there would be no need to write to Johnny at all. He'd soon know; and she would be far away, beyond the reach of reproaches and arguments. Wait for Saturday and hope for the best.

'Yet *another* letter from Marion,' Papa said at the breakfast table on Saturday morning, handing the letter to Ellen with a look of displeasure. 'Has she nothing else to do?'

'I am afraid not, Papa. The tone of her letters has altered since that first one. I think she is finding life at Heatherton very dull and lonely. Papa, on Monday she will have been there a week. And I have not cried once.' It was not the *non sequitur* that it sounded; mindful of Papa's threat and of how, when she cried, her eyes reddened and her nose swelled, Ellen had fought back the tears that threatened as each carefully unenthusiastic letter arrived. Miss Rose, who had been kind, was now never mentioned — had she shown herself in her true colours? Heatherton, in that first letter described as a not un-

pleasant place, had not been referred to again and to Ellen
that sounded ominous. Very bravely she now said:

'Papa, could she not come home?'

'When I decide that she has learned her lesson and is prepared to behave herself,' Papa said sternly. 'And how often
have you written to her, my dear?'

'Twice,' Ellen said. Not quite true, not quite a lie. Anyone
who had written five letters had written twice. And after
Monday evening, posting had been easy. Papa had not issued
the order which Ellen had dreaded — that she was not to go
into the town unaccompanied. It seemed to be taken for
granted that Ellen should do the shopping for little things.
Who else was there to do it? Mamma was incapable now of
making the effort; Ada was almost immobile; Betty had no
time. And Ellen, freed from Marion's pernicious influence,
could be trusted.

'Your daily bulletin,' Miss Rose said, at the Saturday break-
fast-table, handing over Ellen's letter. She no longer bothered
to read them. There was another addressed to Miss Marion
Draper in a different hand but with the same Bereham post-
mark. She would inspect that later.

'Would you mind if I did not come in to lunch, Miss Rose?
Mr. Horridge invited me to lunch with him today.'

'Why should I mind? I take it that you know what you are
doing,' Miss Rose said. From her own letters she looked up,
her monkey eyes asking the questions that could never be put
into words and at the same time saying the thing that was a
secret. Not new; it had happened before, a thing one must
learn to live with, like a hare-lip or a club foot. 'I hope you
have a nice lunch,' she said gallantly.

Successful as his day-long trip to Leicester had
been — what needed to be looked into satisfactorily looked
into, praise for his business acumen pouring in from all sides,
from men born and bred to such procedures — Mr. Horridge
had been anxious to get home. Where thy treasure is, there
shalt thy heart be also.

And Saturday came. Autumn had just breathed upon
summer and there was a crispness in the air; the promise of a
season changing, so exhilarating for those to whom the new
season held a prospect of change, of joy. And in the jogging,
after-Norwich-very-tedious train, he had made his plan.

He handed Marion into the gig, climbed in himself, tucked

in the rug. He proposed to take her to Norwich. There was a Cathedral there which he had seen, but never entered, and would never, of his own volition, have entered. But he had gathered that she liked old things. In Norwich there would certainly be a bookshop, and there was, he knew, an excellent inn called *The Maid's Head*, a very old place with a long history. He had eaten well there on several occasions.

She'd lived such a circumscribed life, poor darling, and he intended to show her the world. He would begin with Norwich.

He mentioned the destination as he took up the reins, and Marion who had imagined lunching at his home said:

'But Edward, could we go there and back before lunch?'

'Of course not. Stormer'll need a rest and a bait. I thought we'd do a bit of sight-seeing, take a look at the shops. We'll lunch at *The Maid's Head*. You'd like that. It's a nice old place.'

Genuine consternation and dark intent mingled in her mind.

'But Mr. Hor ... Edward. I cannot possibly lunch with you alone in a public place. Apart from convention which would condemn me entirely, there is Papa to think of. He has many friends and acquaintances in Norwich. I should be seen and recognised. Someone would tell him and he would be *horrified*. I do realise that in driving with you alone I have not behaved with complete propriety. If Papa ever heard of that he would be very angry indeed.'

Mr. Horridge bore on the rein and Stormer halted.

The moment had come and despite the assurance that had been growing in him these last few days, Mr. Horridge's voice gave trouble again.

'Look,' he said. 'Marion. Well, maybe I have gone a bit too fast. But the last thing ... offend your father. Honourable intentions,' he said. 'Marion, I know I'm no oil-painting, and I'm a bit old; but I'm sound in wind and limb and I love you with all my heart. D'you think you could marry me?'

He'd handled that badly; too sudden, too blunt; too much like a business proposition. But he'd had no time to work up to it, and was no good at making pretty speeches anyway. But he'd done for himself; he could see that by the look of distress on her face.

In fact what he took for distress was intense concentration. Here it was, the proposal, the key to freedom for which she had been angling and hoping. But to be of any use it must be handled properly.

She said, 'Edward, I am most deeply sorry. And honoured, of course, that you should wish to marry me. But it is quite impossible. Papa would never allow it.'

Why not? Because I'm a self-made man? But then so is he by all accounts. Other plans for his beautiful daughter?

'You see,' Marion said, stonily, 'Papa has no intention of allowing either Ellen or me to marry anyone.'

Well, at least she hadn't refused him out of hand.

'Papa holds that daughters must stay at home and provide company and comfort for their fathers. He says that it is no part of a man's duty to bring up a girl in order to provide another man with a wife.'

'I've heard some odd things,' Mr. Horridge said, his voice back under control, 'but that beats all.'

'Papa is a very strange man. I could tell you things . . . ' He noticed that for once her hands were not under control. In their neat little gloves they were plucking away at the fringe of the rug. He put out his own and took them both into a clasp, under which they fluttered like a captured bird. Be still. Trust me.

'You tell me,' he said. 'You can tell me anything.'

So she could now. All danger of the relationship between Papa and herself ever coming under suspicious scrutiny was over and done with. Johnny had given her bicarbonate of soda or boracic powder or some such thing. And Edward must be convinced, here and now.

'I am not at Heatherton,' she said, 'because I am ill or demented. I am there because I was not sufficiently meek. I said a few incautious words and was exiled as punishment . . . '

It all came out. A dam breaking, a boil bursting. The bullying; the jealousy; the prize from Miss Ruthven, Angela's watch, Mamma's piano, the amicable sisterly relationship. Everything ever suffered, everything resented, poured out, as the sun banished that touch of autumn and Stormer, corn-crammed, richly pastured, found something not only edible but delicious in the growth by the side of the road and munched it, jingling his bit.

'So you see,' Marion ended, 'If you really wish to marry me, Edward, it must be done secretly, without Papa's knowledge; and quickly, before I am recalled.' This time no problem of money, or transport, or four to a bed, four to a job. But the human factor ...

'Oh no!' Mr. Horridge said. 'We ain't going to have a hole-and-corner affair.' On rare occasions, under stress, he lapsed into the grammar of his youth. 'We're going to have a proper, slap-up wedding. That is, if you'll have me. You didn't say so yet.'

'Edward, I do. I mean I wish to marry you. There is nothing I wish more. But ...'

'Bless you,' he said. He lifted his hand and placed his arm around her in a rib-cracking hug, at the same time aiming a kiss which, wavering between being deferential on her fore-head and hearty on her mouth, landed ludicrously on her nose. He then tried again and did better and was surprised, though pleasantly, by the way her mouth answered.

He said, tritely, 'You've made me the happiest man in the world. You leave Papa to me. I'll deal with him.'

He would have liked, hearing what the poor darling had endured, to have wrung Mr. Draper's bloody neck. And that was not the half-hysterical thought of the novice. Mr. Horridge had killed a man, in a fist fight, the odds against him since, until disarmed, the fellow had had a shovel.

'Edward, nobody can deal with Papa. In many ways he is not rational. And if you want a proper wedding, you must look for another bride.'

'I want you. And we shall have a proper wedding; red carpet, bells, choir-boys, champagne. And you looking like an angel and your father saying "I do" in the proper place.'

All men were blood-brothers. Papa, Johnny, Edward. Set in their ways and obstinate.

'Unless it is done as I say — in the only possible way — it will never be done at all,' she said.

He hugged her again.

'You've got me now. I don't wonder you're scared of him. He sounds a bit daft to me. But I can handle him. We'll go and tackle him now.'

Deliberately she folded back the rug.

'If you go, you go alone. I have done my best to explain ... I will not be present at a scene. I had enough to last my life-time.' Papa could not humiliate Edward as he had humiliated Johnny, but he would find some other way. And the whole thing would rebound, upon Mamma, Ellen, and even upon Ada and Betty.

'I shall be much obliged,' she said, 'if when you talk to Papa you would avoid mentioning that I had taken drives with you, or visited your house or agreed to marry you.'

'I'm simply going to *ask* him. If you don't want to be there . . . No, wait . . . I'll drive you back to Heatherton.'

You already have, you stupid, you pig-headed . . .

'I can walk back those few steps,' she said. She skipped down into the road and from that lower level looked up.

'If you do this, Edward, I know, I know in my heart, we shall never be married. Never.'

'Don't you believe it,' he said. 'You just wait, sweetheart. I'll be back in no time.'

He rode away to do battle.

Marion stood still in the road, for a moment as physically free as she could ever hope to be. Miss Rose believed her to be out to lunch and would not miss her until late afternoon; she would then send a telegram to Papa and the hue and cry would begin. She visualised the Police wagonettes rattling about; the posters headed REWARD. Papa would do the right thing and offer a reward. Her age, her size, the colour of her hair, the clothes she was wearing. And where would she be, where could she hide, where could she go without a penny in her pocket?

She had said, very boldly, to Johnny, that she would not mind being poor, but she had spoken under the influence of an infatuation. In fact everything in her upbringing and background had been calculated to make her fear poverty — Eat up your rice pudding; there are hundreds of poor little children who would be only too glad of it! We must see what old clothes, what out-grown shoes we can spare for the poor. He couldn't face being poor, poor man, so he died. Nanny speaking.

Even her reading contributed; the books which Papa so sweepingly denounced as rubbish were not entirely concerned with love-at-first-sight against comfortable or exotic backgrounds; the poor were sometimes mentioned, often with sympathy, but invariably as people apart. They lived in hovels — in the country; in slums — in cities. They lived in squalor and died if not of starvation, of fatal coughs.

Johnny knew about poverty and though everything that Johnny had ever said or done was now suspect his words about the competition for jobs, for beds, were remembered.

No. I am not sufficiently brave. Even on the idiot side at Heatherton — and there I shall end if that stupid man who says he loves me and yet would take no notice, isn't careful and a far better liar than anyone so stupid could be — even on the idiot side, they are clean and tidy, they have food, they have beds.

To this am I reduced. Miss Ruthven's best pupil, Papa's dear Marion, Johnny's *chérie*, Edward's sweetheart. And much good it did me!

She swung around and with steady steps and face under control walked back to Heatherton.

Miss Rose, near the bottom of the stairs said, 'Back so soon?'

'Yes. As it transpired, Mr. Horridge had some business to transact and that meant that I should be obliged to wait about.'

In the monkeyish eyes something had changed.

'So after all,' Marion said, 'I shall be able to read to Colonel Fraser.'

'I am afraid not,' Miss Rose said. 'He is in coma — deeply unconscious. One can only hope that he simply drifts away.'

'Without pain. I hope so too. Miss Rose, you must not distress yourself. I know that to lose a patient, having done your best . . . But he was eighty.'

(We shall all be eighty if we live on. And we shall all die. 'Brightness falls from the air; Queens have died young and fair; Dust hath closed Helen's eye.')

'I am not distressed,' Miss Rose said. 'A hopeless case from the first. Nothing to be done, except to see that he was comfortable.'

Thus dismiss the old warrior whose eyes had looked upon horrors and yet retained their candid, blue, almost childish look.

'Is there anything else I can do?' Say yes! Give me something that will take my mind off my failure, my cowardice, my hopelessness.

Miss Rose thought — If you cared to tell it, and I had time to listen, you could entertain me with a story.

She had found time to open and to read Marion's other letter. 'Marion my dearest, my darling, it is now Friday and I have received no letter. Yet to Ellen you have written. I know because Baxter's being closed for renovations she came into the shop. I could only ask as I served her in a whisper. Is it that in that horrible place only letters to the family are permitted? Is it that you have forgotten your Johnny? *Chérie,* having been one as we were so often, to be alone is very painful to me and has a bad effect on my stomach. Mrs. Fenner is insulted if I do not eat well and Mr. Freeman is unsympathetic. Shall you be home on Monday? You said you might be a week away. Shall I on Monday see the light in your window and be taken into your loving arms once more? If so I can contain myself till then. If not, on Sunday I will walk to Sorley if you can meet me somewhere. It would be worth it even for a kiss, but I hope for more! *Coeur de mon coeur,* life without you is not supportable. Please write so that I have a letter early on Sunday. It is a long walk. I am missing you and wanting you all the time.'

Over this effusion, signed, 'Your loving Johnny,' Miss Rose ran an astonished eye. How deep the still waters ran!

The few French words and something odd about the phrasing — Johnny's written English was less colloquial than his speech, informed her that he was foreign; and he was a shop assistant. On certain subjects Miss Rose might hold unorthodox ideas but her class consciousness was rigid. Miss Marion Draper had been engaged in an intrigue not only clandestine but highly unsuitable.

Perhaps worst of all with a man capable of mentioning the state of his stomach in what purported to be a love letter. Disgusting.

Miss Rose now perceived Mr. Draper's purpose in sending his daughter to Heatherton — not as she had imagined, to make things easier for Mr. Horridge, but to get her out of this lout's way. And little as she liked Mr. Draper, she was here in full sympathy with him. Foolish, foolish girl!

She did not destroy the letter. Should Mr. Draper ever accuse her of laxity in allowing Marion to go riding with Mr. Horridge, she would produce this and say — Look what I saved her from! The letter went into the always-locked bottom drawer of her writing-table.

And now here was this foolish, this naughty girl, so dignified, so beautiful, so virginal-looking, saying just the right thing about the old man upstairs and offering to be helpful.

'Your welcoming arms!' They were white arms and slim,

retaining something of a rather touching immaturity. 'Even for a kiss, though I hope for more.' In a less disciplined woman than Miss Rose there might have been emotional tumult. But, as she had schooled others, she had schooled herself.

She said, 'Yes, indeed you could. You could oversee Clarke in preparing the dining-room. Colonel Fraser is not without relatives, and negligent though they have been, once he is dead they will come flocking. I think everything is *clean*, but the room has been out of use for a while and good as she is in many ways, Clarke lacks that little touch which makes all the difference. If you would see to that, it would be very helpful.'

Miss Rose turned and went back upstairs. Presently Colonel Fraser emerged from his coma, not to pain as she had feared — the merciful dose ready to hand. His body had ceased to trouble him, his mind was easy. He had added a codicil to his will — To Miss Eleanor Rose of Heatherton in the County of Norfolk, as a token of her unfailing kindness and care for me, the sum of £4,000 (four thousand pounds). All he owned; a codicil, properly signed and witnessed that made utter nonsense of various legacies to several nephews and nieces who had never cared whether he lived or died.

But for her — a kind of super batman — not enough. He said, 'Not enough, my dear. Never enough,' and with this comment he gave in, surrendering to the final enemy.

Mr. Horridge swung his gig into the wide yard at the Maltings. It was Saturday, nothing much coming in or going out. But from some hidden nook a little boy emerged. 'Hold your horse, sir? Tie him up or walk him? He look a bit hot, sir.' The answer might well make all the difference between a penny and twopence. And Stormer was sweating.

'Walk him,' Mr. Horridge said, twisting the reins about the dashboard and jumping down, lithe as a boy. 'Walk him round, twice, then give him a drink at that trough. I shan't be long.'

Mr. Horridge knew the way to Mr. Draper's office and strode towards it, throwing back the door with such energy that it hit the cupboard on the wall. Very little real business was ever done on Saturday and Mr. Draper, at his battered old desk, was making up the wage piles. He looked towards the door sharply, a rebuke for whoever had entered so clumsily, ready on his tongue. When he saw Mr. Horridge, owner of a thousand acres that grew some of the best barley in England, he stood up, extended his hand and said, genially, 'Ha! Mr. Horridge. Good morning. A beautiful day. Splendid harvest weather. Yours is going well, I trust. Do sit down.'

The curious thing was that all the way from Sorley to Bereham Mr. Horridge had been cherishing his own supremely eligible image. Richer than most; a few shady things in his past lived down and the witnesses to them mainly dead: men of far greater standing than Mr. Draper had indicated pretty plainly that they would find him acceptable as a son-in-law. But now, confronted by the maltster he felt suddenly like an agent, or a tenant farmer reporting on the harvest. The report had better be good, or else . . .

'Doing very well. But that isn't what I came to see you about, Mr. Draper.'

'No?' Mr. Draper waited, attentive and civil. The old desk — Mr. Draper disapproved of fancy furniture in offices — was set at such an angle that by the slightest turn of his head, he could survey his yard. Any visitor seated in the hard wooden chair must crane his neck to obtain the same view. Mr. Horridge craned and drew some assurance from the sight of his gig, the sun bouncing off the yellow wheels, the amber-coloured cob shining.

He said abruptly, 'I've come to ask permission to marry your daughter.'

If that gave Mr. Draper any shock or surprise he concealed it, saying lightly:

'I have two, Mr. Horridge.'

'I mean Marion. Miss Marion.'

'Having seen her once!' There was amusement, mockery, in the question and it provoked Mr. Horridge into forgetting Marion's plea.

'No. Though once was enough. I knew she was the girl for me the moment I clapped eyes on her. But I've seen her since. We get along together. I asked her to marry me and she said she would. So here I am.'

'How very extraordinary,' Mr. Draper said, as though he had just been shown a calf with two heads. But the cold, controlled anger was mounting. 'And how painful for you. Perhaps I am to blame; but I could hardly be expected to make a public proclamation. Mr. Horridge, a short time ago Marion sustained a very severe blow on her head. She is not now in a condition to make the simplest decision for her-self.'

'That's all rot. Marion's as right in the head as you or me.'

'Then why do you suppose I sent her to Heatherton? To facilitate your courtship?' The sarcasm stung, but Mr. Horridge was not going to jeopardise his case by showing ill-humour; he was already regretting having said, 'rot'.

'What I meant was, she's over it. Right as a trivet. And I asked her to marry me and she said she would, subject to your consent.'

'That, at least, was sensible.'

'Then can I have it?'

'No.'

'Why. What have you got against me?' Mr. Draper made no reply but his glance, up and down, said — Everything! Mr. Horridge blundered on. 'I'm a bit old, I know that. But she'd be all right, even when I'm gone. My affairs are in a sound way. You're welcome to investigate. Thorley's is my bank. I'd make one of these marriage settlement things.'

'I wonder,' Mr. Draper said, addressing the wall behind and just above Mr. Horridge's head, 'what gave you the impression that my daughter was for auction.'

Again, but with more difficulty, Mr. Horridge kept his temper.

'I didn't mean it that way. I was trying to explain. I can see that a man wants to see his daughter provided for. And she would be. I'm self-made, in a way; but so are you. Can you give me a reason for refusing me?'

'I can. And your money, Mr. Horridge, has nothing to do with it. I have never held it part of a man's duty to rear and cherish a female child in order to provide another man with a wife.'

'Great God in Glory! If every man thought that where'd the human race be?'

'I am not laying down a rule for general behaviour. I am trying to explain my own position. I look to my daughters to provide me with company and comfort in my latter years.'

Exactly what Marion had said. Poor darling!

In Mr. Horridge a killing rage, very different from cold anger, began to mount.

'Look,' he said. 'I didn't come here to chop logic. I came to ask a question. Can I marry Marion. Yes or no?'

'But I have already given you my answer, Mr. Horridge. And one thing I must make clear. My daughter is now a patient in a Nursing Home. There has been some laxity, into which I must look and I am prepared to believe that you have been under a misapprehension. But if, after this, you persist in forcing your attentions upon a girl who is not mentally sound, you will draw upon yourself no small measure of opprobium.'

Mr. Horridge did not know what opprobium meant, but he guessed it was something nasty.

'And that's your last word?'

'Yes. And now, if you will excuse me, this is pay-day ...' Before him lay a canvas bag, a list of workmen's names, some ticked, and little piles of money.

'All right,' Mr. Horridge said in a voice that would have warned any man accustomed to a rougher world. He stood up, adopting a stance no gentleman would ever have assumed; feet planted wide, thumbs hooked into the top of his trousers. All the amiability had gone out of his face, leaving something basic and dangerous. He said, quite quietly:

'Now, you listen to me. I wanted to do things proper, so I came and asked, and you say no. Man, nobody is coming between me and her. Get that through your thick head. When I want something, like I want Marion, I don't let nothing nor nobody stand in my way. You give me leave to marry her or I'll ruin you.'

Mr. Draper had already foreseen a breakdown in their business association. He said, 'Mr. Horridge, I can buy barley elsewhere.'

'You bloody fool. I never even thought of such a piddling little thing. When I say ruin, I mean *ruin*. I'll go straight out and buy that old boat-building place. I'll start a Maltings. The fellows you give twelve bob a week to, I'll give sixteen, eighteen, twenty. Starting Monday. On every bloody Corn Exchange, every bloody farm within two hundred miles I'll give five shillings over the market price for barley. And what I sell, I'll sell cheap. Give it away. By Christmas this'll be dead and done for. And wherever you go, whatever you do, I'll hound you down, Mr. Draper. Once I get my monkey up ... You poor bloody fool, once I get to work on you, you won't want Marion to cheer your old age, you'll want bread to put in your belly. If it's the last thing I do, if it takes my last penny, I'll see you off.'

In Mr. Draper's smooth cheeks the healthy colour had disintegrated into little islands of scarlet in a sea of pallor. But he did not lose his self-control, or his dignity. And when he spoke it was calmly.

'Against such resources as you command, I am powerless. I have my wife, my other daughter to consider. Very well, Mr. Horridge, under compulsion and without choice, I give you leave to marry Marion.'

'And that's all I wanted.' Why, having gained his point, should he feel deflated, in the wrong? It was something this horrible man did to people. Poor Marion! 'I don't want any hard feelings,' Mr. Horridge said. 'What I said I only said because you drove me.'

'Then we are both in the same boat,' Mr. Draper observed. He stood up and opened the window. 'Hardy!' A man came running. 'Oh, Hardy, something has cropped up which demands my attention. You pay out.' With steady hands he put the piles already arranged, the canvas bag, on the window-sill and handed over the list. 'Tick off each as he's paid. Williams was late on Tuesday. He was docked sixpence. Have you a pencil?'

'No, sir.'

'Then take this one.' He passed over a pencil and closed the window. 'Now, we must discuss arrangements. I imagine that you would wish to be married as soon as possible.'

'It can't be too soon for me.'

'The banns could be asked tomorrow morning. I will call at the Rectory on my way home to lunch. That would allow you to be married on Thursday fortnight. Thursday,' Mr. Draper said distantly, 'is the day on which those establishments which observe early closing have a half-day, and that is convenient for choirmen and bell-ringers. I take it that you wish a full-dress parade.'

'I want the best for Marion, from the very start.' Mr. Horridge then said something that was in fact prompted by considerable delicacy of feeling. 'I know, Mr. Draper that you've been forced into this, in a way. You weren't prepared for it. It's sudden and it'll be expensive. I'll gladly foot the bill.'

He had delivered himself into Papa's merciless hands.

'Mr. Horridge, if you would sit down and for a few minutes forget that you are a rich man while I am comparatively poor, we can pursue this discussion. Otherwise I would suggest writ-

148

ten communication. For sheer vulgarity this interview must be unequalled.'

Mr. Horridge sat down.

'In civilised society it is customary for the bride's family to arrange the wedding — doing their best, according to their circumstances. I am prepared to give my daughter the kind of wedding, and the trousseau which I should have provided had I ever wished her to get married. There will be no bill for you to foot.'

There was no placating him. Detestable man. And Marion had spent her life under the lash of his tongue. No wonder she'd been happy at school, thought Miss Rose very kind, and went stiff at the idea of having to face him.

'What I do feel,' Mr. Draper said, 'is that there has been some flouting of convention. Presumably when you asked Marion to marry you, you were alone.'

'Taking a drive.'

'Most indiscreet. To make amends we must be very careful. Marion must return home immediately. I will make arrangements for her to be fetched this afternoon.'

'Oh, I'll drive her in,' Mr. Horridge said.

'Really, Mr. Horridge, you appear to be incorrigible. Until you are married you will see Marion only when she is properly chaperoned. Hasty marriages cause talk and we must be careful not to give the wrong impression. If indeed it is wrong.'

'God damn you! I never even kissed her till she said she'd marry me.'

'Which brings me to my next point. There must be some explanation for this haste.'

'That was your doing,' Mr. Horridge pointed out, reasonably. 'I know I said the sooner the better; but I could wait for a while. Couple of months.'

'Marion has flaunted my wishes and behaved abominably. Her presence in my home will not exactly give me pleasure.'

It would not, Mr. Horridge could see, be very pleasurable for Marion either.

'So if you could plead the call of business,' Mr. Draper went on imperturbably, 'it would be advisable.'

'I can do better than that. Paris for the honeymoon. You can tell anybody that's interested that I've got a fancy to show Marion the chestnut trees while they're golden. They'll take that from me, they know I'm a bit odd.'

'Ah yes,' Mr. Draper said. 'The rich are allowed their

whims.' He stood up. 'I shall at the earliest possible moment arrange a party in celebration of the engagement. We must put the best possible face on things. You will be overwhelmed with good wishes. I shall not offer mine. In fact I hope she makes you thoroughly unhappy. *She is quite capable of it.*'

Outside in the yard Mr. Horridge quickly recovered. He gave the little boy a shilling at which he gazed incredulously. 'Thank you, sir. Bless you, sir,' he said, and turned cartwheels from sheer joy.

Mr. Horridge thought of Marion's remark that they might not meet again. Look what he had to tell her!! 'Come up, Stormer. Get along! Pick your feet up, boy.' He also thought of Paris, a place to which he had gone in a menial capacity, attendant to two race-horses. On his second visit, as a rich man, he had been a little dismayed to discover that the shops and places of entertainment were less entrancing when you could enter than they had seemed when you could only stand, empty-pocketed, and stare. But with Marion beside him, seeing everything for the first time, all would be made up. 'Come *up*, Stormer.'

At Heatherton he rang the bell so violently and repeatedly that Miss Rose, coming down the stairs, said '*I* will go, Stubbs,' in a voice that boded no good to whoever had rung the bell in that way.

When she saw Mr. Horridge, she thought — Drunk!

He pushed past her, saying, 'Where is she? I've got something to tell her.'

'Miss Draper is in her room. Washing her hands before lunch.'

He charged for the stairs, shouting, 'Marion! Marion!'

Miss Rose took him by the arm, just above the elbow; one of her master holds. It could have been a friendly gesture. Without making any visible effort she sent a paralytic pain running down to the tips of his fingers, a stultifying pain running up behind his ear.

'There has been a death in the house,' she said quietly. 'If you will go into my room, I will call Miss Draper.' But Marion had heard him calling and was on her way down.

'Darling, my dearest, sweetest girl, it's all right. He said "Yes". We're engaged.'

One of her dizzy spells hit her and she tottered. Mr. Horridge, released from that deadly hold, picked her up, hugged her, kissed her, and put her down on one of the sofas.

'I'm a clumsy brute,' he said. 'But what with one thing and another. You all right?'

'Oh yes. It was just ... I could hardly believe ... What happened? Is it true? What did he say?'

'Well, it took a bit of persuasion,' Mr. Horridge said modestly. 'But he came round, in the end.' He had won, he could afford the victor's magnanimity and he never intended to tell her any details.

'I never, in all my life, knew Papa to yield a point.'

'He never had me to deal with before. Darling, Thursday fortnight. And I swear you shall never regret it ... Maybe the next few days ... for you ... I mean he didn't exactly take to the idea, being so sudden. But we'll make up for that ...'

He then became aware of the fact that Miss Rose was there, watching with those monkey eyes. He said:

'Miss Rose, you must be the first to congratulate me, the luckiest chap in the world. I'm sorry about the old boy, but he was oldish, wasn't he?'

Once again Miss Rose found his manner disarming.

'I do indeed congratulate you, most heartily, Mr. Horridge. And, Miss Draper, I wish you every happiness.' Marion looked as though she might be happy, once the surprise had worn off. 'I think,' Miss Rose said, 'that this calls for champagne.'

She kept a modest stock. Sometimes it was ordered medicinally, usually in conjunction with oysters. Sometimes a gentleman patient, feeling his feet on the road to recovery, would demand it, and there were occasions when, at the end of an exceptionally trying day, Miss Rose found a glass of champagne an effective pick-me-up.

When it came it was a better wine than Mr. Horridge would have credited the old girl — or indeed any woman — of choosing.

'Many, many happy years,' Miss Rose said, raising her glass. A sweet, a lovely, an intelligent girl — and surely better married to Mr. Horridge of Sorley Park than carrying on a clandestine affair with a French shop assistant with stomach trouble.

Stubbs came in and whispered discreetly into her ear.

'I knew it,' she said. 'In the last three years nothing has happened in this house without Mrs. Selton trying to divert attention to herself.' She set down her glass and went quickly away.

'Well now, I'll wish you many, many happy years, sweetheart. And if they ain't, aren't happy, it shan't be my fault.'

'Nor mine; I wish you happy, too, Edward.' She gave him her most charming smile. She did not love him. But she knew about love; that forest fire which blazed and blinded and left nothing but devastation behind it. She liked him and would always be grateful to him, always. 'I am not all that you may think of me, Edward. I have faults that you have had no time to discover. But I will try to make you a good wife.'

'You don't have to try,' said Mr. Horridge, coming as near poetic expression as was possible to him. 'All you have to do is go on breathing. You just breathe and leave the trying to me.'

'What did Papa *say*?'

He gave a censored version; the immediate arrangements. 'You mustn't mind,' he said, thinking some warning necessary, 'if he's a bit ... grumpy. He wasn't exactly pleased. But it won't be for long.'

Very faintly, from the other side of the house, from beyond the padded door, came the sound of a scream; and another. But Mr. Horridge was hotfoot after his latest idea.

'A Dean,' he said, 'is a sort of parson. Am I right?'

'A Dean is a church dignitary. Yes.'

'Well, I sort of wondered if you'd like one at the wedding. There's one at Asham they keep on at me about. No kin so far as I know, though the name's the same. But parsons always want money for something, keep the roof on the church or help the poor. I could get him for you, if you'd like that.'

He wanted to give her the moon and the stars. He could give her a Dean.

Now — and for the first time something that she had thought dead for ever stirred. Warmth, a capacity for happiness, for fondness.

'You've given me enough for one day, Edward. I can still hardly believe ... I never dreamed Papa would consent.'

And you were dead right. Nobody but me could have pulled it off!

'Now we've got to talk about the ring. I'd have liked you to choose it. But I don't see your father letting you come to London with me. I'll go up alone, Monday, Tuesday. Give me something to do. What do you fancy? Emerald? Sapphire? Diamond? I do know a bit about diamonds.' That was a modest statement. One of his subsidiary interests in Africa was concerned with them.

'Whatever you choose will please me,' Marion said.

'Then I'll do the best I can in London. And there'll be Paris ...' A whole new world opened before him. He had provided himself with everything a gentleman should have; now he could buy pretty things, expensive things for a lady.

Miss Rose came back. The palm of her right hand was scarlet and stinging.

'Mrs. Selton,' she said, making light of it, 'took a sudden distaste for curry and emptied her plate over Miss Awkright's head. Miss Awkright did not notice, she is as near a vegetable as a vertebrate can be. But unless checked Mrs. Selton might choose a more sensitive target.' The glass was cool to the hand that had done the checking; and the wine was just what she needed on such a day. The idiot side could be very trying, but it was the most profitable side, people would pay more to have a demented relative kept out of sight and given a modicum of care than they would for normal nursing. And whereas medical patients either recovered or died, idiots lived on and on.

After Ellen had ventured a few remarks, met with monosyllabic replies, it was plain that Papa had come home in a bad mood. Something to do with business?

Then, half-way through the meal, Papa said:

'Marion has disgraced herself.'

Mamma put down her spoon very quietly; Ellen's made a little clatter. Papa allowed the moment of suspense to prolong itself. Marion by sheer chance had slipped from his control. Those who were left must be the more rigorously subdued. He filled and emptied his mouth twice before saying,

'She has been playing fast and loose in such a manner that only marriage can retrieve her reputation.'

Sweat broke out on Ellen's forehead and upper lip. Those evenings in the Old Cloister!

'Marriage?' Mamma's voice was quite shrill. She knew her husband's views on the subject. 'To whom?'

'A man of whom I thoroughly disapprove.' Johnny Brisket. 'A cad of the first water.' Johnny Brisket. 'A purse-proud vulgarian.' Johnny could not be called purse-proud, surely. Ellen allowed herself a cautious breath.

'He was here yesterday week; a man called Horridge. If he is to be believed, Marion has been gallivanting about the countryside with him and behaving in such a manner that on a week's acquaintance he proposed to her. And she, without a word to me, accepted him. He was kind enough,' Mr. Draper said with heavy sarcasm, 'to call upon me this morning and ask my consent. I had no choice but to give it.' That was the line he had decided to take — within the family. 'I have informed Mr. Marriot; and the wedding will be a fortnight on Thursday.'

Shocked out of apathy and past caution, Mamma said:

'But that allows no time!'

'Ample, if it is properly used. I shall expect everything to be correct. We will begin with a party — Wednesday I thought a suitable day. I have made a list of those to be invited and I will draft a letter, copies of which must be dispatched so as to arrive by first post tomorrow morning. It would be undesirable for friends to hear first through the calling of the banns. The ostensible reason for this unseemly haste is Mr. Horridge's desire to honeymoon in Paris before the leaves fall.'

'But . . .' Mamma said, and faltered.

'Yes, my dear?'

'What . . . what is the real reason?'

'I was coming to that. Marion has disgraced herself and humiliated *me*. I do not want her about the house. I was never fully satisfied about that counter-jumper fellow. Now, in a week, she has so comported herself as to become engaged. Can you think that a modest woman would have done such a thing? Even with a man of such calibre? The sooner she is married and the responsibility for her passed to other hands, the better.'

Mentally Mamma exonerated herself. She had always tried to bring up the girls to be modest, conventional and amenable. And this had happened when Marion was not even under the home roof.

'I ask you both to remember,' Mr. Draper said, looking from one to another of the two who remained to him, 'that though in public we must put up the best face we can, Marion will not come home this afternoon in a blaze of glory. She has purely by chance and not good judgement, made what, I do not doubt, fools will consider to be a good match. Let the fools tell her so. You bear in mind that she has broken her father's heart.'

Ellen recovered herself and presently found courage to ask, 'Shall I be a bridesmaid?'

'Naturally. Is that not the normal procedure?'

'We shall need others. Has Mr. Horridge any suitable relatives?' She meant suitable in age and size. His sisters would be too old, but he might have nieces.

'No relative of his would be fit for anything except service in a low tavern. But of course you must ask.'

Having thus injected misery into what, for the two women, might have been a joyous occasion, Mr. Draper felt slightly better.

'It'll slide down, Miss,' Betty said, more breathless than usual. The trunk slid down the stairs easily; less easily across the stone floor, Marion lent a hand.

'I dunno,' Betty said, apology in her voice. 'I can remember when I'd have carried it. The truth is I never rightly got over that turn, Monday night. Can't seem to get my strength back.'

'Miss Ellen wrote that you had been unwell.'

'Me and Ada both. Terrible poorly. And they can say what they like about plums. 'S'matter of fact I never had a plum all Monday. Ada did and she's off them for life. I wouldn't say this to anybody but you, Miss, but I know what it was.' She looked round covertly. 'It was the wine. Master said to chuck it out but Ada and me thought we'd just try it. He was right. It wasn't fit to drink. It nearly killed us. It's nice to see you back, Miss. The house didn't seem the same.'

'I'm back only for a very short time, Betty. I am going to be married.'

'Cooo,' Betty said, forgetting her manners. 'Who to?'

How could anyone get married without even walking out?

'Mr. Horridge.'

Betty's first thought was — That old man! Then she remembered the saying — Better an old man's darling than a young man's slave. And Mr. Horridge had given her a nice smile when she had let him in and taken his hat on the evening of the party.

'I do hope you'll be very happy, Miss.'

'Thank you, Betty. I shall be leaving all this,' she indicated the trunk which Betty had opened, and the clothes in the cupboard. 'You may take what you like.'

She then noticed that tucked into the frame of the looking-glass was a tiny folded paper. Inside, in Ellen's writing, 'Welcome home, darling! Wonderful news! We were told not to rejoice, but we do. E.'

In the little half-underground room where love had run its short course and died, Marion stood and thought that though she had failed to free them entirely, she could — as wife of a rich man — do something to mitigate the terms of their servitude. They could visit Sorley; perhaps even stay. Edward should buy a piano upon which Mamma could play. Ellen should have presents, be invited to parties. Papa was sufficiently conventional as not to wish any open rift. She would call for them in that shining carriage.

There were other thoughts too. Very strange. All governed by *if*. If I had not loved Johnny ... If I had not preferred death to facing Papa ... If I had not gone to Heatherton ... If this very morning I had not gone back to Heatherton ... it was all too much for a human mind to deal with.

Mamma said, 'My hand is cramped. And I think I should speak to Ada.'

She walked rather gingerly down the steep stairs to the basement, spoke to Ada and then went on to Marion's little room. She bestowed a kiss of unusual warmth and said, 'Dear, I do so hope that you will be happy. Papa is rather upset. He does not like the idea of losing a daughter, but he will come round in time.'

She went back to the dining-room where Ellen said, 'I have finished the envelopes. There are four more letters ... I must just ...'

'Darling,' she said, down in the little room. 'How wonderful, wonderful! How did you do it? Papa is furious. But we're going to have an enormous party on Wednesday. And then the wedding. I wish somebody would fall in love with me. Mamma is so mortified that there was no time to have the invitations — the wedding ones, I mean — printed, but Papa said ...'

Ada said, 'Eighteen people and seven courses and four days' notice and me lame as a tree. Well, I'll do my best just this once more and then I give in. This time I do mean it, Betty girl. I'll just go to the Workhouse and *sit*.'

'When you go, I go.'

'And for an engagement,' Ada said caustically. 'I really do wonder sometimes whether she can be right in the head. What did marriage ever bring her except misery? She was that gay and pretty, you wouldn't believe. Long before your time, of course. But there she sat happy as a lark supposing a lark had been in a cage for years, and saying she must look out her wedding veil. Well, there ain't much I have to be thankful for with my bones as they are, but I do thank my God I never married.'

'Good evening. Papa.'

'Good evening, Marion.' He could not bring himself to look at her, the instrument of his humiliation.

A profound gloom pervaded the room.

Presently Ellen, mindful of her duty said, 'I understand that the Harvest Festival will be a week early this year, on account of the good weather.'

Mr. Draper mindful of his duty responded, 'It is to be hoped that Mr. Walker's pumpkins will have attained full size.'

Mrs. Draper, mindful of her duty, said, 'I hope so. I always buy one of his for Ada's special ginger preserve.'

It could very well have been almost a year ago except that when the summer had been inclement and the Harvest Festival deferred. And there were houses in which nothing had happened, people to whom nothing had happened between one Harvest Festival and another.

Mamma said, 'The man who brings logs called this morning, Ada tells me. The price for a load is the same as last year.'

'And why not?' Papa asked. A rhetorical question.

Presently, from one of Ada's best offerings, apple and lemon, topped with whipped egg white, crisp and delectable, he took a pip.

'I was aware that Ada's legs had failed. I did not realise that she was going blind,' he said.

The meal dragged along like an animal with a broken leg. Finally, dabbing his table napkin to his mouth and then throwing it aside, Papa said, 'I have something to say to Marion.'

Betty cleared the table. Mamma and Ellen scuttled away.

'Now,' Papa said, still not looking at her, but at some point on the wall behind her, 'I will tell you what happened this morning.' He gave her a stinging, word-by-word account of his interview with Mr. Horridge. 'It was,' he said, coming to the end, 'the most shameless and vulgar use of money as a weapon.' That his own behaviour in the Baxter-Freeman affair had not been different in anything but scope never occurred to him. 'I quite understand that he has found it impossible to find any decently brought-up young woman to marry him. You must not think that he succumbed to your charms or entertains any feeling of affection for you. Far from it. To him you are a bargain; member of a decent family, well-spoken, capable, when you choose, of behaving correctly; but not so choosing. You have made yourself as available as any bought woman. Bear that in mind. That is what you are. A bought woman. And he will never respect you. Had I been a man without a family,' Mr. Draper lapsed for once from strict logic, 'I should have told him to go to the Devil. As it was, I had no choice. So you must marry your guttersnipe who, once the ring is on your finger, will show himself for what he is.'

'He had, at least, sufficient sensibility not to speak of the bargain. He simply said he had persuaded you to give your consent.'

Answering back.

'So it may seem. *Now*. I merely warn you. You are a bought woman. As such you will be treated.'

Like Mamma? Bought by promises, by marriage from the market where music teachers earned threepence an hour? No, I do not, I will not believe it. Edward does love me; he does respect me.

'In the meantime, kindly refrain from putting ideas into Ellen's head. It is unlikely that she will find a man to bid so high for her.'

Ellen, however, stole downstairs when all the house was still and curled up on Marion's bed for a cosy, girlish chat.

'It is a pity that Papa is so cross,' she said. 'Mamma and I are so excited. I have not seen her take such interest in anything. She has everything planned. Miss Bussey is to make your wedding gown and Mamma's dress. That is about as much as she can manage in the time. I'm easier to fit, so the dressmaker at Proctor's will do mine, and the other bridesmaids'. That will keep them busy; so Saunders will do your other clothes and Mamma thought that Nanny might like to do some plain sewing in petticoats and nightdresses.'

'I do not need underclothes. I want the very minimum,

Ellen. A wedding gown is, I suppose, a necessity. I don't want a trousseau bought with *his* money! He said some quite abominable things to me this evening.'

'What beats me is how he ever came to agree to it, feeling as he does about marriage — for us, I mean.'

'Edward can be very persuasive.'

'Do you love him, Marion?'

'I like and respect him. It is not like . . . well, you know . . . But I was younger then.'

'I think you must have a trousseau, dearest; for Mamma's sake. She is enjoying it all so much. On Wednesday, for the party, what do you think? She is going to hire a woman from Corder's agency, for the whole day so that Betty can help Ada. She did not even consult Papa and when I mentioned it she said that he had said everything was to be done properly and that there was nothing improper about hiring extra help. Think of that. Mamma! Oh, and she has found her own wedding veil, all wrapped in blue paper to keep it white, and such beautiful lace.'

'I should have thought,' Marion said bitterly, 'that the very idea of marriage would be anathema to her.'

Ellen said, 'You and your long words. What is anathema? Now, bridesmaids. I suppose we must ask Priscilla Mingay . . .'

Sunday was gloomy, but Monday, once Papa had departed, was gay. The hired carriage made its round and there was obsequious service everywhere. *Rather* short notice — let not our efforts be underestimated — but everything should be ready. The Drapers had always been good, steady customers and Miss Draper was making a splendid match. When she was mistress of Sorley Park she would be able to be extravagant.

Mamma, abandoning restraint, decided to forsake her usual grey and to have Parma violet and not-quite-a-bonnet — more of-a-hat trimmed with artificial Parma violets. Imbued with new life, she mounted stairs nimbly, walked about showrooms, issued concise orders and showed no signs of exhaustion at all. Ellen chatted happily as she collected a handful of samples in sweet-pea colours, for submission to the bridesmaids. It was impossible not to be caught up in the tide of enthusiasm. And why resist it? In a few days she would be married and free. The future stretched out, bright with promise. The past was over and done with.

The past, however, was not to be so easily shuffled off. On neat, rather-too-expensively shod feet it came padding along Alma Avenue and tapped with a well-cared-for hand upon her window.

Johnny; almost forgotten, and certainly, under the pressure of events, overlooked.

Fool that I was not to have written him a final dismissing letter while I was at Heatherton and safe behind the barrier of Miss Rose and her rules.

She let him in the usual way and noted that his temper was surly.

'You did not write, *chérie*.' And for the first time she observed something that he shared with Papa, the ability to use an affectionate term without affection. Papa said, 'My dear.'

'I had no time.'

'I *made* time to write to you. I said I was prepared to *walk* to Sorley to see you yesterday. Unwell as I was.'

'I think I must have missed that letter. Papa ordered me home on Saturday. Very suddenly.'

'But you did not inform me. I said in my letter — which you did not receive — that unless I heard I should come this evening to look for the light in your window.'

Another *if*. If Ellen had not again slipped down to talk there would not have been a light in this room.

He looked ill, thinner and a bad colour. And soon he was to receive a shock. She said, kindly, 'I am sorry that you have been feeling unwell. *L'estomac encore?*'

'Yes,' he said. 'And not this time altogether because of Mrs. Fenner's cooking. Uncertainty and anxiety also take effect. You in Heatherton and between us nothing settled.'

'Poor Johnny,' she said. 'I will give you some brandy.' Brandy was good for shock. She found the bottle labelled as hair tonic and poured generously; and as he drank she considered another *if*. *If* Johnny had never confronted Papa he would not understand what she now had to say; but since he had done . . .

It was very strange to be looking upon Papa as a rock of refuge.

Johnny sipped. 'It has never been so bad,' he said, laying a hand upon the spot where, beneath his elegant waistcoat the pain nagged, like the hidden fox — or was it wolf?, gnawing at the little Spartan boy's vitals. 'But it is better.' The alcohol had its usual effect.

160

'You neglected me,' he said, 'but I forgive you. What matters is that you are safe home and we can make our plans.'

He had briefly hoped that those plans need never be put into effect. For two days he had waited for someone to say, 'How sad about Mr. Draper.' Nobody said it. He had wronged Marion by his suspicion; and of course he had been a fool to suspect her; she did not understand, despite all his warnings, how dangerous the stuff was . . .

She knew that this was not going to be easy. She should have written, casting him off. Yet her reason for waiting had seemed reasonable. Well, now to do it as quickly and painlessly as possible.

'Have a little more,' she said, and tipping the bottle up, emptied it completely. It would not be needed any more.

'Johnny, I have something to tell you. Everything has been altered. Papa has arranged for me to be married to a friend of his.'

The glass fell from Johnny's hand and shattered with what, in the sleeping house, seemed a loud noise.

'*Mon Dieu! C'est impossible!*'

'It is arranged. The date of the wedding fixed.'

'But it is crazy,' he said in a shrill, loud voice. 'How can you be married? You belong to me. In all but name you are my . . .'

'Be quiet! You will rouse the house.'

'I will rouse the house! Let him come down and hear the truth!'

'Very well,' she said. 'Shout away.'

He said, in a much lower tone, 'How could you agree? How can you sit there and say such things?'

'What else could I have done?'

'You could have made a stand. You never did. Never once. I told you again and again. I gave you opportunity. At the Garden Fête, outside the church, when I was of good appearance. But no, it is left to me to present myself in ruined clothes and be confounded. Who is the man?'

'His name is Horridge.'

'Oh yes. I know. Very rich. And soon to be,' he said nastily, 'very much surprised. Your papa also. You never spoke for me, but I will speak for you. First thing tomorrow morning I go to Mr. Horridge and ask how he feels about robbing me of my wife; a woman who, but for accident would now be carrying my child. We shall see.'

She had told Edward on Saturday morning that unless things were done her way they would never be done at all. And hadn't she felt, ever since Saturday, that it was all too good to be true?

Nevertheless, she put up a fight.

'I shall deny it all. Mr. Horridge is in love with me; if it comes to the point I think he will choose to believe me rather than you. He will think — and so will papa — that you suffer from hallucinations.'

And that, Jean de Brissac knew, was all too likely. Always he had suffered from the feeling of being outside the place where rightly he belonged. Looks, intelligence, taste counted for nothing — unless you had money. And that he had never had. Those who had it would combine against him.

He said with a lifetime's stored-up venom.

'That would be possible. Except that I have proof. I have your letters.'

The world gave a jerk and stood still.

For her letters, written with passion and urgency had seemed to have no physical existence, once they had been smuggled out and posted. Then Johnny had mentioned, approvingly, the thoroughness with which Mrs. Fenner, his landlady, cleaned his room, and she had said. 'What about my letters?' 'I read and re-read them until I know them by heart, then I burn them, *chérie*, though it hurts me to do so.' And so, confident, she had written her protestations of love, and her pleas for marriage.

Now to be used against her.

'You kept my letters?'

'A few. Too beautiful to be destroyed.'

'And you would show them?'

'To save you from Mr. Horridge, yes. I must.' He must also, if anything were to come of this whole affair, keep her goodwill. 'Darling, surely you must see. It is your ... our ... only hope. Unless we go back to what we planned and run away and get married.'

'That was my plan. When I believed that you loved me.'

'I do love you.'

'Yet you propose to shame me. Send me back to Heatherton, on the idiot side? That will be the result. Show one of those letters and everyone will know that I am a lunatic. But run along, do your worst, Johnny. I no longer care one way or the other. I will let you out now.'

She stood up. Appearing to accept the worst that he could threaten she seemed to be impregnable.

In a gesture that looked theatrical, but was in fact sincere and desperate, he flung himself down on his knees and clutched her about the thighs. She said, 'Let go of me, or I shall call papa.'

'I meant no harm,' he said, almost whimpering. 'It was to save you. That ugly old man. Marion please, Marion listen. I love you; you love me. Darling, forget it all. Let us go away, hold to our plan.'

She said, and her manner was curiously similar to her father's when he was bargaining for barley.

'And every time I happened to displease you would produce a letter to prove that I had given myself to you, outside marriage; conceived your child. Thank you, no. I would sooner go back to Heatherton.'

'I will burn every letter. Marion, *chérie*, darling ... I wished only to save you, from Mr. Horridge, from your papa, from yourself.'

'As you burned the others?'

'I will bring them here. Burn them before your eyes. Yes, yes, yes ... I did wrong to keep them, to threaten, but you must understand my desperation.' Before his eyes the five thousand pounds, mythical, the product of Marion's imagination hovered. His hold on her tightened. 'Marion, you must forgive me.'

She made a move to free herself. 'How can I think, while you ... ' He got to his feet, looking silly.

'Very well, Johnny. I accept your offer. I would like to see them burn. So many of them have to do with that horrible time.'

'And then you will come away with me? On Wednesday?'

'No. Because on Wednesday Mr. Horridge will give me a ring.'

'Of course! How clever! Thursday then?'

'We can talk about Thursday tomorrow.'

'It must be Thursday,' he said, half pleading, half threatening again. 'If you stay here something will happen. You will be talked round. Or frightened. And you must understand, darling, that while I have breath in my body and a tongue in my head, I shall not allow you to marry any other man.'

'Yes,' she said. 'I understand that.'

She let him out. There was a great moon in the sky. They called it the Harvest Moon because by its light, in a dry season, men could work in the fields, earning the stipulated sum for getting in the corn in the shortest possible time. Outside the back door of Ten Alma Avenue it made the world sharply black and white and when Johnny had climbed the steps and raised his hand in a farewell salute, he looked colossal. Tomorrow by this time, things would be different.

'What people don't understand,' Ada said on Tuesday morning, hammering away at egg-shells, 'is the work that go in to a simple clear consommé. They think if you drop in an egg-shell or two it'll do. There's no short cut, not in cooking. I could've trained you, you know, but there never was time enough. I said from the first this was an awkward house, needing three to run it and room only for two. Not that it matters, these days,' she said sourly. 'These days you just go along to Corder's ...' Mrs. Draper's well-meant action had given Ada so much offence that the sentimental cord was almost severed. 'I never fell down on a job,' she said. 'I grumbled a bit but that didn't mean nothing. I'd never have left her in the lurch. But if she can just go to Corder's ... And I'll bet that woman'll get as much for the one day as I do for four.'

She dropped in the hammered shells. Disgruntled as she was she meant to produce her usual, sparkingly clear consommé.

Tuesday was busy, bustling and happy, for Mamma and for Ellen at least; for Marion it was a yearning towards night as it had so often been, for a differing reason. And when Johnny tapped on the window and was let in, the first thing she noticed was that he was empty-handed.

'I went to the station when the shop closed,' he said. 'I wished to assure myself about the times of the trains. I saw Mr. Horridge, he came off the London train and was met by his man, with his gig. I thought of the ring in his pocket. I laughed to myself.'

'I suppose it has its comic side,' she said. *Where are those letters?*

'Darling, kiss me. You have hardly kissed me properly since you came back ...' And he meant not from Heatherton, but from the sea.

A Judas kiss. But it was demanded of me. Judas proffered his.

Satisfied with his kiss, Johnny said, 'The trains could not be better.' He went to sit down, doing what all gentlemen did if they were careful of their clothes. He lifted his coat-tails; said, 'Oh yes. The letters.' She should have remembered that the pocket in the coat-tail was a repository favoured by men who were vain about their figures.

It was quite a bundle. Did I write so many? It was tied with a blue ribbon.

She had made the grate ready, removing the paper fan, laying a box of matches on the narrow mantel-shelf.

All so sad; though now she could stand aside and look at it dispassionately. There had been love once, reckless, taking no thought, ready to risk anything.

'You light it,' she said. He struck a match, held it to an envelope until it flared and then dropped the bundle into the grate.

'So,' he said, 'you are now convinced? Marion, I have thought about things. It would not be wise for us to leave by the same train. The first for London leaves at half past seven. I will catch it. The next is at half past eleven. You must catch that one. At Liverpool Street Station I shall wait for you, with a cab. What you wish to take with you, you must give to me now. I will take it with mine, so you need carry nothing.'

With the child growing in me and my mind distraught that was what I wanted you, begged you, to say. You would not listen.

'That is not necessary, Johnny. I have made my plan. I wish Miss Bussey to copy some of my favourite dresses. That is an excellent excuse for taking a cab, and a valise. You see?'

He saw that it would spare him the exertion of carrying her gear from here to his lodging, and on Thursday morning from Brewster Street to the Station. And in his present state of health that was just as well. The pain in his stomach nagged and gnawed; he had not eaten a proper meal for more than a week.

'Can you manage that?'

'Oh yes, Mamma and Ellen always sleep on after a party.'

Behind her the packet of letters smouldered. She took up the poker. 'If you had removed the ribbon, they would have burned better,' she said. A single sharp blow broke the charred ribbon, and falling apart, the letters flared. A page writhing like a sentient thing, reared up and bore its message, 'I love you, I love you my darling.' Then it turned brown and collapsed into nothingness.

She felt sorry for the girl, so young and innocent and loving, who had written those words. Deluded fool! And a little sorry for Johnny, fallen from high estate, the lover, the master, now nothing. But he had wrought his own destruction.

She said, 'Now you must have some brandy. It is Papa's very best brought out in readiness for tomorrow.'

She poured; he sipped. He said, 'Your papa, like all Englishmen, judges quality by cost. I have drunk better in a wayside bistro.'

'I am sorry you do not enjoy it. It is the last time you will drink at Papa's expense. Tomorrow we shall be late, a lot of people coming and going . . .'

'Yes. And I have the early train to catch.' He went on drinking and referring to the future. Never again would he be obliged to eat Mrs. Fenner's beef pudding with its, to him, almost-lethal suet crust. He reminded Marion to bring with her everything of value that she owned. Then, narrowing his eyes, he said, 'If you do not come, *chérie*, if you allow yourself to be deterred by any little difficulty, remember I shall come back.'

'There will be no difficulty.'

'Then I shall see you at twenty minutes to two on Thursday at Liverpool Street Station. I can bear this parting because we shall meet so soon.'

Not soon, but certainly. In some murky outpost of Hell where those who betrayed and those who were betrayed, those who lied and those who were lied to would meet and recognise one another and share a common condemnation, the weak as blameworthy as the wicked, the wicked as excusable as the weak.

At the last, at the door, moved by an impulse of pity, she took his face between her hands and kissed him again. 'Goodbye, Johnny. Good-bye.'

For the last time she used the screw-driver on the door. She brushed up every flake of paper from the little grate and put it into the kitchen stove. She replaced the paper fan. She had managed, she thought, well.

'I came a bit early,' Mr. Horridge said, 'because I thought Marion should have the ring on her finger. And I wanted to show you this. I *know* the bride's family make all the arrangements. But this may be worth a look.'

It was worth several. In response to Mr. Horridge's simple, honest letter — claiming no kinship, merely stating that he was about to marry and wanted the wedding to be worthy of his bride, Dean Horridge of Asham had written a most enthusiastic letter.

He was, in fact, a rather unworldly old man who long ago had been excited to learn that he was related to a Joshua Horridge, one of the Protestant martyrs in Mary Tudor's reign. Not only a martyr, a hero. 'He it was who by his courage and cheerfulness, heartened the weaker sort.' 'At the stake Joshua Horridge cried, God Save the Queen, and England from Popery!' For thirty years Dean Horridge had fossicked about in parish registers and country graveyards. But it was only a hobby, and he only an amateur. He had run into a blind alley with Eliza Horridge who had married a man called Crook. She had given her elder son Horridge as a Christian name. Grown-up and in business as a wine merchant, he had, very sensibly, used his Christian name as a surname. He had had two sons; one had carried on the business and prospered; Sir Charles was his descendant. The other had vanished without trace. So now, hot on the trail, Dean Horridge wrote. 'Throughout there has been a tendency — see enclosed — to name boys Edward or Joshua. Your name is Edward; if your father or grandfather bore the name of Joshua it is possible that you are one of what I always call "The Lost Tribe". This would mean that in your blood runs that of a man who was not only a martyr but a hero.' Then, realising that he had not answered this Horridge's letter, he had added a postscript, saying that he would be only too pleased to help officiate at the marriage ceremony. What he enclosed with his letter completely confused Mr. Horridge. It was a section of the Family Tree — the whole now covered several sheets of cartridge paper, carefully pasted together. The idea of being a descendant of a martyred hero did not fire Mr. Horridge's imagination; but he hoped that Mr. Draper would take to the notion of the Dean at the wedding.

Mr. Draper said, 'And I have no doubt that upon

reading this you promptly rechristened your father!' Nasty!

'I didn't need to. My father was called Young Josh. His father was Edward; my old great-grandfather was Old Josh.'

'The Dean,' Mr. Draper said smoothly, 'is to be congratulated. I understand that the bells at Asham cannot be rung, the tower is in such a state that it might collapse.' Again, nasty; but as usual Mr. Horridge endeavoured to stick to his main purpose.

'Can I see Marion?'

'I should have taken a bit of string for measure,' Mr. Horridge said. 'I had to go by guess.' In its dark blue velvet bed gleamed not perhaps the largest diamond to be found in London, but one of the finest quality.

'It isn't new,' Mr. Horridge said, apologetically. 'I tramped about. I wanted something special. And this had a sort of story I thought you might like. Too long to tell now. But they're good. That one in the middle — the best I could find in a day's march.'

The one in the middle was the size of a hazelnut and around it eight others were set, the whole forming a shield shape.

She said, 'It is far too grand.'

'Nothing is too grand for you. After I'd settled for it, I had doubts. Would you have liked a half hoop better? Was I wrong? If you don't like it, we'll change it. If it don't fit it can be altered.'

He watched, as, as though it had been made to measure, the ring, once a mere pendant of a diamond necklace that had made a major scandal and helped to bring about the French Revolution, slipped on to her finger.

'I wasn't too sure; but I must say I like it better now than I did. Your hand sets it off.'

Other guests were now arriving.

This was altogether a more animated party, if only because so few ladies could be seated. Mr. Draper, preserving the necessary good face, delegated to his future son-in-law the dispensing of madeira while he dealt with the sherry. Congratulations and good wishes flew about. The ring was inspected and admired — not always sincerely. Too big; too bright; vulgarly ostentatious.

'How I envy you,' Mrs. Taylor said. 'You will have Marion so near.' Angela was far away in the west country and the little cosy talks between mother and daughter-about-to-become mother, were out of the question.

'You are very fortunate,' Mrs. Marriot said. Her beloved daughter had married a poor curate, had three children, a decaying old vicarage in Stepney and great difficulty in making ends meet. Every now and then, when there were White Elephant Sales, Church Bazaars, Jumble sales, Mrs. Marriot was glad to price certain items low and buy them in. How different would be Mrs. Draper's and Marion's lot!

Apart from the fact that the hired woman was not as efficient as the Agency believed her to be and had to be instructed in a hissing whisper to serve and remove *from the left*, the meal went well. And before it was over the news had spread that the putative bridegroom was not the rich parvenue everyone had thought. Mr. Draper had in the most cool and casual fashion, asked Mr. Marriot if he would agree to the Dean's sharing in the marriage ceremony. 'It appears that after all, he's a kind of distant cousin.'

At that the ring on Marion's hand lost much of its vulgarity.

And the meal was excellent. Several ladies remarked that though they had, from time to time, wheedled a recipe from Ada, the dishes they or their cooks had made, were never quite the same.

'Ada has her secrets,' Ellen said.

And then, into one of those small lulls to which even the most successful dinner-party may be subject, Mr. Marriot said, 'How very sad about young de Brissac.'

He had himself been shocked — half-way through dressing for dinner — to hear what had happened to that amiable and intelligent young man. It had, in fact, rather spoiled his evening and he was not averse to passing his mild misery on.

'What is sad about him?' Lady Mingay asked in her masterful, carrying voice.

'He died, very suddenly. Last night.'

'But that is incredible,' she said — the incredible being what she did not choose to believe. 'I was in the shop myself only yesterday morning, he was then as fit as a flea. What happened? Did he meet with an accident?'

'I think not. Some digestive trouble, I understand. I could

not get much detail from his landlady who came to see me about . . . hmm, hmm. Poor soul, she was very much upset.'

Mrs. Fenner had been upset indeed. She had sent for Doctor Barlow.

'Well, you see, Doctor, he'd had such turns on and off, ever since he lived here. And always got better. He was French, English food didn't seem to suit him. Mind you, the Sunday joint, yes, I'd favour him a bit, with the lean, but with pie-crust, or puddings . . . He'd laugh and say — "Now I take my life on my fork," or some such thing. I've had dozens — lodgers, I mean — and never one I liked so much. But with a pudding you have to treat them all the same.'

'Did anyone else suffer from eating this pudding?'

'No. They all ett it; I ett some myself. Then in the night, he was moving about and I thought to myself — bilious again. But I never heard about anybody dying of being bilious. If I'd known he was dying I'd have sent for you sooner, and if I'd known he'd be dead when you got here I'd have given you time to get your breakfast. But I didn't know. And he was such a nice young man.' She'd had a hard life and tears did not come easily, but a few did and she wiped them away with the corner of her apron.

'At what time was he taken ill, Mrs. Fenner?'

'I couldn't rightly say. I never looked. It was the middle of the night and I heard him, not just moving about, that I'm used to, in the next room. But moaning. So I went and you never did see — well, being a doctor you could have — but I never did. So I wrapped him up and got a hot-water jar . . . I don't suppose you remember my Bill, to the end his hot-water jar was a great comfort . . . So anyway I got Mr. de Brissac one and I said, "Use your chamber-pot, Mr. de Brissac. What's a chamber-pot for?" And he eased off a bit. Then he was sick again.'

'Is the chamber-pot handy, Mrs. Fenner?'

It was. But it was clean and scoured. She had — as was the habit with her kind — cleaned up for the doctor's visit.

'Was there blood in the vomit, Mrs. Fenner.'

The honest answer to that would have been, 'I don't know.' She was more fastidious than one might have expected, and her only thought was to get rid of it. The light in the room was supplied by a single candle, and being alone with Mr. de Brissac, far and away her favourite lodger, in such dire straits, was distressing. The other four men in the house slept like pigs.

But now she felt that Doctor Barlow somehow blamed her pudding, so, giving it an alibi, she said yes, there was blood in the vomit.

With a history of stomach trouble the probability was an ulcer of some long-standing, persistently ignored, suddenly perforating. Already, in his mind, making out the death certificate, Doctor Barlow asked, 'How old was he?'

'That I don't know. I never heard him say. Twenty-six. Twenty-seven.'

As she said this she realised that there were a number of other things she did not know. Who would pay for the funeral for, instance.

After Mr. de Brissac the lodger she liked best was Charley-the-Carpenter. To him she appealed. 'Charley, you come up with me for a minute or two. I've got to make a search and I don't much care . . .'

Charley didn't much care, either, but he went with her.

'What you looking for, Ma?'

'Any sort of paper that'll show who he belonged to.'

No room could have been easier to search. On the top of the chest-of-drawers lay the key to the front door with which Johnny had been entrusted, and the sum of fifteen shillings and fourpence. The bedside table held two books — both in what Mrs. Fenner took to be French, and a gun-metal watch with a pinchbeck chain. His drawers were meticulously tidy; in his cupboard hung his clothes, his boots, all on trees, ranged on the floor, with, alongside, a box holding his boot-cleaning kit. His toilet things were ranged equally neatly on his wash-stand. There was not anywhere a single scrap of paper to connect him with anything or anybody in the world. Yet he had received letters, noticeable because very few letters ever arrived at 18 Brewster Street, and yet not much noticed in themselves because whether they arrived by first or second post, they coincided with the getting of a meal.

Not looking at the bed where the dead man lay, a clean sheet spread over him, Charley-the-Carpenter said, 'Always was a bit of a mystery, wasn't he, Ma?'

'Mystery or not, he's got to be buried,' Mrs. Fenner said.

The parish would have given him a pauper's funeral, but that would have involved a visit from Mr. Mison, the Relieving Officer: and much of Mrs. Fenner's time and energy had been spent in keeping Mr. Mison from her door. When the children were small and Bill was out of work; when Bill was ill for so long; when Bill died, always, somehow she had managed to steer clear of Mr. Mison and the stigma that Parish Relief implied. She still wished not to have anything to do with it, even by association.

So now, most reluctantly and with a renewed sense of the injustice of life, she said, 'On your way to work, Charley, look in at Wilsher's and ask him to come and see me.' Of the two undertakers in the town Mr. Wilsher was the cheaper. She explained what she wanted, the simplest, the cheapest possible funeral; a plain box, no brass, no black plumes on the horses. How much? He said it could be done for five pounds, with five shillings discount for prompt payment. Mr. Wilsher was experienced; most poor people tended to order funerals of unnecessary ostentation and then paid for them belatedly.

'I can lay my hands on that much,' Mrs. Fenner said, feeling as though an invisible wound were leaching away her life's blood. September brought rent day, and rate day, and the purchase of coal for the winter. Coal was cheaper by the ton, and until the end of September, you got it at summer prices.

At some time during the day it occurred to her that Mr. Freeman might contribute towards the interment of his late assistant. So, having served the substantial meal called 'tea' she forced her feet into the shoes that tortured her bunions and trudged along to the shop. There, for a moment, she enjoyed the importance of one who has dramatic and disastrous news to impart.

'Dead!' Mr. Freeman exclaimed. 'I thought he was malingering again. I was going to send Bobbie round . . .' He was also meditating the advisability of giving de Brissac the sack. Baxter's would soon reopen and the tide of trade would shift; he might no longer be able to afford an assistant. Now death had forestalled him.

'What did he die of?'

'Something in his stomach. It burst. The point is, Mr. Freeman, he's dead and he's got to be buried. I wondered if you . . .'

'No, I can*not*,' Mr. Freeman said with some violence. 'I paid him well. More than he's been worth this last month or two. I don't see why I should be held responsible . . . When will the funeral be?'

'On Saturday, if I can fix it with the parson.'

She hobbled on to the Rectory where Mr. Marriot was just beginning to dress for the party to celebrate Marion Draper's sudden engagement.

Mr. Marriot was more upset than Mr. Freeman had been.

'What a tragedy,' he said. 'So young. And so gifted.'

'And very regular at church and anything to do with it.'

'He will be missed.'

'I couldn't let him be buried by the Parish, could I?'

'Oh no. No, of course not.'

Mr. Marriot was not so sharp in taking her meaning as Mr. Freeman had been. But he was nicer. He said she must not grieve unduly; he spoke of the life everlasting. He said Saturday would be all right.

The fine weather broke and it was raining when Jean de Brissac was laid in the Norfolk clay. Mr. Wilsher had given value for money, the horse wore its plumes. There were three wreaths. One was large and lavish, 'From all at 18 Brewster Street.' To this Mrs. Fenner had been forbidden to subscribe; 'No, Ma,' Charley said, 'you've done your lot.' Johnny's fine clothes, la-di-da airs and his reticence had not exactly endeared him to his fellow-lodgers, but his sudden death had sparked off some sentimentality and the same kind of superiority that old Colonel Fraser had left; they were alive, he was dead; they'd drink less in the coming week, but they could afford lilies. The other wreaths were modest. Mr. and Mrs. Freeman had decided that it would look bad not to send, so they sent; a circle of box, sparsely studded with asters. And from the Rectory came the result of a long-standing order; for every church member, except in a few cases, a two-shilling wreath of whatever flower was in season and therefore cheap. For Johnny, dahlias.

At the moment of the actual interment, Marion was having a first fitting of her wedding dress. Miss Bussey liked to have her Saturday afternoons free, but on this order there was not a minute to waste.

After the funeral Mrs. Fenner went home, took off the hurtful shoes, hung up her decent black, the relic of her widow's garb and donned her working garb. Mr. de Brissac's room must be cleared; it was already bespoke. Charley had a friend, anxious to move in on Sunday. She was known to keep a good table and her house was clean; she seldom had a room vacant for more than twenty-four hours.

Mr. de Brissac had arrived in Bereham with one valise; but in his eighteen-month stay he had bought more clothes and she was obliged to fetch up her wicker washing-basket. It was a great pity, she thought, that apart from what he wore in the shop, his things were all so gentlemanly; on the second-hand market worthless. People who bought on that market did not wish for tailed coats, fine linen shirts, lavender coloured gloves, fancy waistcoats. Gentlemen who did want such things, bought them direct. It sounded unkind but the fustian, the best-blue serge, the overalls of any one of her other lodgers would have been worth more and gone further to reimburse her for that wounding four pounds fifteen shillings. Of what value, for instance, was Mr. de Brissac's top hat, nested in a box specially shaped to hold it. Who else could wear these elegant boots, black patent with grey suede uppers?

However, she did, as always, her best. Over the tea of boiled beef, carrots, potatoes and dumplings she said — and in this house her words were heeded — 'It wouldn't hurt any of you to have an extra shirt or handkerchief, would it?'

The macabre little transaction, not an auction, more of a forced sale, netted her ten shillings.

'Put the rest in the shed, Charley,' she said, 'Ikey-Mo should be along tomorrow.'

Ikey-Mo was a melancholy little man who had a little cart, pulled by a melancholy little donkey and he walked the streets of Bereham crying, 'Anyowragbonebottle.' Rags he bought by weight, weighing them on a set of scales at the back of the cart; reliable scales in a way, never registering a value more than twopence. He was already very rich; he owned three of Yarmouth's slummiest and therefore most profitable streets, known as 'The Rows'; he had shares in several fishing vessels and in a kipper-drying establishment. But his way of life was his way of life and he pursued it with the secret satisfaction of despising those who despised him.

He came along with his mournful cry on Monday after-noon. The clothes in which Johnny had put such confidence, lumped down the scale. Twopence! Twopence! In all two shillings' worth. When she offered him the last thing he said, 'Boxes I do not buy. Vot is in the box?'

'A top hat.' She opened it to show him. And there, nested in the top hat which was nested in the box, was what she had been hunting and hoping for. Letters.

'Paper I do not buy,' Ikey-Mo said. 'For the hat, twopence. Vith box. And I vish you good afternoon. Any-owragbonebottle?'

He moved on and with the letters in one hand, the two shillings and twopence in the other, Mrs. Fenner returned to her kitchen where she had already made a pot of tea. It grew cool as she investigated the find which had so nearly eluded her.

There were seven letters, three in their envelopes, four without. Johnny had wished the blue-ribboned bundle to look convincingly bulky. No letter was dated and the paper on which they were written was unheaded. 'Monday, and darling you have just left me.' 'Thursday, my love, and you are now in Honey Lane.' Johnny had, with Gallic good sense, reserved only the letters that would be most useful if ever needed, and they were in no sort of order. But Mrs. Fenner, with very mixed emotions, was able to piece together a coherent story; Mr. de Brissac, had indulged in a violent love affair with a shameless hussy, got her with child and been obliged to marry her secretly.

He had a wife. A widow. It was the duty of widows to bury their husbands. She had buried Bill, unable then to make a down payment or get a rebate for cash. Half a crown every week for fourteen months.

Relief was the first and most powerful of her emotions; but a shocked disgust ran relief hard. How could any woman bring herself to write such things? And then came unholy glee. 'Darling, be a little late tomorrow. I write in haste to tell you that Papa has gone to one of his Maltsters' meetings and will be home on the late train. It will not be safe until half past eleven. I cannot tell you how I long for the moment when I can let you in — and I do not mean merely into the house.'

There was only one Maltster in Bereham and Mrs. Fenner had hated him for years.

Bill had once worked for Mr. Draper, been overworked and underpaid and nagged at. One day he had ricked his back and despite a good rubbing with horse liniment had been unable to leave his bed in the morning, Saturday, pay-day. She had gone down to make excuse for him and collect five days' wages. Mr. Draper said, coldly, 'Fenner. Ah yes, one of those who chose not to take advantage of my medical scheme. So if you need a doctor you must pay.' They'd never been able to spare that twopence a week. Twopence bought a pound of pudding beef, or a large loaf, or a pint of treacle. The children were young then. Mr. Draper had paid her precisely five-sixths of Bill's weekly wage and sent a message. 'Tell him to be back on Monday if he wants to keep his job.' Not a word of sympathy. In fact he had managed to make her feel thriftless and feckless.

Many years later she had had another brush with the horrible man. Bill was dying and despite the fact that she had a heavy cold she had run out for a new supply of the pills which relieved him a little. She had handed the prescription to Mr. Baxter when the door opened and Mr. Draper said, 'Ha, Baxter. I want a large bottle of eau-de-Cologne.' The chemist put down the prescription. It was not right; she'd always paid on the nail and her money was as good as anybody's, and Bill was waiting, alone in the house. 'Here,' she said, 'I was f . . .', then she began to cough.

Over her head Mr. Draper said, 'Never mind about wrapping it. I have no wish to catch a cold.'

Whenever one of her cronies, having eaten his buns and drunk his tea at the Bazaar, spoke sycophantically of the man Mrs. Fenner sniffed.

Now on her own kitchen table she had absolute proof that one of his stuck-up daughters was a shameless hussy who'd had to get married in a hurry.

Mrs. Fenner's mind checked there. A birth was not a thing that could be hidden. Perhaps he knew. Perhaps this would not shock and humiliate him as she hoped. Perhaps he had been paying Mr. de Brissac to keep the secret. Never mind it would give him a nasty jolt to know that *she* knew. And the letters in themselves were enough to give anyone a jolt, leave alone a proud, respectable man like that.

Back to the matter of money, never far from her mind. The Drapers could pay the whole five pounds. She would not mention the discount or the sale of oddments.

And why stop there?

Why stop there? She was now in possession of a secret. People paid to have their secrets kept. How about fifty pounds? In fact had there been no mention of marriage or a baby on the way, the letters themselves were things any father would pay *not* to have shown about.

The more she thought about it the surer she felt of that fifty pounds; and she felt no scruple. Mr. Draper owed her, and the wife of every man he had ever employed, far more than that. She took in, damped down and folded the washing, ready for ironing later on. She prepared potatoes and cabbage to go with the pigs' trotters that were simmering away on the stove. She set the table. When the meal was served she found that she had no appetite; her stomach was churning and rumbling as though she had already eaten some indigestible dish. She drank two cups of strong sweet tea. The letters were in her apron pocket and from time to time she touched them to make sure that they were real.

Peripherally she decided that she did not much like her new lodger; very coarse. Then she thought of Mr. de Brissac's beautiful manners — and look what he'd been up to on the sly! Had she known on Wednesday what she knew now she doubted whether she'd have bothered to . . . But of course, she hadn't wanted the Relieving Officer around . . . And of course, if she'd known then what she knew now the question of who paid could have had only one answer.

She cleared away and washed up. Then she went upstairs and put on her decent black and her painful shoes. It was a funny thing, in her slippers she could walk about, stand, work for hours on end, never feel a twinge. When she had the fifty pounds she would have a pair of shoes made, with the bulges to accommodate the bunions.

It was very rare for her to go out in the evening. Neighbours visited her because nowadays she was better off than most; she could afford tea and cake. In winter she always had a good fire.

Charley-the-Carpenter said, 'Going out, Ma? All dressed up, too!'

'I have a small matter of business to attend to,' she said in the quelling manner she could adopt on occasions.

The new lodger said, 'That was a good blow-out, Ma.' Cheek! Only after six months should he have been so familiar. 'I'm going out too, presently. I'll be late. Can I have a key?'

'No, you cannot, Mr. Sims. Nobody gets a key to my door until he has proved himself to be sober and reliable. I shall lock the door as usual at half past ten and if you are not in you can stay out.' And then because she disliked his table manners she added, 'If my arrangements do not suit you, you can look elsewhere.' Most of them needed a good slapping down to begin with.

Mr. Draper was choosing his cigar when the door bell rang. Betty left the clearing of the table and went to answer it.

'There's a person to see you, sir. She says it's important.'

Betty was showing social discrimination. By Brewster Street standards Mrs. Fenner was all dressed up, gloves, plush reticule, walking shoes, but in Alma Avenue she was a member of the lower orders.

'A person without a name?' Mr. Draper asked. Reproof.

'I'm sorry, sir. Shall I go and ask?'

'No. Show her into the study. And light the lamp on my desk.' The evenings were drawing in.

He had a pretty shrewd idea who the person was. He had sacked a man on Saturday. This was that man's wife and if she thought she would do any good by coming here, to his private residence and telling some piteous tale, she would shortly be shown her error. He was in fact angry with the world.

Lighting his cigar he said, 'We could hardly be worse served. A cook who cannot walk. A maid who cannot remember the simplest instruction. There will be changes here!'

Betty, hurrying in to finish the clearing of the table, thought — And so say all of us! Ada's off to sit in the Workhouse and I've got my eye on a job. One old lady, a staff of four and no basement stairs!

Mr. Draper had a retentive and orderly memory. As soon as Mrs. Fenner named herself he recalled as much of the family history as had been brought to his notice. Fenner; hurt his back; took a lighter job. Dead. Several children. He could guess her errand; a son or a son-in-law seeking employment.

He did not invite her to sit down. He went past her and took the chair behind his desk.

'Well, Mrs. Fenner? If it is anything to do with business, I have an office. As you know.'

'It's private. *Very* private. Nothing to do with business. More of a family matter.'

'Your family?' He was prepared to bludgeon her; she was prepared to blow him up.

'No, yours. You got a daughter named Marion.'

'Miss Marion Draper is my daughter,' he said incisively.

'It's about some letters. Letters she wrote to poor Mr. de Brissac. I found them in his room.'

Her eye was experienced; men sheepishly explaining that they had not come in drunk, they had stubbed a toe on the stairs; they couldn't pay the rent this week, they'd had to send the money home to a poor old sick mother. She saw that when she said *letters* the word did not strike home. But the name did; and it meant more to him than a casual memory of a few lines in last Friday's *Bereham Free Press* – 'Sudden Death of Chemist's Assistant'.

'They were married,' she said with the untutored person's instinctive knowledge that drama, like wit, benefited by brevity.

That shot misfired entirely. Marion was mad enough and bad enough, but she had no opportunity to commit such an act of folly.

'That is absolute nonsense. What put it into your head? Some rubbish your lodger wrote?'

'What your daughter wrote,' Mrs. Fenner corrected him. He did not know. He was at her mercy. Her fingers, encased in wrinkled black gloves moved on the shabby reticule. 'She's Mrs. de Brissac all right. And she had a baby.'

'Really, Mrs. Fenner. You must be out of your mind. Neither of my daughters has ever spent a single hour unaccounted for, to me or to their mother. And you come here with this fantastic rubbish . . .'

There had been *something*; all along his nose had warned him. But no marriage. No baby. Very tentatively he fingered the thought of Mr. Horridge, a vulgar and unscrupulous man, in some way trying to beat him down, to make it seem that in marrying Marion . . . No. No man could sink so low. And yet, the shabby black and the rather insolent manner. . . a hireling?

'What's behind all this?' he demanded. 'Who's paying you to spread this filthy libel? I'll have the law on you.'

As she had avoided Parish Relief, Mrs. Fenner had avoided falling foul of the law. By any standards she was a respectable woman. And of late years she had become accustomed to being the most dominant character in her own circle. To be told that she was out of her mind, her story fantastic rubbish, to have it hinted that someone had hired her to spread filth, when the filth was there, in her hand, roused a temper never markedly placid.

'All *right*!' she said. 'See what you make of them, then she opened her reticule and flung the letters down into the circle of radiance cast by the lamp. As they fluttered they loosed the scent of the oil with which Johnny had anointed his hair; they also offered to Mr. Draper's eyes glimpses of Marion's quite unmistakable hand.

'This will take a little time,' he said. 'You had better sit down.'

The only other chair in the room stood by the wall near the door at some distance from the desk. She sat down, glad to get her weight off her feet; but she badly wanted to watch his face as he read the shocking things his daughter had written, so she tried to edge the chair forward a little. It was heavy, with clawed feet that dug into the thick carpet, and she could not move it unobtrusively; so she leaned forward and watched.

She was disappointed. His face neither blenched nor blushed; his expression did not change. Not a flicker. She herself read slowly and it struck her that Mr. Draper could not really be reading properly, he flipped over the pages so quickly. Half-way through he looked up and said petulantly, 'They all seem to be much of a muchness. Must I read the lot? Shall I learn where and when the ceremony was performed? And what happened to the baby?'

'No. I read them all and there's no mention.'

'Then there must be more. Did you miss any? In some pocket? At the back of a drawer. Tucked into a book?'

Now he seemed to be criticising the thoroughness with which she cleaned rooms between lodgers.

'No,' she said, very positively. 'I looked everywhere. That's the lot. But it's enough, isn't it?'

'More than enough,' he agreed. He put the letters together and then, with the quickest move she had ever seen anyone make, held them cornerwise over the lamp. They burst into flame and turning he dropped them into the grate behind the desk. The paper fan took light and added to the blaze.

Out of her chair, Mrs. Fenner cried, seconds too late, 'No! No! You can't do . . .' Through the smell of burnt paper and the last expiring odour of hair oil she said furiously, 'You shouldn't have done that. They wasn't yours to burn.'

'I only did what you would have done had you had a shred of decency in you.' He levelled his cold, impenetrable stare at her and said, 'I see, now, of course, the object of your visit. Blackmail!'

She could really only blame herself, losing her temper and throwing the whole lot into his hands. She said, shaken and reduced:

'It wasn't that. It wasn't that at all. I just wanted the funeral expenses paid.'

'Then you must look elsewhere, must you not, Mrs. Fenner. I have no doubt that whoever supplied you with those effusions will oblige again.' He spoke with a mocking geniality; and then, as she stood, groping for words, he said, in a different voice, 'Mr. Andrews is your landlord, is he not?'

A vital blow at her most vulnerable spot. 18 Brewster Street, when she and Bill had taken it, had been a dilapidated old house in a street that had gone downhill; bigger than they wanted but cheap to rent. Bill had done a lot of work on it with his own hands; during his long illness and since his death it had been a lifebuoy. It was her livelihood. But, just as she with a few words — 'I shall be wanting your room from next Saturday' — could evict a tenant, so Mr. Andrews . . .

'I think the whole thing had better be forgotten. And I am sure that when you have thought things over, you will agree.' He rang the bell. 'Show Mrs. Fenner out,' he said.

To Mrs. Fenner his treatment of the letters had seemed cursory and incomplete, but he had read every word; every revolting, incredible word. Fornication committed, a child conceived, under this roof. Like Mrs. Fenner, he checked at the thought of the child. How was it possible? Had Marion played that hoary old trick, pleading pregnancy in order to enforce a marriage? She was capable of anything. Like Mrs. Fenner, he was deceived in the sequence of the letters, thinking that the passionate desperate plea for marriage had preceded the signing of herself 'Your wife'. Had the child been aborted? One would have questioned again the matter of opportunity, but a girl who, in a normal, respectable home like this one could contrive to conceive a child, could contrive to be rid of it. Obviously, her capacity for deceit was infinite and he never for a second doubted the evidence which the letters seemed to offer.

Sitting there in the lamp-lit study, he considered the possibility of his wife and of Ellen being implicated in any way. A very sickening thought, and soon dismissed. Neither would have dared; neither was capable of any sustained deception; simple, innocent women, submissive, transparent, desiring only to please. Not a whisper of this unspeakable business must ever reach their ears. But Marion, who, through that man Horridge, had humiliated him, was going to be ground under heel.

As soon as the table had been cleared out had come the pattern books and the samples. There had been hitches. The wedding dress itself was well under way, tacked together. White satin was white satin. But Mamma's choice of Parma violet velvet had revealed that in all Bereham there was not an inch of such material, and London, to whom Proctor's, who supplied material, even when Miss Bussey did the work, had appealed had responded rather too willingly; there were differing shades of Parma violet, and differing qualities of velvet; and Mamma, lately unused to making a decision on any matter, found it difficult to make up her mind. The colour she liked best was not in the finest quality. And she said, doubtless with truth, that after the bride the bride's mother should be the best-dressed woman at a wedding. There was also a little trouble over the bridesmaids' dresses. Ellen wanted pink — hesitating between two shades. Then Priscilla Mingay, who like her aunt had pale, gingerish, almost pink-ish-coloured hair, said that pink was not her colour. And since — they were all aware of it — Lady Mingay's niece was making somewhat of a concession in accepting to act as bridesmaid to a maltster's daughter, her wishes must be regarded. In refuting pink she had not, however, said what colour would be most acceptable. So time, of which they were very short, had been wasted.

And then Ellen, who had good sense, had thought of another thing to be considered. Style. Fashions changed so quickly. Should the fashionable bustle effect be achieved by the gathering, the bunching up of yards and yards of material, an integral part of the dress, or by great bows which could be removed should fashion change?

This is not the kind of wedding I wanted, Marion thought, saying, 'Oh yes' and 'Oh no,' agreeing with Mamma that the best velvet was a trifle harsh in colour, the best colour of poor texture. 'A choice of two evils, Mamma.' After all, Mamma would have to live with it, and wear it.

They were still at it when Mr. Draper came back into the dining-room. On Saturday when he had told Marion about Mr. Horridge's uncouth behaviour he had not been able to bring himself to look at her. Now he did. With curiosity and a prurience, so long suppressed — decent man, good citizen, faithful husband — that he did not even recognise it for what it was.

'That will do,' he said.

'I'll have this one, Ellen,' Mamma said hastily poking a pin through the sample of velvet, the right colour, the wrong quality.

'And I'll write to Priscilla,' Ellen said, holding up between thumb and first finger a scrap of gauze, sea-green. 'And if she does not like it, she must lump it. And I have decided upon bows. Margaret Saunders will be wearing her dress all winter, for balls, and she should be considered. If I see to this, Marion, will you clear up?'

Mamma had already vanished.

'But of course,' Marion said.

'Good night, then; Good night Papa,' Ellen held up her innocent, pink-and-white flowerlike face for the paternal kiss.

In silence Marion began to tidy things away and into the silence Mr. Draper said with soft venom, 'Good evening, Madame de Brissac!'

The world tottered. Under her hands the samples slid about on the polished surface. She reached out and grabbed the back of one of the solid dining-chairs that was pushed under the table. Johnny had babbled on his death-bed. The caller had been his landlady.

Her word against mine.

'Why should you call me that?'

'It is your legal name, is it not? You would deny it? You lying bitch, you strumpet, you filthy whore! Then deny this — "Johnny, we must get married. The truth will soon be obvious, do what I may. And the child must have a name." Deny that you wrote, "I am now in very truth your ever-loving, ever-faithful, ever-yearning wife." Together with other things that I will not soil my tongue by repeating; words so lewd and indecent that coming from the lowest prostitute they would be obscene.'

He quoted with deadly accuracy; the words had branded themselves on his brain.

Johnny had not babbled; he had retained some letters; found by that old woman; read by Papa. The ultimate betrayal.

'What happened to the baby? Did you find some back-street abortionist? And where, and by whom were you married?' These things he must know that vengeance might be taken. And what vengeance!

She gave him truthful answers.

'I had a miscarriage. We were never married.'

The two simple statements had an almost sad dignity about them. It was as though she felt no remorse for her un-speakable behaviour and had not been affected by the names he had hurled at her. That she had had a miscarriage was very likely true — natural or induced; he had first-hand evidence that she had been married.

'How dare you stand there and tell me such lies? You know very well that you were married.'

She said, 'No, Papa,' and inside Mr. Draper something snapped. He jumped up and with the flat of his hand hit her across the face, a stinging, heavy blow which rocked her side-ways. He was at once astonished to find himself giving way to such an impulse, and satisfied at having done so. He realised that he had longed, many and many a time, to strike that inscrutable face.

He did not strike her again and she righted herself and stood upright, her hands no longer holding the chair-back but hanging straight down beside her skirt. Her face, with the red mark showing on the cheekbone was more inscrutable than ever, its expression quite blank. She was not even looking at him.

He perceived her intention to take refuge in Stoic silence as she had frequently done in the past.

'You shall answer to me,' he said furiously. 'I will have the truth. You won't get out of it this way.'

When she neither spoke nor looked at him, he took her by the shoulders and shook her. 'Answer me!'

But in Marion something had snapped too. It was like Yar-mouth again. Give in; let go; turn away.

Presently it dawned upon Mr. Draper that something was wrong. It was not like shaking a living body, though it was soft and warm and yielding. He let go of her and took a step backwards.

She was still gazing straight ahead as though regarding something immensely far away and the controlled calm of her face had given way to a look of profound peace, as though she were sleeping with her eyes open.

It could be a trick; obviously she was the most deceitful creature alive.

'Get out my sight,' he said. 'Go to bed.' If she were fooling she would seize upon the opportunity to escape.

She did not move. On the pale matt surface of her face the red mark flared. It would need some explanation. He found one, and then he did something that came naturally to him. He rang the bell.

All his life he had rung bells and they had been answered; even in his comparatively humble childhood home there had always been at least one servant. Waiting for this to be dealt with by other hands, he looked again at his daughter and reflected callously — One cannot say she has taken leave of her senses: she never had any sense.

Two people answered this summons. Lively, quick and willing, Ellen in whose room, once the servants', the bell actually hung; and lively, quick, less willing, Betty who had heard it ringing overhead and said, 'Blast. What now?' They arrived in the dining-room together.

'Marion,' Mr. Draper said, 'has had a slight turn. She hit her face and appears to be dazed. Help her to bed.'

'Oh, darling,' Ellen said. 'It was so thoughtless of me, leaving you to clear up. I am so sorry. Come along . . .'

The body about which she was placing her arm had been possessed by the chemist's assistant, had conceived. Polluted flesh.

'Let Betty see to it,' Mr. Draper said. 'Betty, see Miss Marion into bed — if she needs help, give it. Ellen, my dear, pour me a little brandy. This has been a shock to me.'

'And all my fault,' said Ellen, beginning the crying that was to last for quite a long time.

Mrs. Fenner walked home, cursing Mr. Draper and herself. Being so often alone in her house she had formed the habit of talking aloud with no listener. She was not given to the use of bad language and never allowed it; but now, as she hobbled along on feet increasingly painful, she muttered. Sly bastard; cheating bugger, she said of Mr. Draper and of herself, bloody fool. Several people, passing her, thought she was drunk. Born unlucky, she said of herself, giving way to an unwonted self-pity; might have known, never did have a bloody bit of luck. Bill, riding high on one of Draper's drays, controlling the two great shining horses with his left hand and waving to her with his right, who'd have thought that he'd be crippled, unemployed, employed in the most menial capacity, sick, dead? Who'd have thought that of four children, two boys, two girls, not one would stay in Bereham to be company and comfort? All scattered, all damned ungrateful to the mother who had, by the sweat of her brow and the strength of her elbow, kept them alive, fed and clothed them? It did not occur to her now — it had never occurred to her, that with nerves over-strained — the rent, the rates, the coal — with a body over-worked and a tongue sharpened by misery, she had said and done things that had alienated her children. For ever. Just as she had thrown those letters at Mr. Draper, so she had thrown their dependence into the faces of her children; who had reacted exactly as she would have done, being her children . . .

Trudging home she denounced the world.

But at 18 Brewster Street there was consolation. As she opened the door Mrs. Fenner smelt the good clean smell of freshly ironed linen and when she entered the kitchen, there was her neighbour, Mrs. Foster, folding the last handkerchief and giving it a thump with the iron.

'Charley said you'd had to go out on business. So I thought . . .'

'That was very kind,' Mrs. Fenner said. And it was, since Clara Foster earned her meagre living by taking in washing and only came in on Mondays to enjoy a cup of tea and a change of occupation.

'And the kettle's just on the boil,' Mrs. Foster said.

'You make the tea. I shan't be a minute . . .' In the passage Mrs. Fenner removed her shoes and immediately felt better. Hanging up the decent black she thought, resolutely — Well, he fooled me, but I let myself be fooled; and I'm no worse than I was when I set out . . . The tough, sour acceptance of the inevitable revived in her, and she went down and cut into, not a cake, but a good substantial meat pie, made and baked alongside the Sunday joint and intended for Tuesday's tea.

Afterwards the two women proceeded with their usual Monday evening's occupation, which was the cutting of news-paper into oblongs, piercing each corner and stringing them to be hung on the hook in the privy. Four lodgers got through an immense amount of the stuff. Presently Mrs. Foster, dismembering the *Bereham Free Press* of the previous Friday, said, 'You marked this. Want to keep it?' It was an announcement of Jean de Brissac's death — 'Suddenly, at 18 Brewster St.' It had been inserted by the undertaker, part of the service and in a way an advertisement since it ended, 'Funeral arrangements by Wilsher and Son.'

Mrs. Fenner had intended to cut it out and keep it, but she felt differently about him now. However, to discard it, having marked it, might look odd. So she said, 'Might as well.' Mrs. Foster folded and sliced and handed over the piece to be reserved. On the social page everything was in alphabetical order under the relevant heading, so it was natural enough that de Brissac in the deaths column should lie alongside Draper in the engagements. Mr. and Mrs. Draper had pleasure in announcing . . .

Like the cloud no bigger than a man's hand that promised Elijah an abundance of rain, a thought rose and hovered on the horizon of Mrs. Fenner's mind. She might put a spoke in *his* wheel yet!

But there was no time to lose. She remembered one of her 'boys' — married and looking the worse for it — who drove the grocer's delivery van. Unless his routine had changed Tuesday was his day for Sorley and its district.

'You know,' Mr. Horridge said almost genially, 'you ought to be in clinko. And that's where you'll end if you ain't careful.'

They had never met before but they had been at home with one another from the first moment. She had arrived just as he was pouring himself the whisky that he took, when alone, instead of tea. He asked her what she'd like, and she said, 'Gin, if you please.' He'd known her choice. Very respectable old ladies in very shabby black always drank gin.

Like Mr. Draper, Mr. Horridge imagined that she had come seeking employment. Households often expanded when the master took a wife. He intended to leave all domestic affairs to Marion, but he'd take her name and address and all particulars; and he'd see how she carried her gin. He poured her a generous measure, noting as she removed her shabby gloves that her hands, though they'd seen some rough usage, were extremely clean.

She then told him her story and about her visit to Mr. Draper.

'You don't go to gaol,' she now said rather primly, 'for telling the truth. And that's all I've done. I reckoned it was something you ought to know, if only to make your own wedding legal. A widow shouldn't go pretending to be a spinster.'

He tipped back his chair, balancing on its back legs, a posture she forbade in her house, bad for the furniture. He swallowed the last of his whisky.

'You make much of a living this way?'

'I told you how I make my living. I take lodgers. Mr. de Brissac was one.'

'And now he's dead and can't contradict you. And you found these letters in his *hat*?' He laughed, finding the hiding-place amusing; an original touch. 'And you didn't save one, or even a bit of one. You handed the lot to Mr. Draper and he burnt them.'

'Like I said.'

That alone was enough to discredit her story entirely.

'How much were you trying to touch him for?'

Careful now, she admonished herself; don't go losing your temper again.

'First of all I was only thinking about the funeral expenses. Five pounds it cost me to bury him and I didn't see why – I mean, with a wife ... And then, I'll be honest with you, I thought it was worth a hundred not to have it talked about.'

A hundred pounds for a girl's reputation! But he was not shocked. He'd lived too long in places where you could buy twenty girls, body and soul, for that much. And always, somewhere in the transaction there'd be an old woman, decently clad in shabby black, ready to do, to say, to sell anything for ready cash.

'Well,' he said, 'I don't believe a word. Not a bloody word.'

And sneaking up behind him came the thought — Suppose I had! Suppose he had! With a more credulous father, and less certain suitor, what a mess a poor girl would be in.

'What made you pick on Miss Draper?' he asked with genuine interest.

'What do you mean, *pick*. She was the one wrote the letters. She was the one married Mr. de Brissac. If you don't believe me, go and ask *him* then. Ask why he set fire to the letters and threatened me with my landlord if I said another word. He'd no right to do that. So then I thought you ought to know.'

Every time she spoke of Mr. Draper, either by his name or simply as *he* the old animosity showed through.

'You don't like Mr. Draper, do you?'

'No. I don't. I never did. And after last night . . . And that's why,' she said, starkly honest again, 'I asked you for a hundred. He as good as said that if I said a word he'd have me out in the street. But if I could offer Mr. Andrews a hundred down and promise fifty within a year, he'd sell me the house and I'd be safe.'

Quite unwittingly she had used the right word. He had been poor, he had lived with the poor long enough to know that safety was the ultimate aim, though safety meant different things to different people; for some it was enough to have the price of a good booze-up.

He brought the front legs of his chair back to the floor and leaning over unlocked and opened the bottom drawer of his beautiful, eighteenth-century writing table. Then, straightening up, he said bluntly, 'I think you are a very wicked old woman and you could do — maybe you have done — a lot of bloody damage. Now you stop. You understand. Can you write?'

'I should hope so. I went to school a full year.'

'Then you take this . . .' He offered her a piece of paper, his best-headed, and pushed across the wide table the silver ink-tray with cut glass bottles, silver-lidded. Then he leaned over again and took from the bottom-drawer a note for fifty pounds, and another, and laid them on his virginal blotter.

'What's your full name?'

'Martha Fenner.'

'All right then.' He tried to recall some of the impressive often valueless legal phrases with which he had from time to time come in contact, thinking that simple statements would have served just as well. 'You write, "I Martha Fenner . . ." and then put it into your own words — what you just told me about Miss Marion Draper was a lie; anything you've ever said about any other young lady is a lie. And you promise never to play such a trick again. Then this is yours. See.'

Nothing but abuse for telling the truth; undreamed-of wealth for putting her name to a lie! That thought combined with all the worry of the last week, and the gin to which she was not accustomed, cracked her self-control.

'Make me out a liar, would you?' she shouted. She took up one of the glass bottles and threw it, straight and true. A quarter of a pint of the best blue-black ink hit Mr. Horridge on the head and from there, as from a watershed, spattered down, splashing everything, including the crisp black and white notes that represented money.

Once it was done she was appalled. Hitherto, in raging temper, she had thrown her own stuff, in her own house, and fretfully borne any damage. Here the damage was frightful. She could not see whether the ink-bottle bounding off on to the floor was broken or not, but she'd ruined his jacket, his shirt, his table. She thought wretchedly of the number of times when she had said, 'That cup will cost you twopence!'

An ill-fated business from first to last. Add this lot to what she was down on already. God help us!

The real, the lasting damage she had wrought was invisible to her; though she did notice that the hand with which Mr. Horridge wielded his handkerchief was unsteady and that where his face was not inky blue it was greyish. Shock, probably. Maybe in addition to everything else he'd charge her with assault and battery.

But she'd learned enough about men to know that to apologise simply put you further in the wrong; and now, shattered as she was, she took her usual strong line.

'You brought that on yourself,' she said, and stood waiting for him to swear. For just as he had thought he had recognised her as one of a type, so she thought she had recognised him; not a gentleman, and under the surface amiability as hard as nails.

But when he spoke his voice was quiet.

'You're wrong, you know. And I'll prove it.'

The violent act, the repudiation of the sum she had hoped for, what she needed to be safe, had convinced him that she was not dishonest. She was mistaken. Somewhere, somehow the most terrible mistake that ever had happened had happened.

He stood up. He said, 'Take that and for Christ's sake keep your mouth shut.' He then flung out of the room and she could hear him shouting for hot water and for somebody to hitch up the gig.

'Take that,' he had said, indicating the money. In the calm and not unsensible mood that always came upon her after an explosion of temper several trains of thought ran side by side. It might be worthless, because of the ink. It might be the price of silence — and if so it had been earned, in a way; she had not run blabbing about and had no intention of doing so. And it had another value; if he turned nasty after all . . . She tenderly blottered the ink-spattered notes on the ink-spattered blotter, folded them, put them into her shabby old reticule. She found her way out of the house and with her mind whirling and her feet hurting, walked along the avenue to the gate where Tom, her ex-lodger had arranged to pick her up. She sat down on the bank. Mr. Horridge, washed and reclad, smashing by in his gig did not see her. He stared straight ahead, his blunt profile like something hewn out of stone. In due time Tom came along.

'You know, Ma,' he said, presently, 'we all thought you made a good thing out of us at fifteen bob. I know different now. Give Elsie fifteen bob and what's to show for it? She ain't a clever shopper and she can't cook worth a spit. Mind you, she's a nice girl. But when I think what you did, rent, rates, washing and grub, oh, them beef puds! And a joint every Sunday. I reckon you're a bloody marvel.'

She said, automatically, 'Language, Tom!'

He said, 'Sorry, Ma.'

Presently she said, 'Tom, do me another favour. Go round by the Station. I want to see about some coal.'

It meant a bit extra for the horse, getting old, getting a bit past it, though he always made a bit of a spurt on the homeward journey. But Tom said, 'Right you are.'

Mrs. Fenner had decided that the best place in which to test this dubious wealth would be at the coal-merchant's shed on the Station yard. There, if the note should be without value nobody would witness its refusal and she would not be ashamed.

It was taken not only without hesitation but with alacrity.

'First thing tomorrow morning; a ton of best house coal,' he said; and he gave her change in *real* money. The old reticule bulged so that she had to hold it, not by its handle, but by its top, the clasp being weak.

She said, 'Tom, I don't want to go straight home. Drop me at Looms Lane. I want to see Mr. Andrews.'

'Wait for you if you like,' Tom offered valiantly, though he wanted his tea.

'No. This may take some time.' Out of the gleaming, the never-to-be-accounted-for wealth, Mrs. Fenner took a sovereign.

'You have this, Tom, and a lot of thanks as well.'

'You can't do that, Ma. Goddammee, you could have had a carriage.' But twenty bob . . . that Elsie didn't know about. 'I don't like to take it . . .'

'Don't be silly, Tom. You can do with it. And I can spare it.' She had practically recovered herself and spoke with much of her usual authority.

'There's a lot wants doing to it,' Mrs. Fenner said to Mr. Andrews. 'And I do see it isn't worth your while — not for five shillings a week. And I can't pay more. Next time you put the rent up I'm out of business and you'll have a house to let. And while you're letting it, with nobody to put a bucket under that drip, it'll be through to the next floor and the ceiling down. If you see what I mean.'

Mr. Andrews saw. A derelict house, bought for twenty pounds thirty years ago, let for half a crown a week. For three shillings, three shillings and sixpence, creeping up over the years to five. On the open market today perhaps worth seventy pounds. The ground floor still waterproof enough to house a store — scrap metal, greengrocery . . .

'If it was mine,' Mrs. Fenner said enticingly. 'it'd be worth my while to mend the roof and have that drain seen to. They're getting a bit funny about drains. Diphtheria they say, though I can't myself see the connection.' The denial was an accusation. There had been outbreaks of diphtheria and, as Doctor Barlow had remarked, they seem to centre on places like Brewster Street.

'How much would you be willing to pay, Mrs. Fenner?'

'I could manage eighty at a pinch.'

'Ninety.'

'Could you split the difference, Mr. Andrews? I've got the repairs to think of. And for a woman like me eighty-five took a bit of clawing together. But I've got it here with me. Right now.'

'As a favour to you; considering how long you have been a tenant.'

She counted out the money as though it had been saved, penny by penny, painfully, over a long period.

'And you'll give me a receipt?' she asked anxiously. 'The deeds or whatever you call them'll do another time.'

Walking home to what was now indeed her own house, her spirit was buoyant and as soon as she had her shoes off she gave the special rap on the wall that informed Mrs. Foster that tea would be ready in two ticks.

Mr. Horridge pulled Stormer to a standstill outside Ten Alma Avenue and committed the anti-social act of tethering him to the front railings, so that he stood athwart the pavement and the gig half blocked the road. He ran up the steps and rang the bell which was answered by Betty who looked as though she had been crying.

'Oh, sir,' she said. No need to ask him in. He was in, 'I'll call Miss Ellen.'

'It's Miss Marion I want to see.'

'But, sir, she's . . . Miss Ellen'll tell you . . .'

Ellen's face looked as though it had been boiled.

'Oh, Mr. Horridge. Something so awful has happened. Last night . . . Last night . . .' She began to cry again, mopping her reddened eyes, her reddened nose with a sopping handkerchief.

Impatiently, almost roughly, he guided her to Mamma's little chair and offered the clean dry handkerchief with which he had provided himself.

'What happened last night? Ellen, stop howling. Howling never did any good.'

Perhaps the uncivil word steadied her. Interspersed with self-accusations — It was all my fault. I shall never, never forgive myself, she told him all she knew.

'You've had the doctor?'

'Oh yes. This morning. But it isn't like last time. She knew me then, when she woke up. Now she is awake and she . . . she isn't *here*.'

'Did she injure herself?'

'Hardly at all. There's the tiniest bruise, here.' Ellen touched her own left cheek. 'But Doctor Barlow said . . .'

'He's only a country doctor. And old. We'll get somebody . . . Can I see her?'

'She won't know you. She doesn't know anybody.' But she rose and led him not upstairs but down. Half-way down the steep stairs he became aware of the kitchen smell; cooking and washing up and old floor-cloths. Servants' accommodation.

In the little room Mamma rose from a chair by the bedside, and she began to cry, too. 'Oh, Mr. Horridge, what a calamity. Just when we were all so happy.'

He had secretly hoped on his way downstairs that the sight of him, his voice might rouse her from her stunned state, or whatever it was. But when he said, 'Marion,' she did not even look towards him. She lay, propped rather high, as Doctor Barlow had advised, and she wore a look of blank tranquillity that he had never seen before except on the faces of the dead. Ellen had plaited her hair, and one plait lay on each shoulder. He saw, for the first time, the scar of her former accident. Her hands lay, slender and limp on the down-turned sheet and on her finger, incongruous in such surroundings, gleamed his ring.

He moved so that he stood, big and solid, immediately in what seemed to be her line of vision. He said again, 'Marion. It's me! Edward!' Not a flicker.

'Doctor Barlow said,' Ellen gulped, 'that the new jolt, coming so soon after, had injured her brain.'

Mr. Horridge said staunchly, 'We'll get a man from London. A specialist. They work miracles these days. Can she eat?'

'She doesn't take any notice. But she will eat if I put food to her mouth.'

'Well, that's something to be thankful for.'

She would accept food if it were held to her lips; and there was one other proof of some kind of sense remaining. Steered across the kitchen and the area, into the downstairs water-closet she seemed to know what was required of her.

Mr. Horridge lifted the hand that wore his ring and kissed it; then he prepared for action.

'Doctors know about specialists,' he said. 'I'll go and see Barlow now.'

Mamma said, 'Would it not be as well to consult with Mr. Draper first?'

Maybe it would. Collaboration would be needed.

'I think he has just come in.' Mrs. Draper, like an animal, knew her master's step. Mr. Horridge made a dash for the stairs.

Mr. Draper, in a fury, was helping himself to sherry. Nobody to greet him; no Ellen to pour for him. The whole house withdrawn, its life centred about the room where that worthless, that depraved, that wicked woman lay. He would lose no time in sending her back to Heatherton, and no question this time about to which side.

Then the door opened and Mr. Horridge came in. A new element seeped into Mr. Draper's mood of rage and shame and self-pity. There was, after all, some justice in the world. What had happened was a judgment on Marion and her new paramour.

Preparing some cutting words Mr. Draper said, 'Ha, Horridge. May I offer you a glass of sherry?'

'No,' Mr. Horridge said uncouthly. 'I could do with a real drink. Whisky, if it's handy. If not, don't bother. Mr. Draper, this is a terrible thing. But we'll get the best brain specialist in London.'

Mr. Draper poured the whisky.

'We must be guided by Doctor Barlow. When he feels a second opinion to be desirable, he will obtain it.'

It was the line to be expected. Mr. Horridge took the glass and was about to drink when the scent reminded him that he had been sipping whisky while that old crone told her tale. He had not believed a word of it; and yet . . . and yet . . . At the end he had believed her to be honest. He'd given her a hundred quid. Could that be construed into disloyalty? Surely not. He'd thought her honest, but mistaken. But he set the glass down, realising that it would be quite some time before he really enjoyed whisky again.

'Doctor Barlow is old to begin with; and stuck away here he can't know about new methods and treatments and things.'

'Doctor Barlow has been our family physician for almost forty years. I have complete faith in him. Old he may be, but I don't suppose that the structure of the human skull has changed since he qualified. Do you?'

'What I meant was,' Mr. Horridge willed himself to patience, 'he can't have the experience. It's likely this is the first case of the sort he ever came across. But up in London a specialist would deal with things like this every day.'

'Doctor Barlow gave me a very lucid explanation of what had happened. But . . .' he paused, 'I suppose that if I oppose your plan to call in some man with new-fangled notions you will threaten me again with ruin. Which would be a pity since

I am now responsible for Marion who seems likely to be a considerable expense.'

'Oh, for God's sake, man, can't you forget that? At a time like this, with that poor girl . . . Can't you see we've got to pull together?'

'It seems to me that you are the one who is unwilling to pull with me. Over the question of marriage you overrode me, Mr. Horridge. With this result, if I may say so. I have said all along that Marion was in no fit state to resume normal life. You thought otherwise; who was right?'

'Well . . .' Ellen, self-recriminatory, had said things about a long fitting and a lot to do and decide upon and she hadn't realised that Marion was still not quite better. 'Shoving blame about won't get us far. What do you mean to do about her?'

'Follow Doctor Barlow's advice and trust that time will do its healing work. And since it is impossible for my wife and Ellen to care for her in her present state, she will return to Heatherton. I have already written to Miss Rose.' He had, more in sorrow than in wrath, done a bit of blame-shoving in that direction, too.

Mr. Horridge caught at the word Heatherton. Nurses as well as doctors, knew about specialists. He said:

'If there isn't anything I can do, then, I think I'll get along.'

'It would be as well if you removed your conveyance. We shall be having complaints from our neighbours.'

Mr. Draper rang the bell but Mr. Horridge let himself out without aid from Betty who panted up in time to take her next order.

'Tell Ada to keep an eye on Miss Marion so that your mistress and Miss Ellen can take their supper at the usual time.'

The mills of God ground slowly, but they ground exceeding small. Marion had defied and deceived him — look at her now! A chemist's assistant had wronged him — where was he? Mr. Horridge had bullied and humiliated him and see what had happened to his grand wedding and his honeymoon in Paris.

'Of course I know. I know the best man in the world. The very best,' Miss Rose said, 'Dr. Hellmutt. I worked with him once; I should probably be with him still, but I was offered a more remunerative post, and he at that time ... But he has made his way since then and is now very well thought of.'

'Would he operate?'

'If he thought it necessary. I hardly think ... I mean by what you have told me, Mr. Horridge. The idea that the human skull is a box so loosely packed that a couple of jolts can, without injuring the container, upset all the contents, is distinctly out-dated.'

'Will you write to him then? I'll meet any train. I'll put him up. I'll pay whatever he asks ...'

And this time for good, Mr. Draper thought, holding the living doll by the elbow and propelling it into the stark room. This time no question of which room, which side. She was a lunatic. That was the only explanation; only a lunatic could have done, could have written, have said ... He removed his hand and Marion stood staring, immobile. Miss Rose went forward and put her hand under the elbow of that white, slim, immature arm. 'Come and sit down, Miss Draper,' she said, guiding her to the sofa and noting that Marion did not sit down all in one piece. Idiots did.

As before she was anxious to be rid of Mr. Draper and did not offer him tea; and when he had gone she went to work, thinking how wonderful it would be if, when Dr. Hellmutt arrived she could present him with proof that she had never forgotten his words, his methods, his attitudes.

She lifted a vase of chrysanthemums, early flowering, coddled, sent by Mr. Horridge and held them under Marion's nose. That good earthy autumn scent.

'You always liked flowers. Miss Draper, Marion. You can hear me, I know. Listen to me. I'm on your side whatever it is. Look, lovely flowers. Smell them.'

Nothing happened.

She tried a book, opened at random. 'You always liked to read.'

Clarke brought in the tea. Miss Rose poured a steaming cupful and placed it and two savoury sandwiches within easy reach of Marion's hand. And watched and waited. Nothing happened.

Ellen, tearful and snuffling, had first said, 'I can look after her, Papa. She is really no trouble at all.' Then, finding him adamant, she had said, 'I think it would be as well if I wrote to Miss Rose. It is rather a delicate matter, but I think she should know.' So Ellen had written and what she said was quite true. Miss Rose tested both statements. A cup of tea held in position was drunk, a sandwich eaten with the usual nicety and presently, conducted to the right place, the doll did what was not required of dolls. As Ellen had written — really no trouble at all, but Papa thinks . . .

Meeting Dr. Hellmutt off the evening train from London, Mr. Horridge knew a doubt. Eyes too big and made bigger still by peculiar glasses; the rest of him too small. Insect-like. And very shabby. A worn old carpet bag his only luggage. A worker of miracles?

In the Station yard where Stormer was tethered, Mr. Horridge helped Doctor Hellmutt into the gig. No weight at all, the elbow sharp. A doctor, to inspire confidence, should look as though he knew enough to feed himself properly, and earned enough to eat and dress well. A firm and hopeful manner was surely desirable, too. Mr. Horridge craved a word of assurance; but all through the excellent dinner, of which Doctor Hellmutt ate little and that little with no sign of appreciation, no such word was spoken. Doctor Hellmutt allowed Mr. Horridge to talk and seemed to listen with sympathetic attention but faced with a question, 'What do you make of that?' he said in his diffident, foreign-accented voice, 'I cannot say,' or 'I shall be in a better position to judge when I have seen the patient, Mr. Horridge.' He neither drank nor smoked and retired early, saying he had some reading to do; and Mr. Horridge was left alone, drinking brandy and going over and over it all again in his mind. Wrong to have forced the pace and thus exposed the poor darling to exertions she was not fit for? Wrong not to have taken that old bitch and run her out of the house? But a girl who could walk through the maze, and all over the house, and then back to Heatherton could surely have stood up to a fitting. And thinking that Mrs. Fenner was, after all, honest, didn't meant that he had for one moment believed her tale. Did it? No! Having reached that conclusion, back his mind went, asking the same questions; giving itself the same answers until, a little blurred with brandy, it produced a thought that was at least a change — If I go on like this I shall have to have *my* head looked at! That, in his semi-drunken state, seemed amusing and he laughed. And was horrified, blaming the brandy. The truth was, whisky was his tipple and he was hardened to it, could drink any amount with impunity. Brandy did not suit him; it and the thoughts, plodding round and round and round afflicted him with something he had never suffered before — a headache.

Doctor Hellmutt made a thorough and lengthy physical examination. The first blow to the skull, though sufficient to cause concussion, was nothing. No cranial damage. The second fall could be dismissed altogether, a mere glancing blow on the cheekbone, one of the most solid parts of the human frame. He tested all Marion's reflexes, and they were perfect. The knee of the leg crossed over the other — not in response to a request but handled by Miss Rose — given a sharp chop with the side of his hand, gave the satisfactory jerk. Useless to apply the usual test for hands — 'Grip my hand as hard as you can,' because Marion took no notice. But when, ruthlessly, he struck a match and brought the flame nearer and nearer to her little finger, the hand pulled away. And her eyes responded normally; the pupils narrowing when he held a light near them, and widening when he held his hand over them and suddenly withdrew them.

'It is not physical; of that we can be certain. It is of the mind, or rather of the will. The area uncharted,' he said. The most tricky area of all, but in this case, he believed, not too difficult. Between them Miss Rose and Mr. Horridge had presented him with some salient facts. The girl had as father a domineering man. Mr. Horridge, so obviously very rich, forty years if a day and not handsome was plainly more likely to have been the father's choice than the girl's. She had accepted him, for what reason, against what inward protest, who could tell?

Mr. Horridge had said, 'We got engaged — officially — I mean I gave her the ring, Wednesday last week. There was a party and she was lively as a grig. Monday this happened.'

Four days, Doctor Hellmutt thought; just long enough for the girl to realise what she had done; to what she had committed herself.

Miss Rose had said, 'There is something I should mention. It struck me: The fact that she will eat only when fed, I disregard. Any young woman, as we well know, can stage a hunger-strike for a week and suffer little damage. But she can and does use a water-closet. She will even close the door. Open it, no. That seemed to be significant to me.'

It was significant also to Doctor Hellmutt. From a situation which she could not face, Marion Draper had withdrawn; but not entirely. She had stopped short of the ultimate humiliation.

And he had noticed, as nobody could fail to do, that great, shining engagement ring.

'We will try,' he said.

He said, 'Marion! Marion Draper! I think you can hear me. Listen. You do not have to marry Mr. Horridge. You do not have to wear his ring. I take it away. It is finished. You are free. You hear me.' He pulled the ring from her finger. 'Look, you are no longer engaged. It is over. I am telling you and you can hear me. Mr. Horridge no longer wishes to marry you and your father no longer wishes you to marry him.'

He talked, he struggled with that errant will until the sweat ran down his face. And all to no end.

Miss Rose said, 'I rather doubted, at first. And had I had the slightest idea that his attentions were unwelcome, I should have rebuffed Mr. Horridge. But it seemed not. She seemed so happy.'

'But there must be a reason. There is always a reason. I am remembering a man in Vienna. A minor government official who one evening *walked* from his office to his home. At the foot of the stairs to his apartment he became paralysed; and the paralysis was genuine. One could tickle the soles of his feet or stick pins into the calves of his legs. But it was of the mind. He had that day been told that the expected promotion had passed him. And if he went up those stairs he must tell his wife. They all laughed at me when I said he could be cured by being given the promotion. If a man sound on his feet could not be, how then could be a man so afflicted? But it was the answer. Equally they all laughed at Columbus, but America was *there*.'

'I never laughed at you, Doctor Hellmutt.'

'No. I am thinking you are the one who did not. So to you I am able to say that with this girl we must go deeper. On a Wednesday she becomes engaged to a man who — you say — is not to her disagreeable. There is a party. She accepts a ring . . . and then . . . You say she was gentle, of sensitive nature. It is possible, Miss Rose, that another man was concerned.'

'There was,' Miss Rose said. And because she knew that Doctor Hellmutt would never question, or criticise her withholding of Johnny's letter, she produced it and offered it; in itself nothing, just a bit of a clue . . .

Doctor Hellmutt read the letter.

'What shop?' he asked, looking up.

'By the reference to Baxter's, the other chemist's. Freeman's.'

'I think,' Doctor Hellmutt said, never sure, always feeling his way in the dark, eyes and hands, the very pores of his skin sensitive as antennae. 'I think I begin to see.'

'Yes,' Mr. Freeman said. 'A Johnny did work here. So what about it? Another foreigner, wanting a job. 'But he's dead and buried and I don't look to replace him. Trade isn't so good.'

'Of what did he die?'

'Stomach trouble. I told him, over and over, take a dose of bismuth but he was a know-all. French. And passed some examination which I never did, so I couldn't tell him anything.'

'When did he die?'

Last week, but which day?

'You any kin to him?' Mr. Freeman asked the question to cover the fact that he really did not know whether it was Tuesday or Wednesday last week. The days went so fast when you were single-handed.

'No,' Doctor Hellmutt said. 'I am no kin. I am merely inquiring. Where did he live? And what was his full name?'

Mrs. Fenner regarded the shabby little man on the doorstep of 18 Brewster Street and thought — Trying to sell something. Or looking for lodgings. But when he raised his battered old hat and asked her if she were Mrs. Fenner she heard in his accent a relationship to Mr. de Brissac's. So he had some family, after all, and they'd heard, and had come to do the proper thing. Magnanimously she decided that she would tell the little man that everything was settled; nothing to pay.

'I am told, Madam, that a Mr. de Brissac lived with you, until recently.'

'Till he died. Come in, Mr. . . .'

'Doctor Hellmutt. It would be great help to me if you would answer a few questions.' She was willing to do that, though she failed to see why he was interested in how Mr. de Brissac died. She asked a question of her own, and Dr. Hellmutt denied being related to the dead man. He asked her one strange question — could it be a case of suicide?

'No, and I don't think that's a very nice question to ask, Doctor Helmet. He died because his ulcer burst. Ask Doctor Barlow if you don't believe me. I don't see why you come here asking such things?'

'I am interested in deaths through ulcers. He had lived with you how long?'

'Eighteen months; but it was nothing to do with the food. I've had dozens of lodgers in my time, they've all had the same food. I have the same myself.'

And then, out came the truth and she saw it all.

'To you did he confide anything of his private life? Did he ever talk of a sweetheart?'

That Mr. Horridge had sent him to test her ability to keep her mouth shut; to see if she'd earned that hundred pounds or not.

Temper again!

'No, he did not,' she said with — it seemed to Doctor Hellmutt — a quite unnecessary force. 'He worked all day; he was home here every evening. Sunday mornings he went to church.' Then she added a peculiar thing. 'You may go back to him that sent you and tell him what I said. Coming here calling yourself a doctor!' She swept a scathing look over him. 'You'd do better to get a honest job of work!'

Practically ejected from the house Doctor Hellmutt remembered a phrase about a lady who protested too much.

To Doctor Barlow Doctor Hellmutt also represented himself as a student of ulcers and the old man, who had few opportunities for such, settled down to enjoy a cosy little professional talk. He was quite positive as to the cause of this particular death; it was not even sudden, he said, when one considered the landlady's evidence. As for suicide; well, granted the young man would have access to poisons, but would a chemist's assistant deliberately choose arsenic, the only one his symptoms conformed with? There were easier ways.

Doctor Hellmutt would very much have liked to proceed to Alma Avenue and question the family — the sister especially — but Mr. Horridge had explained Mr. Draper's attitude towards specialists, and Mr. Horridge had, after all, engaged him.

Over the dinner-table he looked at his host and speculated. A man who wanted to marry a girl would probably have taken an interest in her comings and goings and doings for quite a long time beforehand; and Mr. Horridge did not look the kind of fellow to be very deeply hurt by the idea that before she met him his girl had liked someone else. Indeed the reverse.

He began tactfully. 'I have managed to ascertain, Mr. Horridge, that Miss Draper does wish to marry you.'

'How can you tell that? You said you hadn't got a word out of her.' Mr. Horridge's disappointment with Doctor Hellmutt was growing. Moving about in mysterious ways and producing no result. All he had said was that Marion was in perfect physical condition. And now he proffered the information that she wanted to marry him. Very helpful!

'I have my methods,' Dr. Hellmutt said, abandoning as prime a steak as he'd ever seen or was likely to see again. 'Miss Draper is beautiful, even now. With animation in her face she must have been very beautiful indeed. I expect you had to face a lot of competition from other suitors.'

'You'd think so,' Mr. Horridge agreed. He then told Doctor Hellmutt about Mr. Draper's attitude towards marriage for his daughters. And Doctor Hellmutt, remembering the tone of Johnny's letter, said musingly and innocently, 'In such a climate clandestine affairs flourish. It is just possible . . . After all, Mr. Horridge, you were not an accepted suitor it seems, until you were affianced.' Why should that make him look so angry, so almost dangerous; he had himself given that information last night.

The doubt, the leopard crouched on the branch, waiting to pounce, swooped.

The way she'd leant against him for a moment at the end of the plank bridge; her mouth under his; at the time he had thought it delightful, now he asked, experienced? Her suggestion of a runaway marriage. Because she knew about runaway marriages? He was too much confused to remember that she had made this suggestion on Saturday when, if that old hag's story was to be believed, she was still married to a man who hadn't died till Tuesday. But he did remember Mr. Draper's words — I hope she makes you thoroughly unhappy. She is capable of it.

A thing begins to die long before it shows visible signs of decay.

'We can only try,' Doctor Hellmutt said next morning, to Miss Rose, the one person in the world who had ever seemed disposed to understand him. 'It is a shot in the dark, but it is just a possibility. The landlady knew more than she revealed, of that I am sure. I think Mr. Horridge knows something, also. And, dangerous as assumptions are, it would fit. Women are so strange; so very tough, capable of producing a child a year, for twenty years, but emotionally vulnerable, perhaps because they have so little else to occupy them. Of course we may not have identified Johnny correctly, but let us assume: he loved her, she loved him; she becomes engaged to another man and within a week Johnny is dead. Could it not be guilt from which she has retreated? Could it not even be that in turning away from life she has a desire to punish herself?'

'It sounds feasible,' Miss Rose said.

So he sat himself down before Marion again and made a desperate bid for her attention. 'Marion, listen to me. I know you can hear. What I have to tell you is for your own good. It will make you happy. You are in no way to blame for Johnny de Brissac's death. He was a sick man. If you had never seen him, never spoken to him, he would have died.'

He exhausted himself, repeating the assurance again and again and achieving as little result as he had on the former day when his message was that she need not marry Mr. Horridge.

Finally he broke off and wiping his face on a greyish handkerchief said, 'And yet, you know, I feel she is there. If only one could break through. Find the right word.'

'I have a similar feeling. These last few days, since her return, I look up from what I am doing and except that she does not speak and is not reading it is not so very different from when she was here before. I keep expecting her to smile.'

'We will now join the charlatans who can make respectable gentlemen, wearing their top hats, run about on the stages of music halls and bark like dogs, or perform other antics.'

'Hypnotism?' Miss Rose asked in a sharp, cold voice. 'I disapprove of it.'

'Why?'

'I consider it dangerous.'

'I have used it, often to good effect.'

'That was since my time. And I have read about it. It gives one person too much power over another.'

'My dear Miss Rose, you are so very wrong. I know from experience, no person, hypnotised, ever did or said what, in an ordinary state, he did not will to say or do.'

'Then what about men barking like dogs? Turning cart-wheels?'

'They are — what is the term, *gay-dogs*, Miss Rose. Men who have now and then, wished that they *were* dogs, free of the ten commandments and of the conventions. This I assure you is true. Those who turn cartwheels wish to be children again ... The will is released. I once effected a cure by hyp-notising a woman and allowing her to cry. She had a grief about which she was too proud to cry. Into her it ate like a canker, doing her infinite damage, physical damage. Once released, and having had a good cry, so long needed, she was cured.'

'That may be. I'm still against it.'

'Then I would suggest that you absent yourself. I intend to try.'

'Very well,' Miss Rose said. She had no intention of absent-ing herself.

Doctor Hellmutt sat down and took out his watch, a very beautiful one, solid gold, chased and inscribed, tethered to what looked like an old bootlace. Patiently he waved it, left and right and he was beginning to despair when Marion's eyes focused and began moving, left, right, following the pendulum movement.

'Now,' he said, 'Marion you are going to sleep. You will have the best sleep that you have ever known. But you will hear me. Close your eyes. Good. You need not speak yet. But show me that you can hear me. Move your hand. You are asleep?' She made an affirmative sign with her hand. 'And you can hear me?' She moved her hand again. He leaned forward, tense, intent. 'Now,' he said. He started by repeating what he had already told her — no need to marry Mr. Horridge; no need to blame herself for Johnny de Brissac's death. 'So when you wake up, you will be free and happy. Would you like to tell me what happened on that Monday night? Marion, you are alone, with your papa, just before you fell. Tell me . . .'

'No!'

'Why not?'

'It isn't true. Papa, no! It isn't true. Papa! Papa!'

She began to scream, not loudly, feebly and put up her hands as though to protect her head from blows.

'What isn't true?' Doctor Hellmutt asked relentlessly.

Instead of answering, Marion, still holding her hands defensively, began to rock to and fro, as though she were being shaken.

'What isn't true, Marion?'

She whimpered, dodging blows.

Miss Rose said, 'Really, Doctor Hellmutt, I must protest.'

He waved a hand, signalling her to be silent.

'You are going to tell me, Marion . . .'

'She is going to injure herself,' Miss Rose said. And it seemed likely, for she was now flinging herself from side to side in the high-winged chair. 'If that old wound reopens,' Miss Rose said. 'Doctor Hellmutt, this must stop!'

'We come now to the crux,' he said. 'Be quiet.'

In her own house!

'If you don't stop it, Doctor Hellmutt, I must.'

'Do not interrupt.'

Small, but sinewy and completely determined she pushed herself between them, and said, with all the confidence in the world. 'Marion, wake up. When I say three.' She took hold of one of the uplifted hands and give it three small taps. 'One . . . two . . . three.' Marion 'woke'; the blank stare took possession and under their eyes the look of wild distress settled into tranquillity again.

'Apart from all else,' Doctor Hellmutt said, 'that was a dangerous thing to do.'

'Not nearly as dangerous as what you were doing.' Miss Rose tidied Marion's hair with swift light touches. 'At least she looks peaceful now.'

'So do the dead.' He was not angered, anger served no purpose; nor, in this case, would recrimination. He said mildly, 'It should have been a most interesting experiment.'

'She is not a guinea-pig.'

'As I remember, you were not used to be so squeamish.'

'You used not to be so inhuman. Trying to make the poor girl remember what she saved herself by forgetting!'

'Miss Rose, even you can hardly describe her present condition as being saved.'

'It could be worse — as it was just now. Much worse.'

It was the first time either of them could remember exchanging words.

'Well, well,' Doctor Hellmutt said, 'to argue between us is fruitless now. What is interesting ... As a general rule it takes the person who has imposed the state of hypnosis to remove it. Yet she responded to you. A rarity: I wonder ...' His voice trailed off as he contemplated his next move.

Betty had said, taking her own wages into her right hand, Ada's in her left, 'Ada and me wish to give notice, sir.'

After all he had put up with! Ada immobile, Betty so hard breathing and forgetful.

He said, 'I accept your notice. But I have always made it a rule not to employ anybody under notice. It is never satisfactory.' He produced another month's wages; thirty shillings for Ada, always grossly overpaid, a pound for Betty. 'And I should be glad if you would leave my house tomorrow.' That should teach them, living on the fat of the land, giving notice.

Betty did not mind at all; she could go to her granny's. Ada was a bit upset, the cord, actually her lifeline broken; the Workhouse, so often spoken of as a resting-place, where one could sit, a bit far away. 'And there's all my stuff,' she said, rather helplessly.

'Don't you worry. You and me, Ada, we'll do the thing properly tomorrow. We'll have Jarvey's cab. I'll go round first thing in the morning and it can take you to the ... to where you want to go, and me to my granny's.'

'Not too early. There'll be breakfast.'

'Oh no! Well, if you're daft enough to make it, I shan't carry it up. Leave the house tomorrow he said and I take that to mean first thing. Come on, I'll help you up and you can get your stuff together. And after this no more stairs, Ada.'

The brisk bright woman at Corder's Agency said, 'But of course, Mr. Draper, we shall do our very best to accommodate you. Unfortunately, just at this time of the year ... There is that stupid firework factory at Layham, twopence an hour and a wagonette to take them out and bring them home. And the clothing factory is even a greater threat.' To you, Mr. Draper and to me. 'Now let me look.' Briskly, brightly she leafed through her book. 'I could offer you a good daily woman, quite reliable and honest. Unfortunately she will not cook.'

'That would be better than nothing.'

'And I will immediately begin to look out for what you require; a cook who can do some housework and a good house-parlourmaid.'

To tide over, Ellen began to cook and that seemed no bad thing, since she cried less, her grief and remorse eased by the attention that cooking demanded of her inexperience. Papa extravagantly praised the simple dishes she produced at first, 'Very nice indeed, my dear. As good as I ever tasted.' But the daily woman left at six because she had her family's tea to prepare and it hurt Mr. Draper so much to see Ellen bringing trays up from the kitchen that he undertook to carry them himself. And sometimes he, like Betty, breathed hard when he reached the dining-room. Then, after the meal, since they used the dining-room as a living-room, the table must be cleared. With that he also helped and in the kitchen urged upon Ellen the desirability of leaving the used crockery for the woman to deal with in the morning.

'But it looks so messy. I'd sooner do them now than have them staring at me while I make breakfast,' Ellen said.

'Then I'll help you.'

Clumsily and with unnecessary vigour, he began to wipe up, and in his hand his claret glass divided itself into two; the bowl and the stem. Looking at the pieces he said, 'Now how did that happen? It just came to pieces in my hand.' For the first time since the disaster Ellen laughed.

'They all say that,' she said.

He dropped and smashed a plate, and irritated with himself took it out on the general situation.

'I hate to see you at that filthy sink.'

'These old soapstone sinks are difficult to keep clean,' Ellen said. 'There are new ones now, made of a kind of porcelain.' Mr. Draper missed the significance of that remark.

Then Corder's Agency produced Flossie, neat and nimble, if a bit pert; but no cook yet. Perhaps next week.

Ellen turned her serious attention to cooking, and aided by the book which Ada had left in the dresser drawer embarked upon more ambitious dishes. She had always been practical and good with her hands, and there was far more satisfaction to be gained from preparing food than from the making of shell-boxes. Weighing and timing and trying to decipher the recipes in Ada's book, some in writing originally almost illegible and some on cuttings from papers and magazines, and all soiled by much handling, by spilled grease and gravy, Ellen could forget, sometimes for an hour together, that Marion was in Heatherton, unlikely ever to come home again and that it was all her fault.

One evening Mr. Draper came home holding fastidiously on a loop of string two brace of partridges, the first of the season, sent to him by a farmer whose barley he bought. The new girl was in the dining-room, laying the table and he held out the birds to her. 'Take these down and hang them up,' he said. She recoiled as though he had offered her vipers spouting venom.

'Oh, sir, I couldn't. I really couldn't. I never could touch a dead bird, not even when our poor little old canary died.'

He controlled his tongue and did not say — You damned fool! — but his eyes said it and made her wonder whether she wanted to stay in this place after all. Carrying the birds he stamped down to the kitchen and there was Ellen, flushed from the stove and wearing a large white apron with a bib.

'My dear,' he said, eyeing it with disapproval, 'surely this is carrying things a bit too far.'

'I am frying chicken for supper, Papa. It spits. Muslin, even with frills, would not offer sufficient protection.'

It was a plain statement of fact but there was something almost sarcastic about *even with frills*, unlike Ellen; unlike her too, the firm voice, the businesslike manner.

'That simpering fool upstairs cannot touch a dead bird,' he said. 'But hung in the outside safe they'll keep till the new cook arrives.' He began to move to the outside meat-safe on the area wall which in this narrow house served as a game-larder. Ellen looked up from the pan and said, 'She will not be coming, Papa.'

'What!' he said, halting. 'Has Corder's let me down? That woman promised.'

'And she kept her word. A woman came, to be interviewed. I sent her away.'

'You did *what*?'

'I sent her away. She was not clean. I took one look at her hands and knew that I should never fancy anything she had touched. Nor, I think, would you.'

'You had absolutely no right,' he began, and stopped himself. When scolded Ellen always cried and lately she had cried enough tears to float a battleship. 'It was hasty, my dear. She could have been told to wash.'

'Do you want to be cooked for by a woman who only washes when told to?'

Again that note. 'Well,' he said, 'I'll take these to the poulterer and have them dressed.'

'That is not very wise. One can never be sure of getting one's own birds back. I have never plucked or dressed a bird, or even seen it done, but I shall find out. Ada's book is very informative; though, as I suspected, she kept her secrets to herself. One day I must visit her in the Workhouse and pick her brains.'

In Mr. Draper's body the healthy blood turned into something hot and gluey; as he hung the birds in the safe he could feel it, thick and heavy in his neck, in his temples. Ellen's dainty little fingers dabbling in a dead bird's entrails; Ellen saying in that positive way that she would visit the Workhouse; Ellen implying that she was going to cook for ever: Ellen sending a cook away!

He said, coming back into the kitchen, 'You obviously have no idea, Ellen, how it hurts me to see you in the kitchen.'

'The kitchen,' Ellen said placidly, prodding the frying chicken, 'would be quite pleasant, with a new sink and a new stove, and the window made to open, and some bright matting on the floor.' These were words which he was to hear again. And again.

Mounting the stairs, going towards his sherry, he thought querulously — what happened? What did I ever do to merit such affliction? Once he had had three pretty dolls, velvet-clad, kid-slippered, softly spoken, sweetly smiling. One he had broken in the — surely unblameworthy — process of trying to shape it to his needs; one had broken herself, flinging herself into filth and obscenity, emerging as an idiot, sitting out an idiot's life at Heatherton; and the third, busy, intent, almost bustling, wearing a great ugly apron was down there, dealing efficiently with fried chicken and speaking authoritatively. What had he done? What had he ever done, except work for them and cosset them, cosset and protect them?

He was in this mood, pouring his sherry when Doctor Hellmutt rang the bell.

Doctor Hellmutt had had considerable trouble with his host.

'Seeing him won't get you anywhere,' Mr. Horridge said when Doctor Hellmutt said it was essential that he should talk to Mr. Draper. 'He'll just chuck you out. I tried to explain to you — he didn't want anybody else called in. He'd sooner see her sit there for ever than married to me. There's the bit I didn't tell you; I never meant to tell anybody.'

He told it now: and then, two brandies the worse, said, 'when I sent for you I hadn't reckoned with all this raking over and ferreting out.' One side of his mind warded off the thought that there was anything to rake over or to ferret out; the other side ... Mr. Horridge said, 'When I sent for you I reckoned you'd do something. Once I saw a man ... somebody'd given him a clout on the head and there was a dip in his skull you could have laid an egg in. He was as good as dead. But along comes a man — they called him Doc but whether he was or wasn't, who'd know? He was drunk twenty-four hours a day and he didn't have nothing but an ordinary penknife, but he set that chap right in no time.'

'But this is different. I can see, Mr. Horridge that you think I have not earned my salt. This is not — I told you — a case for surgery, so simple, so easy ... But this morning I was near, very near finding the answer. Mr. Draper is concerned. I was left with the conclusion that he struck his daughter.'

'Well, all right. Suppose he did and I wouldn't put it past him, what good will seeing him do?'

'He could give me the key. He was there when it happened. He knows why it happened. I regret, Mr. Horridge, to go against your wishes in this matter, but to see him is essential. I would avoid mentioning your name and allow him to think that I had been called in by Miss Rose, but that in the circumstances might be unwise. He might move his daughter and she might not be so well-cared for elsewhere.'

'Mention me then,' Mr. Horridge said sourly. 'I'll drive you in and wait for you at *The Rose and Crown*.'

'It's a Doctor Hellmutt, sir,' Flossie said.

'Bring that,' Mr. Draper indicated his untouched glass, 'and the decanter and a clean glass into my study.' He went into the hall and shook Doctor Hellmutt by the hand, his superficial geniality of manner restored. Doctor Barlow had not mentioned his intention to seek another opinion, or warned him of this man's coming. Still never mind. To this caller, a professional man, though unimpressive in appearance, he not only offered a seat but lifted the chair forward.

'I am sorry to disturb you,' Doctor Hellmutt said, 'but there are a few things I need to know.'

'Naturally. Anything that I can tell you. A glass of sherry?'

Doctor Hellmutt refused. He also refused Madeira.

'Light this lamp before you go,' Mr. Draper said. In rooms with more favourable aspects there was still daylight enough for a conversation to be held, but the little room was growing dark.

'And now, what can I tell you?'

'I would like to know exactly what took place on that evening, Mr. Draper.'

'But I told Barlow what happened. Surely he . . .'

'Doctor Barlow was not present, Mr. Draper. You were. If you could tell me — it may be a very small thing, something you do not regard as worth reporting.'

Really, Barlow could have spared him this, Mr. Draper thought, his blood thickening again. The old man was getting doddery.

'You will understand, Doctor Hellmutt, that the memory of that evening is most painful to me, but . . .' Lucidly and concisely he said what he had always said, would always say.

'And no word was spoken between you?'

'No. My daughter was tidying things away and I was reading my paper, as I have just said.'

'There had been between you no difference of opinion?'

'Most certainly not.'

'Mr. Draper, you wish your daughter to be restored to a normal state of mind?'

The true answer was a resounding NO. Marion had got what she more than deserved; she was where she should be.

'She is my daughter. How do you expect me to feel?'

'If she is to be restored,' Doctor Hellmutt said, 'you must be truthful with me, Mr. Draper. No, no. Do not anger yourself. It is understandable that you should tell an acceptable story. In time it will seem to you to be the truth; but it is not the truth that I must know *now* if she is to be recalled before it is too late. Withdrawal can be progressive.' And what might that mean? A grubby little foreigner, coming here and as good as accusing him of lying. What the hell had come over Barlow?

'You can tell me,' Doctor Hellmutt said in his most insinuating voice. 'What you tell me I shall use, but I shall not reveal it. You see, I know that more happened than has been told. I have tried to reach her — she is not yet so far away — but on two very reasonable assumptions, I failed. This morning, in a state of hypnosis, she became extremely distressed. She screamed. She said, "No, Papa," again and again, and acted as though defending herself from blows. Did you strike her, Mr. Draper? You may have had reason. But did you?'

Mr. Draper controlled himself, the thick, the outraged blood painful again in neck, in temple. Hypnosis, that flapdoodle! And yet how dangerously close to the truth.

'Doctor Hellmutt, I gather from that remark that you have had access to my daughter. By whose authority?'

'Mr. Horridge engaged me — but that is irrelevant. What matters is the poor girl's state of mind. I can release her.' Doctor Hellmutt clasped his fragile hands together and hammered them on his sharp, threadbare knee. 'If I could know what it was that made her retreat. I beg of you, Mr. Draper, consider again. The girl's whole future is at stake.'

The effort to persuade the father was as physically exacting as the effort to reach the daughter. Wielding that grimy handkerchief again he thought — both very strong characters, very resilient. It was no trivial thing . . .

Mr. Draper looked upon Doctor Hellmutt with contempt and rage; a fellow who did not even possess a clean handkerchief, a goggle-eyed little runt, setting himself up as a saviour. And so nearly right!

'I have listened to enough of this rubbish,' he said. 'And I am severely displeased by the whole affair. Mr. Horridge had no right to call you in without consulting me; Miss Rose had no right to admit you. I will overlook the impertinence of

213

your ridiculous suggestion that I struck my own daughter. I forbid you, absolutely, to go near her again. I wish you good evening.' He stood up, tall and bulky behind the desk.

Doctor Hellmutt remained seated. He said patiently:

'May I explain what you regard as rubbish? This is of the mind, of the will. Something she could not face. Something you will not speak of. Is it too painful? Perhaps I could talk to her sister . . .'

Of all the infamous suggestions! Have Ellen involved in this!

Mr. Draper had never been given to violence; words, honed to hurt had always been his weapons. But Marion's seemingly stupid, stubborn lie had made a breach in his self-control, not yet mended. But he made the effort to master himself, to master the situation.

'I shall most certainly not allow you to speak to my younger daughter. I have wished you good evening, Doctor Hellmutt. I now ask you to leave my house.'

'But I must know, Mr. Draper, and you only can tell me. Something happened, something was said. We will discount the blow, if indeed you struck it. A young woman of that quality would survive a smack on the face. She is, in effect, hiding from something and so are you, Mr. Draper. It must have been something of an extraordinary nature.'

'I have asked you, civilly, to leave my house,' Mr. Draper said. 'Unless you do so I shall be obliged to throw you out.' A pleasant thought; take the little man by the collar, run him through the hall, boot him down the steps.

'But what good would that . . .'

Too much! Mr. Draper reached out and Doctor Hellmutt reached up with one of his small thin hands and applied to the big man's elbow the hold he had taught Miss Rose — the surest way of quelling the violent. He held the pressure as long as was necessary and then released it. Mr. Draper comforted his momentarily paralysed arm, felt the pain in his hand and behind the ear subside.

'I regret,' Doctor Hellmutt said, 'When one is small . . . Now please sit down and tell me what was so horrible?'

Mr. Draper's response was surprising. He held out both arms, slightly crooked.

'Do it again,' he said. 'Both sides, Doctor Hellmutt. You will get no word out of me.'

It was, though Doctor Hellmutt could not know, almost an

exact duplication of Marion's challenge to Johnny to do his worst.

He said, 'I had no wish to hurt; only to help,' but he knew that there was no help to be found here. So he stood up. Mr. Draper conducted him to the door. At the top of the kitchen stairs Flossie banged the gong.

Waiting at *The Rose and Crown*, Mr. Horridge had drunk some more brandy. When Doctor Hellmutt appeared, defeated, smaller and shabbier than ever, Mr. Horridge said, 'Well, you've been long enough. I reckoned he'd have chucked you out before this,' and led the way to the waiting gig. In the gateway, wide enough to accommodate a much larger vehicle, the hub of the left wheel missed so narrowly that Doctor Hellmutt was alarmed.

'Well, get what you wanted?'

'Only in a negative way.'

'Whatcher mean, negative way?'

He sounded truculent and at the corner, a sharp one, skirting the Guildhall, the gig swayed dangerously and the horse seemed to know that the hand on the reins was not as reliable as usual.

'I wonder,' Doctor Hellmutt said, 'if you would allow me to drive a little. It is now many years since I handled the ... ribbons.' The word was well chosen; a horsy, slangy, making the request seem casual.

Taking the reins from Mr. Horridge he thought sadly about the word that he had needed, so badly, and could not find.

'Whatcher mean, negative way,' Mr. Horridge asked again.

'I meant that Mr. Draper gave me no information. But his manner confirmed my suspicion that on that Monday evening something of a cataclysmic nature occurred.'

Cataclysmic. Something to do with earthquakes. Of course. Mrs. Fenner! ('So last night I walked round there ...') How blind not to have seen the connection before. How wrong — perhaps — to make too much of it now.

'Something from which he is himself hiding,' Doctor Hellmutt continued, half to himself. 'Pressed, he became very angry and threatened to throw me out.'

Mr. Horridge gave a bark of mirthless laughter. 'And did he?'

'Oh no. I am accustomed to dealing with violent people. I

am inclined to think that Mr. Draper will shortly have a stroke.'

'I hope he has a dozen.'

After that conversation lapsed. Mr. Horridge brooded, veering this way and that, for almost the first time in his life unsure of his own feelings. Doubt, having pounced, clung on; but love was persistent too; the one bred self-pity, the other self-hatred and to him both emotions were new and difficult to handle. Both had some connection with the little man now seated beside him and after a long silence he said, 'Well, I suppose you've done your best as you saw it. There's a good train up at eleven-thirty in the morning.'

Doctor Hellmutt had been meditating some other avenue of approach; difficult to find since he was now forbidden to see the patient, and had, he sensed, alienated Miss Rose who might, perhaps, at a pinch, have defied Mr. Draper up to the point of allowing him secret access. Now he was being dismissed by the man who had engaged him. So he had failed. But he did not blame himself; self-recrimination, like anger, was futile and the toleration which he tried to extend to all men included Josef Hellmutt.

He said, 'I am sorry not to have helped more. There was cause, there was effect. The effect we see; the cause we seek. And in this case there is a conspiracy of silence to keep the cause hidden.'

Next morning after a breakfast at which Mr. Horridge ate even less than his sparrow-appetited guest, he wrote a cheque for the stipulated fee, twenty guineas. His eyes were bleary and his hand unsteady, but he remembered that cheques should be put into envelopes; the gentlemanly way.

'I feel I cannot accept it,' Doctor Hellmutt said, 'I have done you no service and I have enjoyed your hospitality.'

Mr. Horridge, with no intention of being rude, glanced at the scruffed old shoes which three vigorous polishings, the first they had ever known, had failed much to improve.

'Go on, man,' he said. 'When I sent for you — best man in the world, Miss Rose said, and she should know. I hoped you'd *do* something. Put it at the lowest you've told me there's nothing to be *done*. All this running round asking questions, what could you expect but bloody lies? Still it took up your time.'

Doctor Hellmutt saw the look and did not in the least resent it. He wanted this poor puzzled man to understand that in calling him in, he had done his very best. And only through money could that assurance by conveyed.

He said mildly, 'Mr. Horridge, I am in no need. I ask large fees because I have learned that people value everything by price. I make quite astonishing sums of money. The fact that I look like a tramp is due to carelessness. And over this sorry business, so unsatisfactory to you, I have learned . . . If you wish, send the money to Wakingham, an asylum for the mentally afflicted. They are in need. I will write the address for you.'

'But you'll be out of pocket. Train fares.'

'No. On this line I have a first-class pass for any journey. One of its Directors had a little boy with such a stammer that he was inarticulate and thought to be simple-minded.'

'And you cured *him*?'

'Most simply. Born left-handed, made to use the right. Allowed to use the left, as Nature intended and no longer chided . . .'

'I have, Miss Rose, been dismissed. I am forbidden to see this patient again, and now the gig waits to take me to the Station. So I am come to say good-bye.'

'Yes,' she said, 'I had a letter from Mr. Draper this morning. Doctor Hellmutt, I am sorry about yesterday. It was simply that I could not see her so distressed. She was such a gentle, intelligent, companionable person. You never saw her as she was. If you had you would understand me and what I did.'

'I am understanding,' he said, 'she is the daughter of her father. Last evening he and I came — not to blows, to grips. I put the hold on his one arm, and then he offered both; he challenged me, he said "Do it again on both arms and you will get no word out of me".'

Miss Rose stared. She had said that Marion was gentle and intelligent; and he had likened her to her father, insensitive and stubborn. Was it just possible that Doctor Hellmutt's work with various forms of dementia was having an effect upon him? It *was* possible. After all, hypnosis!

'I am sorry to leave the poor girl as she is, and I shall always think that but for your prejudice against hypnosis we could have reached the truth. But at least I comfort myself, she is in good hands.'

'I do the best I can for all my patients. Suiting treatment according to their condition and their need. And now, if you are not to miss your train . . .'

On the sunny walls of Sorley Park, figs, late plums, early pears, late pears ripened and under the glass so did the great black grapes. For Mr. Horridge walking across to Heatherton, bearing offerings became more and more of a duty.

'Any change?'

No; never any change. Looking very beautiful (looking bloody daft?) Marion sat.

In that October he took to hunting. He could afford to hunt three times a week and made quite a name for himself; *reckless* fellow. He also attracted a good deal of sympathy; *poor* fellow, the wedding all arranged and now the bride-to-be senseless in Heatherton. There were several pretty girls and their mammas willing to do a repair job, *eligible* fellow.

Then November closed down, the whole world wrapped in yellow-grey flannel and he began to feel the call of the sun.

'Any change?' he asked, having deposited his offering to a lost love — the late, brown-skinned pears, the last chrysanthemums, in the hall.

'None at all.'

'And you can't think of anybody else to *try*?'

'I told you at the time, Mr. Horridge.'

'Yes, I know,' he said; and the brandy fumes reached out towards her; she thought, I shouldn't like to strike a match within a foot of him, he'd flare up like a Christmas pudding.

'Things like this,' Miss Rose said, looking towards Marion, 'happen, Mr. Horridge. And must be accepted. The great thing is that she seems happy.'

'Yes.' His mind caught at a phrase. 'In a negative way.'

'That is true.'

'It wasn't what I meant . . . I mean, it should have been different . . . We'd have been in Venice now.'

'Yes, it is all most unfortunate. You may think me unduly interfering, Mr. Horridge, but I truly think that you would do well to get away for a time. A complete change of air and scene.'

'I was thinking about it. There's business in Africa that could do with a look over. I'm useless here. Or so,' he looked at Marion again, 'it seems.'

'You know,' Miss Rose said, 'that you can trust me to take good care of her. And to let you know should any change manifest itself.'

'Yes, I know.' It was what he didn't know, might never know that weighed heavy, dragging down his shoulders, dragging down his face, so that nowadays shaving was becoming a tricky business with new furrows and folds to negotiate.

'If there's ever any question of money, anything that'd make her more comfortable, special food or anything like that,' he said humbly, 'here's the name of my London chap. He'll let you have what you like.'

'I think we can manage without that, Mr. Horridge. Still it was a very kind thought. Thank you.' He was the best of them; best of a bad lot.

They were within the ambience of Christmas again.

'And this year the Bazaar will be without a contribution from this household,' Mr. Draper said with sad reproach. Mamma had started one of her little shawls but she knitted very half-heartedly and half-way through had got in a muddle and had to pull a lot out. Ellen had said bluntly, 'I have no time for such things these days.'

It was true. The woman at Corders had done her best and sent three women in rapid succession. One get very drunk on the cooking sherry; one was caught red-handed in the act of passing a basketful of stuff from the store cupboard to a ragged little boy at the top of the area steps: one, sober and honest, had an alarming epileptic fit. It was very strange, but when Ada was hobbling about and Betty panting about there had seemed to be no shortage of proper staff. What had happened to all those splendid women, sober, honest and not prone to fits?

With Christmas looming and Ellen still in the kitchen, Mr. Draper was driven to make what was, with one exception, the major concession of his life.

'There is no help for it,' he said, 'Ada must come back. I will buy her a wheelchair.'

'She would not come, Papa. Ada is quite happy in the Workhouse.' That was true, the rule that bore most hardly and was most resented — the segregation of the sexes — did not bother Ada at all; and after a lifetime of making intricate dishes she enjoyed even porridge, however watery or lumpy, so long as it was prepared by somebody else.

'How do you know?'

'I went to see her. I always knew she had secrets that were not in her book.'

Up came the hot thick blood. The Workhouse, the pest house; worse than old Nanny's hovel, about which he had spoken.

'I was wondering, Papa, if you could let me have a little extra money. I usually make so many Christmas presents; this year I must buy them.'

This manifest evidence of dependence at least in one sphere, soothed him and he clicked his sovereign case three times.

'Will that do, my dear?'

'Amply. It is most generous of you, Papa.' But was it? Do I not work? Should I not be paid? And if you knew what I propose to do with some of this, you would have a fit, Ellen thought.

'Miss Draper, here is your sister to see you,' Miss Rose said in such a bright, normal manner that entering the room, Ellen expected some spectacular change to have taken place. No change had taken place. And as Papa had always said, when Ellen had asked about making a visit — What was the point in visiting someone who would not recognise you? But Ellen was making a visit of inspection. A few sharp glances gave her the welcome information that Marion was as well-looked after as though she were tended by Ellen herself. Perfectly clean, hair beautifully arranged, freshly laundered lace at throat and wrist. A beautiful doll. Kissing its placid face, Ellen began to cry.

'You must not distress yourself,' Miss Rose said. 'As I have reported regularly, there is no change. But she seems happy.'

'Yes. Excuse me, I did not intend to do this . . . But seeing her reminds me . . . It was all my fault, you see.'

'Your fault?' Miss Rose asked alertly.

Ellen explained how she and she alone was to blame for this dreadful thing. She had ceased to blame herself aloud at home, partly because she now thought it less often — in bed, at night, just before she went to sleep — and partly because it was so ill-received. Papa had ceased to say, tenderly, 'No, no my dear, you must not blame yourself,' and now said, impatiently, 'Rubbish, Ellen. Morbid rubbish.' Mamma's response was surprisingly reasonable, 'If you are to blame, Ellen, then so am I.'

Miss Rose said, 'I think you are too hard on yourself, Miss Draper; you could not possibly have foreseen. When she left here she was fit for anything. After all I am a trained nurse and I did not hesitate to let her help me with tasks far more onerous than putting away a few patterns. It may not have been a swoon at all, she may simply have stumbled, something you could not have prevented even had you been there.'

'I never thought of that.'

Then think of it now and go away and begin to forget: it is the sufferers from remorse who hang about over graves.

'You know,' Ellen said, dabbing her eyes gently and stealing another look at Marion, 'it is quite *possible*. The edge of the carpet does not quite reach to the sideboard. If it had rucked and she caught her toe she would have fallen forward and struck the back of that chair.'

'A most likely explanation,' Miss Rose said.

'You know, Miss Rose,' Ellen said impulsively, 'I know now why Marion said you were so kind. So kind and understanding. You have greatly relieved my mind. Nobody knows what a burden it has been . . . I brought a few little things.' A large bottle of eau-de-Cologne, bought from Baxter's shining newly-opened shop; six fine lawn handkerchiefs, a box of chocolates. Ellen had not dared to spend too much, having absolutely no idea of what Jarvey's cab would cost. 'And these,' she said, lifting paper shrouds, 'I made myself, mincepies. I made the mince-meat too, from out old cook's secret recipe. She even told me about pastry . . .' Miss Rose had offered a verdict of Not Guilty and Ellen would return tit-fortat. 'Not to use a rolling-pin,' Ellen said, 'a glass bottle, full of water as cold as you can get it.'

'I never heard of that,' Miss Rose said. 'Miss Draper will enjoy the mince-pies. She enjoys her food.'

'It is a little early for mince-pies, but I am afraid I shall not be able to come again before Christmas. For one thing I am very busy, for another, there are . . . little difficulties. Mamma should not be left alone much.'

'You must not bother, Miss Draper. As you see, a visit means nothing to her. And I shall report regularly.'

One thing that had bothered Ellen was that the same person did the looking-after and the reporting and could hardly be expected to give herself an unfavourable report. But now she was reassured.

She kissed Marion again and a button on her cloak caught and pulled out a strand of the glossy chestnut hair. Miss Rose tucked it back — as though, Ellen thought, Marion were her favourite doll, or a pet dog whose coat had been ruffled.

'I cannot say,' Ellen said, in the hall, 'how very grateful we all are to you for looking after her so well . . .' Reality dealt its next-to-final-stroke. 'It is all so sad, is it not?'

'Life is full of sad things, but full of compensations, too.'

'That is true.' They shook hands, Ellen remembering how gently that hard little hand had dealt with Marion's hair.

One of life's sad things; with its compensations; and perhaps I am not to blame . . . The kitchen window had been made to open, bright matting laid on the floor, during the annual holiday this year a new sink and a new stove were to be fixed. Papa would go on trying to find a cook but Ellen did not intend her new status to be threatened; if necessary she would resort to sabotage.

On the idiot side old Mrs. Selton had heard the cab arrive. Rescue at last, the rescue for which she had been prepared every moment of her waking day. Fully dressed, even to the ebony and gold ear-rings in her shrivelling ears, she had waited for one of her letters to spur somebody into action.

When this cab drove away and hope knew one of its temporary collapses, she fell into a tantrum. Miss Rose, called in to deal with it, was a little rougher than usual because self-control is an expendable commodity and she had expended hers during Ellen's visit, calling Marion 'Miss Draper' and 'she'.

She used other terms when they were alone together. She said, 'My pretty one', 'My dear one', she said, 'My darling' and 'My love'.

The magnificent novel of Henry VIII's first Queen

NORAH LOFTS

THE KING'S PLEASURE

Katherine of Aragon

—a proud Spanish beauty who became
Queen of England

From the moment of Katherine's betrothal to Arthur, Prince of Wales, she looked upon herself as the future Queen of England. But Arthur died just after their marriage and it was as the wife of his brother, Henry VIII, that she went to her Coronation.

This delightful, richly tapestried novel tells of her life with Henry— the many happy years; the birth of their daughter, Mary Tudor; her popularity with the people and, above all, her constant and unswerving love for the King. But after nearly twenty years, Henry—his eyes affixed firmly on the ambitious young Anne Boleyn—repudiated their marriage, submitted Katherine to the humiliations of a 'trial' and banished her from his life.

The King's Pleasure is a brilliant re-creation of one of history's greatest tragedies. A story which will impress Katherine in the reader's mind as a noble woman and a great Queen.

"Enjoyable ... and informative" *Daily Telegraph*
"This is everything that a good historical novel should be" *Guardian Journal*

THE FINEST HISTORICAL NOVELS
ARE IN CORONET BOOKS

Catherine Gavin

☐	14984 1	THE FORTRESS	40p
☐	12946 8	THE DEVIL IN HARBOUR	40p
☐	02317 1	THE CACTUS AND THE CROWN	40p
☐	04354 7	THE MOON INTO BLOOD	30p
☐	12611 6	MADELEINE	40p
☐	15116 1	THE HOUSE OF WAR	40p

Jane Aiken Hodge

☐	02892 0	WATCH THE WALL MY DARLING	30p
☐	10759 6	THE ADVENTURERS	35p
☐	10734 0	HERE COMES A CANDLE	25p
☐	12790 2	THE WINDING STAIR	35p
☐	15029 7	MARRY IN HASTE	25p
☐	16228 7	GREEK WEDDING	35p

Norah Lofts

☐	15111 0	THE KING'S PLEASURE	35p

Alison MacLeod

☐	15885 9	THE TRUSTED SERVANT	30p
☐	15807 7	NO NEED OF THE SUN	35p

Anya Seton

☐	15701 1	KATHERINE	40p
☐	02713 4	AVALON	35p
☐	15700 3	THE TURQUOISE	35p
☐	01951 4	THE WINTHROP WOMAN	40p
☐	15683 X	THE MISTLETOE AND SWORD	30p

Mary Stewart

☐	15133 1	THE CRYSTAL CAVE	40p

Rosemary Sutcliff

☐	15090 4	THE FLOWERS OF ADONIS	40p
☐	15682 1	SWORD AT SUNSET	50p

Nigel Tranter
The Robert The Bruce Trilogy:

☐	15098 X	THE STEPS TO THE EMPTY THRONE	40p
☐	16222 8	THE PATH OF THE HERO KING	40p
☐	16324 0	THE PRICE OF THE KING'S PEACE	40p

Marian Palmer

☐	15814 X	THE WHITE BOAR	40p

All these books are available at your bookshop or newsagent, or can be ordered direct from the publisher. Just tick the titles you want and fill in the form below.
CORONET BOOKS, Cash Sales Department, Kernick Industrial Estate, Penryn, Cornwall.

....

Please send cheque or postal order. No currency, and allow 7p per book (6p per book on orders of five copies and over) to cover the cost of postage and packing in U.K., 7p per copy overseas.

Name ....

Address ....

....

....